Just A Normal Mummy

BABY BOOM!

About the author

Helen Wallen is a blogger, funny lady, mother of two, and all round gin, wine and cake enthusiast. Formerly a copywriter/PR-type person, she is now dedicated to growing human beings in her uterus and blogging about life with babies, toddlers and beyond.

Helen's award winning 'Just a Normal Mummy' blog is the inspiration and basis for her witty, and hilariously honest, debut fiction title – *Baby Boom!*

HELEN WALLEN

Just A Normal Mummy

BABY BOOM!

HODDER

First published in Great Britain in 2018 by Hodder & Stoughton
An Hachette UK company

1

A CIP catalogue record for this title is available from the British Library

ISBN 978 1 473 66171 4
eBook ISBN 978 1 473 66172 1

Typeset in Sabon MT Std
by Palimpsest Book Production Ltd, Falkirk, Stirlingshire

Printed and bound by CPI Group (UK) Ltd, Croydon, CR0 4YY

Hodder & Stoughton policy is to use papers that are natural, renewable
and recyclable products and made from wood grown in sustainable forests.
The logging and manufacturing processes are expected to conform to the
environmental regulations of the country of origin.

Hodder & Stoughton Ltd
Carmelite House
50 Victoria Embankment
London EC4Y 0DZ

www.hodder.co.uk

For Tim.
Thanks for being awesome.
(And sorry for always talking about my fanny
on the Internet and stuff.)

CHAPTER LIST

PROLOGUE

Baby-Group Politics
(and how to avoid them)

Today, I went to my first-ever 'Baby-Group'.

Please don't be fooled by the name. This is not simply some 'Group' containing 'Babies', oh no. That's what the Universe wants you to believe, like when they told you childbirth was a 'constructive pain' . . .

Baby-Groups are DOG EAT DOG. For some they're wonderful; for others . . . nothing short of BRUTAL. It's just the way it is, like some kind of social experiment where new mums of every kind congregate because society very clearly tells you that if you don't Baby-Sensory the living shit out of your newborn you're going to die cold and alone in a pile of discarded Sophie the Giraffes (or something).

The pressure is real, people.

1

And I can tell you right now: it's TERRIFYING.

I've given speeches on branding to rooms full of hundreds of people; I've delivered PR presentations to the marketing directors of international companies; I've been within licking distance of Jennifer Aniston, and once stroked Justin Bieber's face before throwing up on his security guard's foot at a drunken press event. But today? I almost shit myself walking into a room of exhausted-looking new mothers, because I'd have to make real-life conversation with real-life people I don't know, while somehow looking like I've got my real-life shit together and have actually slept longer than twelve minutes and changed my underwear more than twice in the last week.

(Which I have. *high fives self*)

I had imagined a room full of open-armed mummies holding babies, smiling and chatting and welcoming new faces with hugs and songs and kindness and magical sleep goblins . . .

But actually, most women had come in pairs or small groups of NCT chums, and kept to themselves. And the few lone mums without the support of a 'mummy-buddy' had holed up near the back, their heads down, seeking solace in their iPhone screens, trying not to blink too often in case they fell asleep through sheer exhaustion. Which I fully sympathised with. As I took another glug of my double-shot latte, and pretended to be checking my emails while secretly looking at funny cat videos on Facebook . . .

I decided to spend most of the hour observing the mums surrounding me. (In between waggling some foil fish at my three-week-old son. As he slept. And occasionally regurgitated a bit of breast milk on to my chest. Which I took as a sign he liked it. Obviously.)

I managed to break it down into five main types of mum you find at Baby-Groups . . .

1. The Slummies

Floaty, tie-dye, baby-wearing ladies who carry around little pots to catch their nappiless baby's shit in. Yes. In an age where five-year-olds do their own online banking, and you can 3-D print bionic limbs, people are actually carrying around infant faeces in pots. These women are wrapped in several metres of fabric which they refer to as a 'sling' and seem to be covered in lots of knots. They also smell a bit like lentils and have never quite discovered the art of matching colour to skin tone . . .

2. The Yummies

Yes. They're wearing actual lipgloss. And their hair has been brushed. Today. And despite their

3

children being under three months old, their waists appear to be about the same size as most people's forearms. And it appears they have no, I repeat, NO sick permanently piled on their left shoulder. They're probably not for you. You overheard one of them talking about her AGA . . .

3. The Crummies

They seem to be able to produce home-made baked goods from about their person at any point. While this in itself is skilful, with a three-week-old child permanently clamped to at least one of their body parts, how exactly in the name of fuck do they have time to decoratively ice cupcakes? They're feeders. If you can't say no to cake, you can't be friends. Trust me.

4. The What-the-Fu . . . -Mies

One appears to have no actual baby with her, another appears to have far too many, and – I shit you not – I'm fairly sure I spotted one newborn that appeared to still be attached to its umbilical cord while the mother carried the rotting placenta around in a Sainsbury's plastic carrier bag. Again, probably not for you.

5. The Normal-Mummies

Messy bun, eye bags, slightly crispy black leggings, with optional small amount of poo in fringe. Doesn't pretend to know the words to the nursery rhymes, looks like a complete twat trying to do that weird finger-to-thumb thing for 'Incy-Wincy Spider' and will be heading to the pub straight after for a large gin and tonic. Boom.

whispers that last one is me . . . see you in the pub . . .

#BabyGroupPolitics

Chapter 1

PISSY WRIST

'Shit.' said Emily.

As she sat on the loo, with her pants stretched awkwardly from one ankle to the other, feeling slightly undignified and more than a little exposed in the middle cubicle of Angel Public Relations unisex toilets.

Why the hell hadn't she waited until she'd got home? WHAT ON EARTH possessed her to use her lunch break to buy a couscous salad, a packet of diced coconut, and a double pack of Clear Blue pregnancy tests? Well – she'd only bought the coconut because she overheard one of the girls on reception say it made you thin and it sounded easier than actual real-life exercising – but she didn't even like couscous . . . And the pregnancy tests? Why was she doing this NOW? At work. Ten minutes before a whole agency brainstorming session about a luxury towel brand.

Yet here she was, with her Ted Baker pencil skirt hoisted up round her waist while her own lukewarm urine dribbled into her shirt sleeve.

Excellent, she thought to herself, pursing her lips and using her other (non-pissy) hand to hold back her mane of thick blonde curls.

The box said it took two minutes. Two minutes to show

a clear result. Well, frankly, two minutes felt like a bloody lifetime while you were sat with your vagina out listening to Brian from accounting trying to politely cough his way through a spot of IBS.

No. Not exactly ideal. But here she was: pantless, pissy wrist and all, watching in slight disbelief as two very distinct blue lines in the 'pregnant' window slowly appeared and stared back at her.

'Shit.'

'Hello?' Brian said tentatively from the sink area.

FUCK OFF, BRIAN.

'I'm fine. Thanks,' she called back at him.

Emily took a deep breath and tried to block Brian out as she fixed her gaze on the little white stick that was telling her her life was about to change quite a lot from this point. Probably. Right?

What did this mean?

OKAY, she knew what it 'meant'. Obviously. But what did it really MEAN . . . Did she need to call her doctor? Find a midwife? Stop eating cheese?

I mean – anyone could take or leave Cheddar, but Camembert? That was going to take some serious commitment. Just thinking about it now was making her crave a Brie-and-bacon sandwich and a large glass of Pinot Grigio.

THIS IS RIDICULOUS. IT'S NOT ABOUT CHEESE. PULL YOURSELF TOGETHER, EMILY. YOU'RE CURRENTLY SITTING WITH YOUR FANNY OUT AND PISS DOWN YOUR ARM WITH SIX MINUTES TO GO UNTIL A MEETING ABOUT TOWELS AND

YOU'RE THINKING ABOUT SOFT FRENCH
CHEESES.

She took another deep breath.

A smile grew across her face. She couldn't help her
teeth from showing. There were a lot of teeth.

But she was just so happy.

(And semi-naked . . .)

And her mind was racing.

However, in the interest of somehow pulling her shit
back together so she could think creatively about towelling, Emily reassembled herself, quickly snapped a picture
of the pregnancy-test result on her iPhone and then
wrapped the test in loo roll, popped it back into the packet
and into her handbag.

Pants and pencil skirt now firmly back in place, she
fired a WhatsApp message off to her husband Paul with
the photo and a caption simply saying:

You're going to be a daddy . . .

Swiftly followed by:

But can't talk now.
Got to go brainstorm the shit out of
some towels.
I love you.
I can't stop grinning.
Everyone is going to think I REALLY
like towels.

9

And with that, Emily checked her phone was on silent, took a final deep breath and, confident she was now alone, finally left the shelter of the middle cubicle.

As she washed and dried her hands, she imagined laughing in the future about finding out the happiest news of her life at the same time as Brian from accounting had the shits in the loo next door to her . . .

Emily shook her thoughts away, composed herself and left the toilets. She quickly made her way back through the open-plan office attempting not to make eye contact with anyone (especially not Irritable-Bowel-Brian). It felt like her news must be pasted all over her face and might burst out of her any moment. It was almost disappointing that no one so much as glanced at her as she returned to her desk.

Focus, Emily.

She sat in front of her Mac and pulled up the briefing document she'd prepared for the brainstorm.

She stared at the screen. It was impossible to concentrate. All she had to do was press print, but it was so hard to think about towels now that she knew she had a human growing inside of her.

MY UTERUS HAS AN ACTUAL TINY PERSON IN IT.

It was an utterly insane feeling.

Just then, her eyes met her colleague Matilda's. Matilda was a senior account manager who sat directly opposite her. She was a bit of a bitch, actually. Emily was fairly sure she was after her job, so she would literally be the *last* person on earth she'd let know it could be up for grabs, even temporarily, in about nine months' time.

'Everything okay?' Matilda suspiciously raised an eyebrow in Emily's direction. Which irritated Emily way more than it should do.

'Yes. Everything's great, thanks,' Emily snapped. Attempting to remove the persistent grin from her face.

'It's just you were gone quite a while.' Matilda responded with her eyebrow still suspiciously raised. 'And now you're grinning like some sort of lunatic. Had some good news?'

MEDDLING. BITCH.

'I just really like towels,' she retorted as she pressed print.

Matilda rolled her eyes and looked back at her screen.

Just then Natalie, the managing director, called everyone in to the large meeting room for the brainstorm.

'Right. Let's get going everyone. Got those briefing documents, Emily?'

Emily rose to her feet, grabbing the warm sheets from the printing bay on her way to the meeting room.

Right.

Don't think about what's in your uterus.

Think towels.

Towels.

Fucking towels.

Chapter 2

MOLLY, MOLLY, MOLLY

It had been a pretty ordinary Friday for Molly.

She'd been clock-watching since lunchtime. Which seemed to have the annoying effect of making the afternoon drag even more . . .

She'd spent the week temping at a shitty building site, where she'd mainly been sat in a shitty Portakabin, wearing shitty shoes she couldn't walk in.

She was so bored.

And so so cold.

And just wanted her trainers.

But at least today was her last day. And who knew what wonderful dreams and delights the temp agency would have in store for her come Monday . . .

Molly had a rule to never temp in any one place for more than a week. That way, if it was totally awful, she only had a maximum of five days to deal with it. And there was always the excitement of something new every Monday morning. Not that it ever actually 'was' exciting. It was mainly data entry.

But hopefully, whatever next week had in store, it was something that didn't involve her sitting in a cardboard room, in November, with only an underpowered fan heater for company, in the middle of a building site in High Wycombe.

Saying that, she'd managed to remain fairly enthusiastic throughout the week. She'd done a lot of printing, handed out the occasional lanyard, answered the odd phone call, but had mostly spent her days sending fairly explicit text messages to her boyfriend Tom.

Well. For £6.75 an hour what did they expect?

Anyway. She couldn't help herself.

She fancied him so much it felt impossible to go longer than an hour without some kind of contact with him. Even if that contact was a slightly out-of-focus picture of her left boob as she photocopied some risk assessments.

Tom
Seriously.
You are going to get me fired!

Molly
Who cares.
Get fired. Let's go to India.

Tom
I thought you wanted to go to Vietnam?

Molly
Yes. After India.

Tom
And how will you be paying
for this trip exactly?

13

If you're secretly minted you
better tell me now . . .

Molly
Being rich is for losers.
I'm more of a pay using a credit card now,
think about it later kinda girl . . . lol

Tom
Ahh yes. I remember now ;)
Excellent tits too.

Molly
Ha. Well . . . I need to copy some
public liability insurance documents
in a minute so,
if you play your cards right,
I'll get a snap of the other one
so you can have a matching set.

Tom
That's my girl . . .

Molly put her phone away and looked ominously at the large pile of paperwork the site manager had dumped on the corner of the desk.

She let out a deep sigh.

Seriously. What am I doing?

The truth was, she didn't really ever know what she was doing. Not for very long, anyway. Molly really did live one day to the next. Or at most week by week. She didn't have any desire for a 'career' or anything in her life that involved any kind of ambition or application. It just wasn't her thing.

She'd much rather spend her days without the boring ties of a 'real job', scanning component lists for £6.75 an hour, renting a tiny room above a shop on the high street, and cutting her own fringe.

She was only twenty-nine, after all. She had her thirties for all that 'responsibility' stuff, right? Who would want some boring 'serious' job that meant you couldn't piss off to India for a few months if you fancied it? Right?

Reluctantly, she grabbed a wheelie stool, kicked off her shoes, and positioned herself between the scanner and the stack of paper that sat on the desk.

She yawned, rolled her head around her neck, and decided to suck it up and get on with it. It was 2.34 p.m. So, in two hours and twenty-six minutes she'd be out of there. Twenty quid richer than if she walked out now.

Another twenty quid in the India fund . . . Although it was more likely that twenty quid would be going into a Wagamamas-on-a-Friday-night-before-going-home-and-having-sex-with-Tom fund, but either way it was worth it.

She glanced back at the clock: 2.37 p.m.

Just then the desk phone rang.

Molly stared at it for a couple of rings, then decided it was far too much effort to deal with any real-life people right now. She had scanning to do.

And scan she did.

15

For TWO. BASTARD. HOURS.

She could not face any more. But she was so close . . . Perhaps she'd go to the loo. That had to burn through a few minutes.

Plus, while she was there she'd give Tom a little gift to take with him into his Friday afternoon sales meeting . . .

And send him a picture of her fanny.

Chapter 3

THAT FRIDAY FEELING

So here she was. Again.

Sat in that bar. Again.

On her own. Again.

On a Friday afternoon.

Waiting for 'him' to decide it was 'safe' to come meet her.

Again.

Liz had placed herself neatly on a high stool at the end of the bar, in an oh-too-familiar shady corner, in front of a gin martini with her back pressed up against the wall. That way she could casually survey the door, observe the room, and avoid any awkward eye contact with the bar staff.

She'd done this every Friday – same time, same place, same seat, same pretend recurring meeting in her diary – for as long as she could remember.

She sometimes wondered what the staff behind the bar thought of her, sat in the shadows, pulling olives off a cocktail stick with her teeth, being careful not to smudge her freshly applied lipstick. Attempting to play it cool, and not to check the time on her phone every few moments as her glass slowly emptied.

As the alcohol pumped round her system, an angry voice would begin sounding in her head . . .

Why the fuck am I doing this to myself? Am I really so worthless that I can't do any better than being someone's dirty secret? Someone's bit on the side? A filthy lie?

She hated it.

She knew she was better than this. She hated him. But she loved him. So much. So much it made her accept what she was doing. She loved him in spite of the lies, the deceit, the sneaking around . . . She felt like shit every second she was away from him. But then she felt like shit when she was with him too . . .

She shook the dark thoughts out of her head and finished off her second gin martini. Her thoughts turned to how she'd get off the bar stool she had so gracefully managed to perch herself upon only a short while ago, without flashing part or all of her vagina at the table next to her.

She caught the barmaid's eye and tapped her glass to signal another round. The barmaid smiled and nodded in understanding. Or was it a smirk? Was she judging her? Laughing at her? Or worse – pitying her?

Who gave a shit – she looked about nineteen. She probably didn't even have to wear a bra. And she had amazing eyebrows.

Liz always envied other women's thick eyebrows.

If you grew up as a teenager in the era of the Spice Girls, and spent most of your pubescent years relentlessly plucking at your brow line so it remained only one-hair thick, then you were destined to live out your days suffering excessive eyebrow envy . . . And spend the rest of your life painting, powdering and pencilling them back in.

One day she'd tweet Geri Halliwell and tell her what she'd done to her and her poor sparse brows . . .

Her eyes flicked down to her phone as it lit up with a message.

> It's me.
> I'm trying to leave.
> I'm so sorry.
> Karen called and I got stuck.
> I'll try and be there in the next half
> hour
> but you know how it is.

Liz turned her phone over so it was face down on the bar and mulled over the last sentence. 'You know how it is.'

Yes. I know exactly how it is.

Her fresh martini arrived. She stared at it for a few moments then swiftly downed it in one, ignoring the small dribble that had escaped and made its way down her chin.

She'd leave the drinks on his tab. He could pay the bill then. The shit.

She picked up and waved the tab card in the general direction of Eyebrows. Who was becoming more blurred by the second. Moments later she appeared with the bill for Liz to check and sign. Which she did. With little regard to the total. And added a twenty-pound tip. Nice to be generous, she thought. Even shits can be generous.

19

'Everything okay?' said Eyebrows.

'Not really.' Liz became suddenly aware of the effect of the martinis, as she drew in a long breath and blinked slowly. 'Men are dicks. If you want my advice? Stay away from all penises. For ever. Until you're dead. Or a lesbian.'

'Oh right. Cool. I meant was everything OKAY with your drinks?' Eyebrows laughed a little as she took the signed bill and held Liz's gaze for a moment before shuffling off.

Liz decided the best strategy was to pretend that none of that just happened. She was done. She avoided eye contact with anyone as she awkwardly clambered down from the bar stool. She no longer cared if the table opposite got an eyeful of labia. Or that her lipstick had faded. Or that her usually perfect sleek bob was starting to look a little dishevelled. Also, how had the barstool got so much higher since she'd been sat on it . . .?

He wasn't coming. Why prolong the misery?

She'd get the train, switch off her phone and spend the rest of the night in her pyjamas with her cat. She was fairly sure that if she started drinking water now and ate some pasta when she got home she'd escape a hangover. In fact, she'd got some tuna pasta salad in the fridge she could use up . . .

Fucking hell.

When did I become the pissed-up cat lady who eats leftover tuna pasta salad in her jogging bottoms on a Friday night while sobbing after getting stood up . . .

Chapter 4

SUPER SPERM

Emily had ignored Matilda's rather unsubtle and consistent brow raises as she'd begun shutting down at twenty-nine minutes past five. It was Friday. And she now had a very important reason to get home. And remove the wee-covered plastic stick wrapped in loo roll, which was probably soaking urine into the lining of her designer handbag, as soon as possible.

She'd glanced at her phone as she headed out of the door and saw that Paul had responded with a fairly impressive series of emojis. Possibly all the emojis his phone contained. In fact, she wasn't sure he hadn't downloaded some kind of additional emoji pack specifically for the occasion.

Needless to say, the ridiculous grin she'd been trying to suppress since lunchtime was still spread across her face as she drove home and parked in front of their pretty Victorian terraced house in Spring Gardens Road on the outskirts of Wycombe town centre. Paul's car was parked opposite. He must have left work early.

Emily did everything she could to stop herself squealing as she bleeped the lock on her Fiat 500 and skipped up the front path.

Before she could turn the key in the door, Paul opened it with a grin so wide it made hers seem pathetic.

Emily couldn't help it; she burst into a flurry of happy tears and just hugged and hugged and hugged him.

'Why are you crying, you doughnut?' Paul said, laughing a little. He stroked her face and affectionately kissed her forehead. 'Right, my beautiful pregnant wife, get in here now so we can pop open the bubbly and you can watch me drink it all.'

'Dick,' Emily said, as her tears turned into snotty laughter.

'Have you told the girls yet?' Paul called from the kitchen as the familiar sound of a popping cork rang through the house.

'Not yet.' Emily removed her work shoes in the hall and took her phone out of her bag. 'I was in that bastard towel meeting for about two hours! Two hours of my life I will never get back. Although I mainly spent the entire time grinning like a twat.'

She headed to the lounge and curled herself into the left-hand corner of the sofa like she always did, as Paul brought the drinks tray through.

'Besides,' Emily continued, 'I wanted to see you first. This one is all about us. I can't believe that we're actually going to have a baby. It's nuts.'

'I know.' Paul placed the tray down on the coffee table, and gently put his hand on her stomach as he sat down next to her. He looked at her intently. 'But it's amazing. And it will be amazing. We will be amazing . . . Now, text your mates. Stop getting soppy. And shut up while I get pissed on both our behalves.'

Emily gave him a playful poke in the ribs.

She started a new WhatsApp group, adding her two best friends, Liz and Molly, and titled it:

'You'll never guess what?'

She knew she wouldn't have to wait long. So she picked up the glass on the coffee table in front of her and took a sip.

'What is that?' She pulled a face.

'It's alcohol-free wine. I grabbed it on the way home.'

'It's rank.'

'It's your life now, preggo,' Paul joked.

Emily threw him a look. But its impact was lost as she still couldn't stop smiling.

'Sorry. But it is.' He continued. 'That, and being my taxi driver, not being able to see your own vagina and avoiding Camembert.'

'Do *not* even start me on Camembert. I'm in mourning . . .' Emily sniffed at her glass suspiciously.

'But you're fine about your long-lost vagina?' Paul said, laughing.

Just then, Emily's phone buzzed.

Liz
????

Molly
??? Don't leave us hanging, you cow!

23

Emily's grin came back.

Emily
So . . . it's early days but . . .

Molly
But WHAT!! You're killing me.

Liz
Spit it out, lady.

Emily
*sings along to classic
Spice Girls anthem*
. . . When Two Become One . . .
(Although it's actually more like
one become two . . .)

Molly
OMG

Liz
I knew it!!

Molly
Totally amazing!! I'm so happy for you!!
How far along are you??

Liz
Are you sure you're not just fat?

Emily
BITCH

Liz
JOKING. ;)

Emily
I've literally just found out!
Got piss on my hand in the loos at
work doing
the test. Then had to pretend to be
excited about towels.
Matilda was being a DICK.

Molly
Matilda is a DICK.

Liz
Hey. Maybe she's just misunderstood?

Emily
Ever the lawyer Liz!
ANYWAY.
Can we talk about ME please ☺

Molly
LOL x we're super happy for you
darling!
Give Paul a big kiss
and tell his penis well done from us.

Liz
lol. And me.

Emily
LOL
Love you guys xx

'How are the girls?' said Paul.

'Great. Happy for us. They send their congratulations to your penis.'

'My penis says thank you,' Paul responded, nodding his head downwards in acknowledgement.

'Have you told anyone yet?'

'No. I wanted to wait until I'd seen you.' Paul sipped his champagne. 'I'll call my folks later. And text Matt. Right now, I'm happy sitting here listening to you talk about how much you miss soft cheeses. After four and a half hours of knowingly being pregnant.'

'Ha! Well so long as I can substitute with the odd tub of ice cream, I'm sure I'll do just fine.'

Paul smiled and topped his glass up.

'Hey,' said Emily, 'Text Matt now. I want to hear what he says. Just please promise me that you won't make any shit jokes about having super sperm or anything wanky like that.'

'I love you, but I'm afraid I can't make those sorts of promises.'

Chapter 5

#FORKDICKS

It was almost 5.30 p.m. on Friday evening and Molly had just arrived home.

She'd climbed the stairs up to her one-bed flat above Wookie's Tattoos, ignoring the empty boxes up one side of the steps, and the excessive volume of death metal blasting through the wall on the way up. She turned the key in the lock and stepped inside. It was a mess. It was always a mess. And Molly had left it a mess as she'd walked out of the door this morning, running late, as always.

She liked to think of it as organised chaos.

Organised chaos that possibly harboured some kind of biological weapon, given how long that glass of orange juice had been on the windowsill, but she didn't care. Her discarded beverages may have grown their own furry blue winter jackets, but she could find everything. And it wasn't like she spent any real time there. Her time was for enjoying life, not washing up cups and putting her pants away properly . . .

And right now, time was for getting herself ready for a date with Tom.

Lovely, beautiful, wonderful Tom.

She smiled just thinking about him.

Molly and Tom had almost reached the six-month stage in their relationship. Not that they were 'labelling' it a relationship. Neither of them were really label or relationship kind of people. But this was the longest Molly had ever stuck with one guy, and not had her head turned . . .

She loved that Fridays had become their night. That they'd got past that awkward stage of trying to impress each other and find new and exciting things to do, that now they could just grab some food, hit a few bars and head back home.

She'd never had that with anyone before. She wasn't sure if Tom realised that. Realised that she really liked him. *Really* liked him. She didn't go to those levels with her amateur photography efforts in building-site Portakabins for just anyone, you know.

She couldn't think of anyone she'd rather eat noodles and have sex with. And *that* was actually a pretty rare thing for her . . .

Just then her phone went . . .

It was Emily, one of her best friends. She'd added her and her other friend Liz to a WhatsApp group:

'You'll never guess what?'

It didn't take a genius to work out what 'what' could be. Emily had been married for two years, never stopped talking about having a baby, and had pretty much picked out her nursery décor by the time she'd arrived back from her honeymoon . . .

Emily was pregnant. She'd just found out. Molly fired

a few messages back to her and smiled at how happy and excited she was for her wonderful friend.

She began to wonder why Liz was also replying . . .

Normally she was out seeing her 'mystery man' on a Friday straight from work, and if she was responding then it really could only mean one thing . . . Molly opened a new chat window.

Molly
Hey sweetie – you not out with 'him'?

Liz
No.

Molly
Is everything okay?

Liz
No.

Molly
Did he stand you up again??

Liz
Well, I'm about to eat leftover pasta in my pyjamas while downing a bottle of wine and crying about how shit my love life is . . .
So . . . Yes.

Molly

29

Oh . . .
Hey. Why don't you come out with
me and Tom?
We're only going to Wagamamas?

Liz
Oh yeah. Great.
I'd just love to spend the night
eating ramen and watching you two
sucking face while feeding each other
Ebi Katsu.

Molly
Wow. I'm impressed you
know the names of stuff.
You're like a Waga-Pro.
I just point at the menu and ask for
wine.

Liz
Ha. Well. Despite my Waga-Pro
status, and as much as I like wine,
I'm in my pyjamas now.
And I know you don't really want me
there.
Although I appreciate you pretending.

Molly
I'm not pretending.
Just come!
It'll be fun.

We'll get drunk and judge the people
who ask for forks . . .

Liz
Dicks.

Molly
#ForkDicks.

Liz
LOL.

Molly
Seriously though – are you OK?
How's things with him?

Liz
Shit. It's shit. He's a shit.

Molly
You know you can do so
much better than him.

Liz
I know.
Look, have a great night.
I'm turning my phone off now before
he tries to call me.

Molly
OK. Love you. xxx

Molly frowned.

31

She had no idea why someone as smart, funny and brilliant as Liz would want to waste her time with some dickhead who stood her up most Fridays and was clearly never going to leave his wife.

For a moment, Molly felt almost guilty for being so happy. And that Emily was so happy.

It played on her mind as she peeled her clothes off, stepped into the shower and began scrubbing the memories of the week's Portakabin-scanning-hell from her hair and body.

Feeling refreshed, Molly twisted the shower off, quickly opened the door and grabbed a towel from the floor she thought was probably quite clean. (Hopefully.)

She made the quick dash to her bedroom and stood wrapped in the towel in front of her wardrobe as she perused her outfit options for this evening.

Hmmm. Skinny jeans, boots and a top that showed just enough cleavage to be enticing, without the chance of a nipple reveal if she had a few too many vodkas later . . . Perfect.

She glanced at her phone as she sat down on her bed and pulled her make-up bag and hairdryer in front of her. And smiled at a message from Tom to confirm they were on for 7 p.m.

As she started lining her eyes with thin black flicks, she had a revelation: Tom had loads of cool, single mates. Liz had to like 'one' of them, right? And surely anything was better than spending your weekend in your PJs, crying into some cold conchiglie at thirty years old . . .

A smug smile appeared across Molly's face as she brushed mascara through her lashes. Yes. This was genius.

She'd get Tom on board tonight and they'd formulate a plan. This was what Liz needed for sure – someone to distract her away from that lying dickhead and get her having some fun again.

And with that sorted, Molly set about blow-drying her mid-length wavy brown hair, brushing her fringe into place, and considering what colour bra and knickers Tom would most appreciate tonight . . . Perhaps no knickers?

Maybe she'd send him a photo and find out . . .

Chapter 6

LAST SATURDAY CLUB

An entire week had passed, and it had felt like a month . . .

It was an odd thing, Emily thought to herself, to have the miracle of life going on right there inside of you, and just to carry on day-to-day, trying not to think about what was happening inside your womb. Trying to subtly study the backs of pre-packed sandwiches and switch to decaffeinated teabags while convincingly acting like the experiential campaign for a large Swedish furniture store in Southampton was the most important thing you had going on in your life right now . . .

She quite genuinely 'felt' pregnant now. There'd been more than one untimely dash to the work loos (thankfully, not after Brian had recently vacated) and a fair few pukey-pull-overs on the morning commute . . . Which was not quite the beautiful start she'd had in mind for her unborn child.

She wasn't glowing. If anything, she looked slightly grey. And angry. And really fucking wanted to eat cheese.

Physically nothing had happened to her body shape yet, which was almost disappointing . . . if anything, she'd lost a bit of weight from gagging every time she smelled cucumber.

But thankfully, Friday had come back around again and tomorrow she would get to see her best friends properly.

She couldn't wait to see them.

And hug them.

And show them her itemised Pinterest boards for the new nursery. They'd LOVE that.

Right now, it was twenty past five and, despite feeling Matilda's witch-like bitch-stare burrowing into her forehead, Emily thought 'screw it'. She'd had enough of shuffling papers around on her desk while pretending to work, it was time to get the hell out of there and get back to her sofa, her husband and her slipper-booties.

'Have a lovely weekend,' Emily barked in Matilda's general direction avoiding any eye contact. And marched down the office as quick as her mid-height black court shoes would allow her.

She reached the glass entry door and began rummaging for her car keys in her handbag with a sense of relief. She'd made it through another whole week . . . Only thirty-six or thirty-seven more to go . . .

Emily slowly felt her eyes peel themselves awake.

She hadn't even remembered falling asleep last night, but clearly she'd made it into bed somehow. She certainly wasn't ready for it to be morning again already.

The back of Paul's head slowly came into focus and she became aware of his deep still-asleep breathing.

It was really quite loud. And really quite annoying.

Quite a lot of things had become really quite annoying recently.

Right now, it was annoying that Paul could sleep so deeply and completely while she had woken up, sat up in bed, flicked Saturday-morning television on, and begun a series of light huffs and sighs in his direction without him so much as stirring. Arsehole.

It didn't matter that she knew this was her hormones on overdrive, and that he was exhausted from a tough week of travelling and working his arse off. No. What mattered was that she'd only changed their bed on Thursday and he was snorting and dribbling all over his pillowcase like a drunk on a park bench.

Emily upped the volume of her huffing, but it still had no effect.

Instead, she decided to get out of bed (as noisily and angrily as she could), and go for a shower in the hope she'd re-emerge clean and back to being an entirely reasonable human who just happened to be growing another human inside them again.

As she stood up, a horrible and oh-too-familiar wave of sickness washed over her as she tried to get her brain to fully communicate with her only-just-woken-up body to get to the bathroom. NOW.

Emily moved as fast as her legs would allow her, and made it just in time to the bathroom sink.

'FUCK THIS!' Emily shouted when she'd finished emptying the contents of her stomach.

She kept the water running until the sink was clear and

gently splashed her face. She looked up into the mirror above the sink. Was she imagining it or was her face getting wider? Seriously. Pregnancy was actually increasing the girth of her face. She began to wonder why the actual fuck she'd allowed Paul's sperm to do this to her.

This time last week she was so happy she could cry. Now she smelled permanently of sick, her face was turning into the moon, and she couldn't be in the same room as legumes without gagging.

SERIOUSLY. FUCK THIS, said Emily again. In her head, this time.

She was going to see her girls. She was going to put expensive make-up on her newly ample face. She was going to laugh, and have fun, and discuss with them her idea to start a pregnancy blog in the hope she'd get a free iCandy pushchair and maybe a holiday to the Bahamas complete with a nanny. Although, perhaps some washing powder and a maternity bra was more realistic . . .

Yes.

It was time to pull her slightly vommy-self together and spend some well-deserved girl-time with her two wonderful best friends.

It was 'Last Saturday Club' after all: an agreement they'd all made when they left sixth form, to try and meet on the last Saturday of each month. They'd choose a different location each time . . . cafes, pubs, or just at each other's houses. But so long as they all showed up. That's all that mattered.

Emily heard her phone vibrate on her bedside table.

She stepped back into the bedroom, grabbed it and perched on the bed while Paul continued to snort last night's red wine into her White Company sheets.

Molly
You better not be vomming
and trying to bail on us preggo!
See you at 11
xx

Emily smiled. And considered her response for a moment.

Emily
Not only am I vomming,
but my face now has its own orbit.
Be careful not to eat or
drink too close to it
as any wayward crumbs may be
sucked in by its gravitational pull!
I'll be there though.
First rule of Last Saturday Club is . . .

Molly
. . . miss it and YOU'RE A DICK.

Emily
We may need to update these rules
☺
Also – I can't help but remember

> when you missed several
> years of LSC
> while flouncing about Asia
> trying to find your inner peace
> or some shit?

Molly
Second Rule . . .
We don't talk about Last Saturday Club.
Talking about it MAKES YOU A DICK.

> **Emily**
> This kind of proves my point.

Molly
WE DON'T TALK ABOUT
LAST SATURDAY CLUB.

> **Emily**
> Whatever.
> Me and my giant face will see you at
> 11.
> Xx

Molly
Xx

Molly always knew how to make her feel better.

They'd known each other since for ever. She was the first friend she'd made when she started secondary school in Marlow, aged twelve. They'd met on the first day, on the school bus travelling from High Wycombe bus station, and had bonded over a mutual appreciation of *Just Seventeen* magazine, Body Shop products and Damon Albarn. And had pretty much been inseparable since.

Emily had always admired Molly's ability to not give a shit about anything, yet be one of the most kind-hearted, generous and loyal people she'd ever met.

Liz had joined the school in lower sixth, and was the perfect addition to their little friend group. All three ladies were entirely different but were the best of friends in spite of it.

Over a decade later, they were all still the closest of friends. And all had taken their lives in utterly different directions. Not that it mattered. What mattered was that they made time for each other . . . Especially now their lives were all changing.

This Last Saturday Club was the first one where it was going to be different. Really different.

Now, said Emily to herself, I just need to gather the energy to get me and my giant face there, without throwing up in my hair.

Chapter 7

DECAF. THAT.

Emily walked in to the little coffee shop off Wycombe high street, smiling in anticipation. Her big blonde ringlets were casually pinned on top of her head, and she paused at the entrance as she scanned the seating area for her friends.

Liz was there first, as always, her hair and lipstick perfect as she sat rather seriously in front of a tall latte. Liz's face lit up the moment her eyes met Emily's.

Emily weaved her way through the tables and push-chairs, and immediately dropped her handbag as she reached her friend to give Liz an intense hug. She wasn't sure why but her eyes welled up slightly. It just felt so lovely to see her.

'Are you crying?' Liz said with a smile.

'It's the hormones!' Emily laughed back at her as she dabbed her eyes with her fingertips.

Liz smiled again and rolled her eyes a little. 'What do you fancy to drink? I would have got you a coffee but I didn't know if you were off it in your . . . erm, delicate state . . .'

'There's nothing delicate about this I can tell you. I had to throw up in a bin on the way out of Sainsbury's car park just to make it here!'

'You make it sound so special!' Liz said, laughing.

'Can you just get me a glass of cold water?' Emily said, peeling her coat off.

'Of course. Caffeine is overrated anyway.'

'It's really really not.' Emily pulled a sarcastic face.

Just then, Emily spotted Molly ungracefully shoving her way across the cafe. She looked like she'd spent the night sleeping in a skip.

'Sorry, sorry, sorry!' she said as she reached them. 'I literally got out of bed ten minutes ago! I probably would have been here early but Tom stayed last night, and he's just so horny when he wakes up, and—'

'Can I just stop you there,' Emily said. 'As much as I'd love to hear about your pre-coffee shag, I'm actually in a very delicate condition here and that may well force me to throw up in a bin. Again.'

'Urgh. That sounds terrible,' said Molly, hugging her friend. 'Liz, if you're getting the drinks in . . .'

'I know, I know, large gingerbread latte with extra cream,' she said with a smile as she made her way to the counter.

'So tell me honestly. How have you been?' Molly looked intently at her friend. 'Can you feel anything yet? When do you get a bump? I want to hear all about it!'

'Well, I feel like shit. I have no bump, no appetite, and I can't stomach avocados any more, which I'm incredibly sad about,' Emily replied straightforwardly.

'Wow. I'm sure there's some kind of online club or society you can talk to about your avocado betrayal . . .' Molly said smiling.

'I'm not actually ready to laugh about this!'

'Love you . . .' Molly cooed back. 'Anyway, where's Lizzy-tits? I need that gingerbread latte.'

'Okay. I still love you, but please can you just not talk about gingerbread lattes otherwise I might be forced to stab you to death with the accompanying gingerbread biscuit.' Emily said, breaking into a smile.

'Cool. I both understand and accept that,' Molly said, laughing.

'Gingerbread latte for the horny unwashed one, water for the one with the enormous face!' Liz interjected placing the drinks down in front of her friends.

'So girls,' Emily began, 'I want your advice on something. I've decided I'm going to start a little blog to document my pregnancy. A week-by-week rundown of how I'm feeling, how my body's changing, how Paul's feeling maybe, how we're prepping for the baby. The stuff we're doing and buying . . . You know, that kind of thing. What do you think?'

'Are you just trying to get free shit?' said Liz, dryly.

'Well, a bit. But honestly, I thought it'd be really lovely when the baby grows up and we can show him or her how they started out in life, and all the wonderful things we did before they were even born . . . And get a free pushchair. Obviously.'

'How much do pushchairs even cost?' added Molly.

'You could easily spend a grand,' replied Emily.

'A. GRAND.' Molly's mouth dropped open in astonishment. 'Seriously? A thousand pounds . . . Are they made out of frigging unicorns or something? I could go to India for three months for that! Wow. I had no idea.'

'I know,' said Emily. 'Motherhood is expensive. But it's also amazing, and wonderful and worth every penny. I'm actually looking forward to shopping for this beautiful little person. It's starting to feel so real now.' She rubbed her tummy. 'I think it'd be nice to share this stuff with other people who've just found out they're pregnant too. Don't you think?'

'Hey – if I knew I'd need to take out a mortgage just to push my kid around, I'd wanna know ASAP that's for sure!' joked Molly.

'Well,' added Liz, 'I think if you're going to do it, then you should actually be "real". There's enough bullshit out there on the Internet as it is making out it's all a breeze.'

'Well, for some people maybe it is?' said Emily, slightly irritated by Liz's negativity.

Liz leaned in a little and lowered her voice. 'Do you want to know what's real? I went for a coffee with my sister and my two nieces a few weeks ago. I headed up to get our drinks from the counter, and in the meantime, while my sister breastfed her five-week-old, Clover, my darling two-year-old niece, decided to take the opportunity to remove her trousers and curl off a turd the size of a Toblerone in the middle of Starbucks. Knowing full well her mum was entirely incapacitated and could only look on with utter embarrassment as she started prodding it with a Tombliboo. And shouting, "Look, Mummy. Bum poo. Bum poo. BUM POOOOOO . . ."

'*That*, my friend, is the magical reality of motherhood. All the other shit you read about with actual sleep and floating about in fucking kaftans is total bollocks designed to LIE to prospective parents in order to ensure they get pregnant in the first place.'

As Molly hid behind her drink, pretending not to be laughing at the phrase 'bum poo', Emily decided to ignore Liz, and not worry because clearly this wasn't the sort of thing that would ever happen to her anyway, and dream about her iCandy.

Also, she'd google what a 'Tombliboo' was later when she got back home. She may need to add it to the baby-items list . . .

45

Chapter 8

IF AT FIRST YOU DON'T SUCCEED . . . TEMP.

It was a few weeks later: 9.07 a.m. on a dark mid-December Monday morning, to be precise.

Molly had been in the queue at her regular temp agency for about twenty-two minutes now. Not that she was counting or anything . . .

She sat quietly observing as the waiting area filled up with people who looked young enough for her to have given birth to. Everyone seemed to be a teenager, except her. Why was that?

Surely not everyone in the South Bucks area who'd developed all their pubic hair had a job, did they? It wasn't like she couldn't get a more serious, steady job if she wanted to. She was here out of choice, right? She needed to be able to drop her life at any moment so she could see the world, take off on an adventure . . . Being here was totally by design, Molly reminded herself. A little unconvincingly.

But watching the teenage girls with their heavily make-up-ed faces and the sixteen-year-old boys in front of her in the queue with their unironed shirts, skintight jeans, and slightly greasy, floppy haircuts obscuring their eyes as they fixated on their iPhones, was making her feel uncomfortable today.

They paid no attention to their surroundings as they sat, heads down, waiting for Amanda, the amply-busted-temp-staff recruiter, to call them over and send them off for a day of photocopying or scrubbing pots in a hotel kitchen somewhere.

Molly had done this nearly every Monday. Every Monday for the last two years. It suited her. It wasn't like she hadn't got an education . . . She'd been to university. Three universities, in fact. After failing her first year twice, she'd ended up back in High Wycombe, studying jewellery design right here in her hometown. She'd scraped a 2:2, and headed off on a gap year. Which became a gap 'three years', and after she'd returned she'd just sort of done 'this' . . .

Besides, it was easier to keep under the pay threshold of having to pay back her student loan, and fantasise about heading back across the world than it was to face up to being a proper grown-up. That sounded boring and shit. And expensive.

But hearing her wonderful friend's news about having a baby, and seeing how sorted she'd got herself – nice little house, nice little job, nice little family on the way – Molly couldn't help but wonder, as she sat breathing in a toxic amount of Lynx Africa in the waiting area at Blue Diamond Catering and Office Staff . . . if she should give more of a shit.

Most of the people around her hadn't learnt to drive yet.

They couldn't even buy alcohol legally.

They were probably getting a few days' work in around college so they could buy vape pens off eBay to impress girls wearing tiny slogan-based clothing, and lie to their parents about not having started having sex yet while they borrowed their mum's Volkswagen Passat. If they actually could ever get out of those ridiculously skinny jeans with their penises still intact, that is . . . An erection would probably split a seam if they got excited enough, Molly thought chuckling to herself.

'Molly Andrews?' Busty-Amanda's voice infiltrated her brain just as it was wandering into strange teenage erection territory. 'Molly?' Amanda said again, slightly more arsey the second time around.

'Sorry. Yes. That's me. I was miles away,' Molly said smiling and expecting a friendly smile back. She didn't get one. Busty-Amanda didn't have time for smiling. Busty-Amanda was very busy and important.

'Right – I've got four days in a school in Marlow, working as a kitchen hand. Seven quid an hour, ten o'clock to two o'clock starting today? Okay?'

Molly couldn't quite respond. As she'd risen to her feet to approach the desk she'd suddenly had a rush of nausea. She'd just stood up too fast, she was sure, but right now she was doing her best to get her eyes to focus and not throw up down the rather-well-exposed cleavage bobbing around in front of her.

'Are you okay?' Busty-Amanda asked insincerely, watching Molly attempt to steady herself as the colour began to return to her cheeks.

'Um . . . Yeah . . . I just got up too fast. I'm fine now. Can you say that again?' Molly managed with her hand on her forehead.

Busty-Amanda looked quite put out by that idea. But somehow summoned the strength to repeat herself. 'Four days. Ten till two. School kitchen. Marlow. Okay?'

'Sure. Which school?' Molly said, still feeling slightly faint.

'The primary school next to the train station,' Busty-Amanda snapped back at her impatiently.

'Ah, okay. For a second, I thought you were going to say the secondary school near the high street. I went to school there, so that would have been a bit awkward,' Molly joked. 'Yeah. That would have looked great, wouldn't it? – serving up pasta bake to my old chemistry teacher while I had apple crumble stuck in my hair or something!'

Molly's attempt at friendly banter was met with Busty-Amanda's professional resting-bitch-face.

Ignoring her, Busty-Amanda turned and reached for a freshly printed work roster behind her. She signed it and handed it over the desk. 'Right. Take this. Ask for Mike. And I'd recommend you tie your hair back.'

I'd recommend you go get laid, you miserable cow, thought Molly as she smiled in response.

As she turned to walk out, she noticed none of the teenagers had moved an inch. They were motionless, staring at their phones. It was quite eerie. What were they looking at?

Probably porn, she thought to herself. Hopefully the stitching on those jeans holds up . . .

And with that she headed out the door and crossed the road to the bus stop outside Argos. She knew the buses pretty well by now. She'd catch the 9.26 a.m. to Marlow high street, grab a coffee, and wander down to the school after a decent caffeine injection.

She felt better now. The brisk winter air was filling her lungs. And she'd worked out that for her sixteen hours of probably-very-minimal effort, she'd get £112 and Friday off. With Christmas less than two weeks away.

Excellent.

All she needed to do was stop thinking about teenage erections before she entered a primary school and she was on to a winner.

Chapter 9

BASTARD

Liz's lunch meeting had cancelled just as she'd got across London in a black cab. (Of course. Bastards.) So she'd had the cab turn around and headed back to the office to get through some admin while she had the chance.

She was expecting the usual quiet tapping of keyboards and muffled tones of meetings behind closed doors, but as Liz strode swiftly down the corridor she could sense an uncommon commotion in the boardroom.

Anticipation formed an uncomfortable little knot in her stomach. Had she somehow missed an important email? She was aware she'd been distracted lately. And was hoping this wouldn't be the moment where her colleagues realised she wasn't actually as perfect as she made herself out to be.

It was exhausting keeping up her flawless facade at work. But it was also the one thing that kept her sane. Her reputation as the firm's 'ice queen' who never fucked up, never had a day off, never felt emotion, and never let anyone into her personal life (*bar the one obvious person, that is, but she had been very careful to ensure no one knew about that*), had served her well. And she wanted to keep it that way.

The knot in her stomach quickly untied itself as she reached the door of the boardroom and was met with a sea of party hats, banners and a table of party poppers complete with a ridiculously sized rectangular cake with '40' piped on to it.

'Quick, get in. He'll be back from lunch any second!' a voice from behind her shouted as she promptly tucked herself between Hayley, the two senior partners' PA, and Gerald, one of the newer faces to have graced the corridors of Hoare & Stanton Family Law Attorneys . . .

Yes. Gerald. He must have been working there for almost six months now. She remembered the day he started. It was July and there was a crazy heatwave, and the air-con had decided to pack up. There'd been a lot of sweating. There'd been under-boob moistness while she was wearing a pastel-coloured shirt. And her fringe had gone slightly kinky on one side. It was dreadful.

But no one was sweating now. Thankfully.

Liz looked around the room, which was tightly packed with fully grown men and women, mostly above the age of forty, poised with party poppers and wearing brightly coloured cardboard cones strapped to their heads with cheap elastic. How ridiculous they all looked, she smirked. Then her gaze landed back at the side of Gerald's face. She'd never really looked at him before; she'd never really stood this close to him before. He had a kind face, she thought. And allowed herself to smile a little. And he smelled nice. She breathed him in a little.

'Did you just sniff me?' Gerald's words snapped her

back to reality like a punch in the face. A now very hot and red face.

Liz couldn't muster a response as her cheeks burned. Why was her usually brilliant brain not providing her with some kind of smart and witty comeback? Why was it allowing her to humiliate herself by just standing here mute with her face on fire and her mouth gaping open . . . ?

Gerald turned to face her and smiled. It was all Liz could do to smile back at him and laugh a little to relieve the awkward tension that was hanging there between them.

A loud 'shush' filled the room and the whispers and titters simmered down to silence.

Thank fuck for that. Liz felt her face finally beginning to cool down.

'SURPRISE!' came the cheer as the ribbons from party poppers streamed through the air and the crowd gently dispersed.

Liz finally saw who the surprise party was for. And it hit her like a knife in the stomach.

Not only was it 'him'.

But 'she' was there.

His wife.

The adrenalin was pumping so hard round Liz's body, she could no longer hear the cheers and pops, just the thudding of her own anxious heart, while her brain tried to make sense of what her eyes were showing her.

He had his hand in the small of her back. Gently

guiding her into the room. She looked happy. Comfortable. Relaxed, even.

So did he.

What the fuck?

What was he doing? Why would he do this? Had he planned this deliberately on a day he knew she'd be out of the office?

Her mind was shouting a thousand panicked questions.

Just then.

She noticed.

She saw.

She saw the shape of her body. Her slightly awkward movements and the way she sat to avoid pressure on her belly.

She was pregnant.

Very pregnant.

Liz's stomach was churning and she could feel her eyes beginning to steam up. She needed to get out, right now.

By the time she'd managed to catch her breath, she was choking back ugly tears in the ladies' toilet. She had no idea if anyone had seen her leave. Or if 'he' had even noticed she was there.

She couldn't get her mind to process what was going on. What she'd just seen.

She needed to get her shit together.

She took a few deep breaths, folded a paper hand towel in two and dabbed away the black smudges from beneath her eyes.

All she had to do was make it to her office, then she

could just pretend she had an urgent personal matter and get out of there.

To the nearest bar, where she planned to do tequila shots until she could no longer feel feelings.

Or her face.

Chapter 10

CHRISTMAS DON'T

December was a seriously shit time to be pregnant, Emily was beginning to realise.

It was the last Thursday before Christmas, and tonight was the night of the office Christmas do, and in the immortal words of baby Jesus himself – she just couldn't be arsed.

She was ten weeks pregnant now.

And she was feeling every single nauseous, exhausting, vomit-encrusted one of them.

She still didn't have much of a 'bump'. It was incredibly disappointing . . . If anything, she just looked a bit chubby. And bloated. Or like she'd eaten an enormous roast dinner. Which she would if she could guarantee she wouldn't projectile-vomit it straight back up afterwards . . .

And she just wasn't in the mood for squeezing herself into a sparkly body-con dress while people looked at her like she'd eaten a few too many mince pies. What if she squished the baby? Apparently, it was only the size of a kumquat now. Emily began to wonder if the entire kumquat was spread across her face as that was still the only part of her that seemed to have noticeably expanded . . .

How would she explain why she wasn't drinking? And,

quite frankly, how could she survive the party without the numbing effect of alcohol?

At last year's party, Charles from the London office got a bit 'overexcited' by the vodka luge, and decided it would be a good idea to erotically pleasure it as the studio manager filmed his antics on the company GoPro . . .

It turned out he'd been drinking since lunchtime, after finding out his wife was leaving him, and the entire ordeal ended up with him regurgitating a large quantity of vodka and a selection of recently consumed festive canapés over the managing director's shoes.

It was as epic as it was terrible.

Emily had absolutely no desire to witness anything like that ever again, especially not while sober.

So she'd been putting 'Project Migraine' into operation since around 10 a.m. this morning, which mostly consisted of her spending a lot of time sipping water, rubbing her temples while wincing, and drawing sharp intakes of breath every time a phone rang within six feet.

Matilda had glanced up a few times, but seemed entirely disinterested by Emily's discomfort.

'So, what you wearing tonight, then?' Matilda's question came a little out of the blue as she began putting her scarf and coat on to head out for some lunch.

'Erm. Well. I was thinking black, mid-length and maybe some sparkly accessories, but I think I may have to play it by ear to be honest. I've had a migraine coming on all morning . . .' Emily gave her temples a slightly dramatic double-handed rub. She was rubbish at lying. But she felt she'd managed to lay some convincing foundations for her planned no-show this evening. 'How about you?' Not that she gave a shit.

'I've not really decided yet,' Matilda replied. 'Either short and black, or sparkly, red and knee-length . . . You can't really go wrong with a little black dress, can you, but it's just a bit boring don't you think?'

NO. YOU BITCH.

'Well. You can't beat a classic.'

Matilda threw her a tight-lipped smile, turned on her heels and headed off for lunch. Maybe she'd choke on it.

Time to deploy part two of Project Migraine.

Emily wandered down to Natalie's office. She rapped her knuckles gently on the open door. Natalie signalled her to come in as she finished tapping out an email.

'Hey, Emily. Close the door behind you if you need to. How are you, sweetie?' said Natalie warmly as she pressed send and turned her body to give Emily her full attention.

Emily left the door open. She didn't want this to take too long.

'Well, I'm not too great, actually. I've been suffering with these dreadful headaches the last few weeks and today I'm in agony. I think I need to head home and try to sleep it off if I've got any chance of making it tonight . . .' Emily tried to make her face look as ill and pathetic as possible to back up her story. Which wasn't really that hard, considering she'd had to make a run to the loos only half an hour ago after someone had begun eating a rather pungent tuna and cucumber sandwich in her vicinity . . .

'Oh darling, that's dreadful.' Natalie was genuinely concerned. 'You really haven't seemed yourself the last few weeks, actually. Are you sure there's not something else going on? Have you been to see a doctor or anything?'

SHHHHHHHHHHHIIIIIIIIIIIIIIIIIIIIITTTTTTTTTT.

Did she know? No. That's impossible. She's just being concerned. You need to answer her now or this will start looking weird . . .

'Err, no. I'm sure I'm fine. It's just been a full-on couple of weeks. I'm really looking forward to some downtime over Christmas.'

'Oh God, tell me about it! And hey, just take it easy this afternoon. Head home and get a bit of rest. Don't worry about tonight. The important thing is you look after yourself, sweetie, okay?'

Emily resisted the urge to pump her fist at how awesomely Project Migraine had worked out.

'Sure. Sorry to be such a let-down. I'd be rubbish company anyway. Thanks for being so understanding,' Emily said as pathetically as she could manage.

Natalie smiled and nodded as Emily stepped out of the door and headed back to her desk. She packed her things away with a huge sense of relief, and began to fantasise about a nap, a takeaway curry and mostly not spending the evening having her shoes puked on.

She wasted no time getting herself out of the door, and driving back home to her little house. Once parked up, she quickly made her way inside, out of the cold, and into her lovely warm living room.

She pulled her phone out as she closed the front door behind her and sent a quick message to Paul to let him know she'd be home for the night.

Managed to escape! Woohoo!
No tonic water and pukey shoes for me.
Staying put on the sofa tonight.
Hurry home.
Love you.
xx

And with that, Emily kicked her shoes off and chucked her coat down on the floor on top of her handbag as she sunk into her usual left-hand spot on her comfy, slouchy settee.

When Emily opened her eyes she felt quite disorientated. She hadn't meant to fall asleep on the sofa.

She got herself upright and rubbed her eyes.

She suddenly became aware it was dark.

How long had she slept?

She picked up her phone from the living-room carpet. Wow. It was nearly six o'clock. She'd been asleep for hours.

She rubbed her eyes again and let a series of messages from Paul come into focus:

Paul
Hey babes.
How you feeling?
I thought you were going out tonight
so I made plans with Matt!
Sorry!
I can't really cancel on him now –
he's probably already at the pub.
I'll try not to be too late . . . but don't
wait up for me.
Give bump a kiss for me too.
Love you.
xx

She knew she had no right to be angry with him but Emily couldn't help but feel a little rejected.

He's not an arsehole – he's just going out for a few drinks with his best mate because he thought he'd have the night off while I was at my Christmas party.

But now he knows his pregnant wife is sat at home alone on the sofa while he prances about getting pissed and deliberately not committing to being home at a particular time simply because HE IS A SELFISH BASTARD.

Although he wasn't. And Emily knew that.

But she felt like shit, and had no control over anything that was happening to her body. And right now she didn't have the energy to be rational.

So instead, Emily changed into her pyjamas, made

herself some potato waffles in the toaster for dinner, and set about watching the last three episodes of *The Walking Dead* she had recorded. The ones that she and Paul had promised each other quite explicitly they would be watching together this weekend.

But right now she'd decided she gave no further shits about that, and instead spent the evening texting her husband all the key plot developments and character deaths just to fuck with him . . .

Initially, it had felt really good. But now that he'd stopped reading them, and hadn't responded in over an hour, she just felt a bit silly. And embarrassed. And had a little weep to herself on the sofa for acting like such a bitch.

Chapter 11

A MOLLY-JOLLY CHRISTMAS

It was 10 a.m. on Molly's first-ever Christmas morning with something close to a 'proper' boyfriend in her life.

And it felt amazing.

Molly had never been that bothered about Christmas.

Christmas Day always had a slightly depressing edge to it since her mum had died. She knew her dad would be fine. It had been over five years ago now and he'd just got on with life . . . they both had. And it was sweet how much effort he'd put into making Christmas a special day. But it somehow always ended up the same – the two of them pissed, eating a partly microwaved, fairly average roast dinner in front of his ancient television, watching crap festive telly in paper crowns and bad jumpers . . .

But this year Molly was determined to make things a little more Christmassy.

Because this year she had Tom.

And she couldn't think of a more wonderful way to celebrate Christmas than with her two favourite men in the world, in her home, while she cooked a festive extravaganza and they Christmas-ed the living shit out of Christmas.

The only small problem being that, in typical Molly fashion, she'd left it all to the last minute, and had to fight off a surprisingly feisty pensioner with a stick for the last turkey crown on the shelves in M&S on Christmas Eve, and make a few veg substitutions after under-estimating sprout demand in Tesco . . .

But hey. Her turkey, tinned sweetcorn and 'alternatively blanketed piggies' feast would still be epic.

And, failing that, she'd just get everyone shit-faced and feed them cheese and Quality Street. Those were every-one's favourite bits anyway right . . .

Molly grabbed her phone and started a new chat window with Liz and Emily:

> Happy Christmas you filthy animals!
> I know I say this every year,
> but this year I mean it more than ever
>
> . . .
>
> You beautiful ladies are my best friends.
> And the best people I know.
> And I'd be no one without you.
> And obviously now I've got an actual
> real-life boyfriend you'll have to
> deal with me saying his name in
> every conversation and talking about
> our amazing sex life in
> VERY GRAPHIC DETAIL.
> But I know you secretly love it.
> HAPPY CHRISTMASSSSSSSSSS!
> PS: how do you cook a turkey?

Emily
Love you too, you nutter!
You may go down as the first person
in history to be serving raw turkey for
Christmas lunch!
JESUS WOULD BE PROUD.
Just google it!
And have a drink for me ☹

Molly
Ha – I will!
And I'll be thinking of Baby Jesus
the whole time, obviously.
ARE YOU STILL ALIVE, LIZ?

Emily was right. It was probably time to start googling those turkey recipes, considering Tom and her dad would be here in two hours. She'd also got a Christmas-tree-vajazzle kit off Amazon for Tom's benefit later, but probably best to see how long the parsnips took her before she made any festive-fanny-décor commitments right now . . .

65

Chapter 12

BEING PREGNANT AT CHRISTMAS IS SHIT

> Pregnant at Christmas.
> What an absolute shit.
> No boozy parties,
> just excessive amounts of Smarties.
> While only your dressing gown will fit.
>
> Pregnant at Christmas.
> What a twatty idea.
> Sod the festive magic,
> while you're feeling this tragic.
> Fuck Band-Aid . . . fuck champagne . . .
> fuck fucking reindeer.

Emily was NOT feeling festive.

She'd come to realise that being pregnant on Christmas Day was probably some of her worst planning ever.

After watching Paul and his parents sink about twelve glasses of Buck's Fizz before it was even mid-morning, and silently fuming as they scoffed cheese in front of her like some kind of pissed-up-cheese-flaunting wankers, she'd decided it simply wasn't fair.

She'd become painfully aware that without alcohol,

Christmas Day morning at the in-laws had very little purpose. Paul's family didn't like to open any presents until the afternoon, and dinner wasn't scheduled until 2 p.m. *TWO. P.M.* There were only so many Twiglets and glasses of Shloer one person could consume.

She was almost twelve weeks pregnant now, and finally her 'bump' was beginning to emerge.

She'd tried her best to squeeze her rounded tummy into a sparkly party dress, but it just wasn't happening. Not without either busting a seam or the use of some kind of industrial-strength corset capable of hiding her oversized uterus up inside her ribcage or something. Either way, it was incredibly uncomfortable and absolutely did not appeal to her right now.

So she'd opted for option B – the oversized comedy festive jumper and leggings. Complete with flashing Rudolph nose and an excessive amount of polyester.

It wasn't quite as glamorous as her first choice, but it was certainly easier to get in and out of during the frequent loo trips. During each of which she'd jump on Facebook in the hope something in her news feed would cheer her up, only to find pictures of more smug pissed bastards with their morning alcohol and excessive cheese eating. The shits.

Without booze, she just wasn't enjoying Michael Bublé on repeat in the same way she usually did, and if Paul's sister sang at full volume to the high bit in Mariah Carey's rendition of 'All I Want For Christmas' one more time she was going punch her in the throat.

67

Every time she tried to feel festive she just got angry.

She knew Paul had noticed. But she also knew that he needed to be the dutiful son, and spend some time with his family, as well as looking after her and listening to her ridiculous teary rants about missing prosecco . . .

No one was letting her do anything. Paul's mum had insisted she sat on the sofa as she buzzed around her with a cooking apron on, plumping and dusting things in between bastings like some kind of festive bee on crack.

She'd even ordered in every type of adult soft drink known to man, purely to give Emily something nice to drink in the absence of wine, which was really sweet. Even if her fridge did look like she was launching a festive juice bar to service the entire neighbourhood . . .

'If you're tired, why don't you go for a nap, babes?' Paul said soothingly as he sat down next to her.

'I'm not tired, I'm bored,' Emily grumbled. 'I want to get twatted and belt out Mariah while spooning Alpine soft cheese into my face but your fucking baby won't let me.'

Paul threw his head back and laughed. 'It's *our* baby. And you're doing an amazing job keeping it safe for us. If you really want to, then have a small glass of prosecco. One isn't going to hurt. And if it makes you happy and shuts you up, I'd say it's well worth it!'

Emily smiled. He was right. A few sips of fizz on Christmas Day wasn't the end of the world. She was being a bit of dick about it.

'Okay,' she announced firmly and rose to her feet.

She wandered into the kitchen as Paul followed after her. She was a little terrified to touch anything, as Paul's mum furiously stirred, chopped and prepped things she wasn't sure she even recognised . . .

She spotted the open prosecco and glasses by the sink and headed over, careful not to disturb anything. She poured herself half a glass and sipped it triumphantly.

Weirdly, and rather disappointingly, it didn't feel quite as wonderful as she had hoped . . .

In fact, after about four sips she felt slightly ill and racked with guilt. She tipped the rest down the sink and decided she felt so guilty she'd probably have to go and have a small cry and take that nap now.

Just then her pocket buzzed. It was Molly.

Seeing her friend's messages cheered her up instantly. At least dinner here was not likely to give everyone salmonella poisoning or be accompanied by tinned veg and hotdog sausages. Emily smiled to herself.

And with that, she finally felt a bit Christmassy . . .

Chapter 13

ARNEE LIZ IS BACK

Liz knew that her friends were busy.

And happy.

And she hadn't really wanted to bother them and bring them down with all the crap she had going on in her life right now.

Besides, she'd barely looked at her personal phone the last couple of weeks. It was a pathetic stream of grovelling messages, and emails and voicemails and missed calls (and every other form of communication you could access via a mobile phone) from a certain giant shithead she had no interest in having any contact with ever again for the rest of her life.

She'd worked from home since 'that day', and then on Christmas Eve she'd driven herself down to near Winchester to stay with her sister for the festive period. It felt good to have a change of scenery. And distract herself by spending time with her nieces.

Tiny children made it easy to forget that being an adult is mostly shit and full of disappointment. Toddlers are brilliant, amazing balls of energy and innocence that can keep your mind off even the shittiest of shits just by being themselves. Liz had enjoyed being reminded of that. And that there's absolutely nothing wrong with having jelly and cheesy puffs as a key part of your diet at breakfast, lunch and dinner . . .

Despite the crap going on in her personal life, it really had been a wonderful Christmas, with all the attention on the children and away from her. It was exactly what she needed.

But tomorrow was New Year's Eve and she'd promised Molly and Emily that she'd go to Emily's New Year's gathering. Emily had insisted on calling it a 'gathering', rather than a party, which was a little concerning and did imply that instead of alcohol they might all be forced to have smoothies and eat tofu. It was the kind of ridiculous shit that came up on Pinterest if you searched for 'how to still have fun on NYE when you're pregnant'.

Hmmm. Hopefully unlikely though, Liz thought to herself. But perhaps she'd sneak in a hip flask of gin and pack some crisps in her handbag just in case . . .

Liz headed up to the spare room she'd been staying in and lifted her suitcase on to the bed. As she began packing her clothes neatly into the bottom of the case, reality started to creep back into her head . . .

She knew she was going to have to face it all soon.

New Year's Eve vegan smoothies aside, it was only a few days until she'd be back at work. Back in the same building as 'him'.

And sooner or later, she was going to have to find the

71

strength to speak to him without losing it. And/or violently assaulting him.

'Arnee lizzzzzzzeeee . . .' came the small but surprisingly piercing call from the bottom of the stairs.

'Yes?' Liz called back, quite happy for the interruption.

'ARNNEEEEE LIZZZEEEEEE. Hideee-Seek!!' Clover's voice filled the house. It was impressive, for a two-year-old.

Liz decided the packing could wait.

She'd learnt very quickly that when a two-year-old calls you for a game of hide-and-seek you better drop whatever you're doing and try your best to convincingly 'not' find them.

Even while they stand in plain sight, 'hiding' with their hands over their eyes. It's an Arnee's duty.

Liz opened the door to her flat and felt pleasantly relieved to be home. Her cat, Jasper, appeared at her feet, weaving and purring round her ankles as she made her way inside. He was fat and spoilt from a few days of tinned salmon and treats from the lady across the hall who'd been looking after him.

The journey back had felt long. Her neck and shoulders were stiff from the increasing anxiety she'd felt as she'd headed up the motorway. But that feeling had swiftly dispersed as she'd got back into the familiar surroundings of her apartment in Wooburn Green.

Despite being utterly in love with her nieces there came a time in every auntie's life where they needed to go back

ARNEE LIZ IS BACK

to somewhere quiet, calm, and both glitter and Ninky Nonk free.

Liz's flat was as immaculate as she was. Minimal, monotone, modern and not a cushion out of place.

She wheeled her suitcase into her bedroom and flung herself backwards on to her well-made bed. The cat followed suit, nuzzling at her hands and curling up on the bed next to her.

She sighed deeply. It was going to take a lot of mental strength to get through the 'gathering' tonight. She could quite honestly drift off to sleep right now and not wake up again until the next afternoon. But a promise is a promise. And this was technically the 'last' Last Saturday Club of the year, so her friends weren't going to let her get away with missing it.

Liz sighed and sat herself up. She pulled her phone out of the zip pouch at the front of her case. She knew Molly and Emily had been trying to contact her. She'd felt bad ignoring them but she'd needed the space.

But now, it was time to finally make contact with them again before they started sending out search parties:

I'm back . . .
Sorry I've not been in touch.
Needed some time away
from everything.
Will explain tonight . . .
Or will just get so drunk
I don't care any more

and lose the power of speech
via tequila.
Right now I'm thinking option B!

Messages sent; Liz got on with unpacking. It didn't take long for the responses to come flying back.

Emily
OH. MY. GOD.
I must have sent you about 30
messages!!
I'm very glad you're not dead.
Are you okay???
Is it him?
I'm sorry things are shit, babes
are you sure you're okay to come
tonight?

Liz
Definitely not dead.
I'll be okay.
Don't worry.
Want to see you guys tonight.
I've missed you.

Molly
I didn't think you were dead.
But I'm still glad you're not if that
counts ☺

Liz
Very touching.

Molly
I will fill you with excessive alcohol
and make sure your New Year starts
with an epic hangover.

Liz
I know I can count on you xx

Molly
Can't wait to see that bump Emily!

Emily
Well.
You can't miss it now.
I pretty much look like someone's
stuck sequins all over a potato with
giant knees.
And no ability to see their own pubic
hair any more.

Liz
Ooh. How festive.

Emily
Ha! See you at 7.
BE. ON. TIME. MOLLY.

Chapter 14

NEW YEAR'S TEARS
(AND UNEXPECTED DALE)

Liz picked Molly, Tom, and Tom's unexpected friend 'Dale' up in a taxi. Liz knew taking charge of the travel was the only way she could guarantee Molly would get there by midnight.

They smiled and made chit-chat during the journey, but there was an elephant in the room. They just needed to get to Emily's house, and Liz could talk to her friends and kick that big grey bastard out.

The taxi pulled up outside and Emily opened the door as her friends emerged from the back seat, looking glamorous and sparkly, and clutching bottles of alcohol.

Molly strode up the path first, enjoying the unfamiliar sensation of arriving somewhere on time for once. Liz followed directly behind with Tom and Unexpected-Dale a few paces after her as they headed into Emily's house.

Tom had clearly been briefed as he took himself and Unexpected-Dale off to find Paul and disappear into the lounge, leaving the three women in the kitchen.

'So . . .' said Emily, passing both her friends pre-poured glasses of prosecco and deciding to get straight to the point. 'Are you okay, Liz?'

'Not really.' Liz took a large glug of her drink. Then

released a long sigh before allowing the words she's been storing up for so long to pour from her.

'I'm not really okay at all. In fact, I'm shit. Totally shit. He's a lying, cheating, dick-bag of a man, who didn't even have the decency to let me know that instead of *leaving* his wife, like he'd absolutely promised me he would be, he would instead be impregnating her. Several months ago. And parading her around the office like a fucking pregnant trophy to symbolise how awesome his really quite pitifully sized penis is, just so absolutely everyone could know just how shitting perfect his life is. And the worst bloody part?' Liz continued, choking back tears.

'She's beautiful. She looks happy. They looked happy. I had her pictured in my head as this sour-faced, sad, lonely woman who was angry that her life was a farce, and I very quickly realised that that's not her at all.

'That's *me*.

'It's all been utter shit. All of it. And even though a part of me knew it was bollocks, I just kept believing him and thinking that if I gave it another few months it'd be over between them and we'd be able to be a real couple. A proper couple. Not the dirty, disgusting secret we'd become, so he could shag me while she carried his fucking child inside her.

'It makes me feel sick every time I think about it. I can't believe I've wasted two years of my life with that prick. I'm so ashamed of myself.' Liz's head dropped as she let the tears flow down her face.

Her friends both grabbed and hugged her.

'Look at me, Liz,' Emily said gently. 'You have absolutely nothing to be ashamed of. All that shame is on him. You know now. Now is the time to get the fuck away from him and find someone who makes you feel as wonderful as you really are.'

Liz nodded as Emily held her gaze intently.

'Has he tried to contact you?' Molly asked.

'The only thing he hasn't tried is sending a fucking carrier pigeon,' Liz said, managing to smile through the tears. 'But I've ignored him. I don't even know how I've done it some days, but I've stayed strong. I haven't even read the messages. I don't want to. I don't even want to give him a chance to explain, because what is there to explain? He used me. He made an idiot of me. Why would I want to go back to that? I'm so much better than that. I should've done this ages ago. But now I really know I can. Because I am. I'm stronger and better than all of this. I just need to keep believing it.'

Molly handed Liz a tissue and topped up both their glasses from the open bottle on the side.

'Honestly, you really are,' Emily said, smiling at her friend. 'We've always known that. You've always known that. This is the end of all that shit. This is it, sweetie. You're the strongest person I know . . . I know you can do this. And we're there for you one hundred per cent.'

'Right. Fuck this. I propose a toast,' Molly announced suddenly and triumphantly. 'Goodbye to this total dick of a year. And goodbye to that total dick. Next year will be the year that my beautiful, smart, quick-witted friend finds both love and happiness. Now – FUCK HIM. Let's get twatted.'

'You are the voice of sheer beauty and eloquence, Molly,' said Liz, feeling her tears drying up and the weight lifting from her shoulders. It felt like she could breathe properly for the first time in two weeks. 'Thank you, ladies. I love you both.' Liz embraced both her friends again before wiping the last few tears away and raising her glass. 'Now – let's get twatted.'

The three friends clinked glasses and sipped their drinks.

'Clearly, I shall be allowing you ladies to enjoy all the twattery on my behalf for obvious reasons . . .' Emily was a little underwhelmed by her virgin mojito (she'd found the recipe on Pinterest) ' . . . but you know I'm with you in spirit.'

'Now, more importantly . . .' Molly gave Liz a playful nudge. 'What do you think of Dale?'

'Well, he's got a tattoo of a monkey holding a spoon on his face, Molly,' Liz said dryly.

'What? He's hot! He's in a band!' Molly hoped that this might be the turning point for Liz.

'Molly. I'm not fifteen,' Liz responded tersely. 'And I'm sorry, but I generally prefer men who own their own car and don't live in their parents' garages . . . And don't have badly drawn wildlife tattoos on their faces.'

Chapter 15

NEW YEAR, NEW YOU TOO

It was almost midnight.

It had been a great night. There had been a lot of people, a lot of laughter, and thankfully not a tofu smoothie in sight.

Emily was absolutely exhausted, but had decided she would be making it to midnight regardless. It was strange being the only sober one . . . she'd only seen her friends drunk when she was drunk. This was new. And, quite honestly, it was a revelation to learn that no one was as funny or as interesting as they thought they were . . .

Molly had spent most of the night sucking Tom's face off in between stints of bad dancing and random conversation. It was a little sickening. But you couldn't help but be happy for them. They were like a couple of horny teenagers who honestly didn't care what they looked like or what other people thought. You were torn between being slightly jealous of them and wanting to throw up.

Liz seemed relaxed for the first time in for ever. She'd even been flirting outrageously with Unexpected-Dale. The attention was clearly making her feel good about herself. As she should.

It was gone half eleven. Liz watched from across the

dining room as Emily headed into the kitchen to pour champagne for the New Year's toast, while Molly sat down on the stairs suddenly looking very pale.

Liz pushed her way across the room to get to her friend. 'Are you okay, sweetie? Too many cocktails?'

'No. I've barely drunk. I just keep feeling sick at the moment. I think I'm coming down with something,' Molly responded, pressing the back of her palm to her head.

Liz frowned. 'Let's go to the loo. It's nearly midnight so let's hurry.'

Liz held Molly's hand as the two friends headed off to the upstairs bathroom.

Molly put the toilet lid down and sat taking a few deep breaths as Liz closed the door behind them and began rummaging through Emily's bathroom cabinet. She quickly came across what she was looking for and turned to face her friend.

'Do it,' she said intensely as she passed Molly a pregnancy test. 'Don't worry about anyone else right now. You don't even have to tell me if you don't want to. Just do it.'

Molly was shocked. She hadn't even considered she might be pregnant. She and Tom weren't really that careful, so it was possible. But . . . she'd know, wouldn't she? Although, come to think of it, she couldn't even remember when her last period had been . . .

Shit.

Liz could be right.

Molly looked down at the packet, then back up at her friend and nodded.

Liz smiled gently back at her and left the bathroom closing the door behind her.

Molly took in a breath slowly.

She knew her friend was right. She just needed to piss on this bloody thing, see it was negative, and get back downstairs to get wankered with her friends.

Yeah.

It's not that hard, Molly said to herself as she stood up and lifted the lid on the toilet. Just rule it out and get back downstairs like nothing happened . . .

She hoisted up her dress, ripped open the packaging, pulled off the cap and did her best to not wee everywhere.

Like nothing's happened . . . Like nothing's happened . . . Molly kept repeating as she placed the test on the back of the toilet and pulled her dress back down.

She continued to stare at it as the result slowly appeared. She looked at the packet again. A cross for no, two lines for . . .

FUCK.

How could this have happened? Could the test be wrong? That was probably it, right? Oh God, but what if it wasn't? What if she really was . . . PREGNANT . . .

Molly knew she wouldn't have to say anything.

Liz would know from her face the second she walked down the stairs that she'd just discovered she was pregnant.

She had no idea how she felt about it. Other than shocked.

Molly wrapped the test up in toilet paper and put it

in the bin. She added some more loo roll on top to make sure it stayed buried.

As she left the bathroom, she was relieved that Liz had rejoined the party and wasn't there waiting for her. As she reached the top of Emily's stairs she'd heard the countdown to midnight begin.

She quickly jogged down the stairs and back into the room, avoiding any prolonged eye contact with anyone, finding Tom just as midnight struck.

'Hey, babes – Happy New Year,' Tom said, as he pulled her close to him and kissed her passionately. 'I wanted to wait until this moment to tell you something. Molly, I love you. I really do. I'm totally in love with you.'

FUUUUUUUUUUCCCCCCCKKKKKKKKKKK, Molly's mind screamed.

'I've got something to tell you too . . .' said Molly.

Tom stared back smiling at her lovingly.

He was so beautiful. What they had was so perfect, perfect just as it was. Right now. Just the two of them. The *TWO* of them.

'Just . . . that I love you too,' Molly said. 'Can we get out of here? I just want to be with you.'

'Sure,' Tom replied, and kissed her again.

Molly kissed him back. Knowing there was a lot she was going to have to tell him very soon . . .

Chapter 16

THE MORNING AFTER
THE TEST BEFORE

Molly had seen her phone continually lighting up on her bedside table as she lay on her side in bed.

Tom was still fast asleep next to her. But she'd woken up early with a head full of thoughts and questions.

She knew it was Liz messaging her.

She knew what she was going to ask her. But maybe the test had been wrong? She'd just go get another one, and when that showed she wasn't pregnant it'd be fine. This probably happened all the time, right?

She couldn't ignore Liz all day, though . . .

> **Liz**
> ANSWER YOUR PHONE.
> I know you're getting my messages
> . . .
> Are you okay?
> Did you do the test?
> If you want me to fuck off just tell me, you don't have to tell me what the result was.
> I honestly just want to know you're okay?

Molly

Hey – I'm fine.

Reckon that test might have been a dud or something.

Gonna get another one and do it later.

Don't worry.

Liz

As in it was negative?

Okay, cool – well, let me know if you need anything.

I'm here if you need me, sweetie

Molly

Not exactly . . .

Just let me get another one.

Okay.

Liz

Okay. Xxx

Molly knew she wasn't ready to tell Tom about any of this yet.

She crept out of bed and slipped on some comfy clothes. She really couldn't care less what her face or hair looked like. An off-centre ponytail and the remainder of last night's mascara was the most she could manage right now.

The whole world below (or at least High Wycombe high street) felt like it was shut down. As Molly descended the steep stairs down to the street the usual traffic and people sounds were absent and the road empty. It was

New Year's Day, but luckily the big Tesco had its doors open. Complete with a few resentful staff, who'd much rather be in their pants playing with their kids and eating leftover ham . . . but right now Molly was very thankful they were there.

She moved swiftly through the shop, head down, praying no one would notice her heading to the pharmacy aisle and perusing the surprisingly large selection of pregnancy tests.

She didn't have time for this. She grabbed one each of the two most expensive ones and swiped a packet of croissants as she made her way to the till. She pretended to be on her phone as the teenage checkout boy beeped it all through. She didn't want to make eye contact; she didn't want to feel judged. Especially not by someone whose main hobby was probably wanking in front of the Xbox Santa got him for Christmas . . .

Back at her flat, Molly let herself in quietly, glancing through to her open bedroom door and now empty bed. Tom was up but in the shower. Probably wondering where she was . . .

She shoved the pregnancy tests into her coat pocket and headed through to the kitchen clutching the croissants. She'd warm them and make them some coffee.

'Morning, beautiful,' said Tom chirpily, as he headed out of her bathroom, looking ridiculously attractive with only a small towel tucked around his waist, and his dark jaw-length hair gently falling over his face, made black from being wet.

'Morning.' Molly was aware she was staring at his toned and tattooed body lustfully. She loved every inch of him. And he loved her. He'd said the words last night. Right after . . . The reality of the situation smacked her in the face again.

'Do I spy croissants?' Tom said, moving behind her and kissing the side of her neck affectionately.

'Indeed you do. This year we're starting out classy.'

'Ha. Well, after my classy breakfast, would it be okay for me to take my classy bird back to bed and do classy things to her for the rest of the day?' Tom's hands moved smoothly round her waist.

'If you never use the phrase "bird" in association with me or any other female human ever again, I might consider it,' said Molly, laughing, and taking herself swiftly off to the bathroom.

Tom laughed as she closed the door behind her and felt the intense sense of anxiety she'd woken up with return.

She needed to not get distracted by the prospect of mid-morning sex with her ridiculously hot, and slightly damp, boyfriend. She needed to get on with this.

Molly pulled the tests out of her pocket, and quickly scan read and opened them both up. She managed to do both of them, just. There's only so much wee you can produce on demand . . . She placed them both on the sink and stood patiently next to them, distracting herself by staring at the timer on her phone and thinking about Tom's toned stomach . . .

Okay.
Two minutes were up.
Molly picked up the first one . . .
FUCK.
And then the second . . .
DOUBLE FUUUUUUCCCCKKKK.

Chapter 17

THUNDER. STEALING. BITCH.

So. Today was the day.

The day Emily had thought would be incredibly exciting and liberating. But in reality was utterly terrifying and was making her feel as though she wanted to throw up. Although most things were still making her want to throw up so that wasn't anything new . . .

Today was her first day back at work after Christmas, and it was the day she was going to tell work she was having a baby.

She'd taken an extra couple of days' leave so she could have her twelve-week scan and spend a few more days with Paul. But today work and real life was starting up again properly, and it really was all becoming very 'real'.

She'd been playing the scenario over and over in her head for the last week. She'd grab Natalie, casually, before she headed into the 10 a.m. management meeting and just tell her not to worry but she was having a baby. Just like hundreds, thousands, probably even millions, of women do every day, and now it just happened to be her turn. And that was that. Natalie would be amazing about it, she was sure. But her stomach was still doing flips every time she thought about saying the actual words out loud.

Plus, once she'd got that bit out of the way, then it was the announcement to the wider agency. And that was the part she was really dreading. The thought of the inevitably smug look on Matilda's face was already making her jaw tense up.

But she'd arrived now, parked her car on the verge opposite the office entrance, and turned the ignition off. A few deep breaths weren't stopping her heart from pumping or distracting her from the overwhelming sensation to go for a wee. Again.

She felt utterly exhausted from a night spent tossing and turning as her mind would not switch off from the task ahead. But now it was time to suck it up, and get this done.

As she walked down through the office, smiling and greeting a few colleagues on the way down she noticed there was a huddle around Matilda's desk, where Matilda sat beaming amid a swarm of interns who were hovering around her like skinny, flat-chested bees round a bitchy honeypot.

'What's going on?' said Emily as nonchalantly as she could muster.

'She's just got engaged!' squawked skinny-bee number one, gushing as if she had known Matilda her entire life, when in fact all she'd done was bind proposals quite close to her for the past six weeks.

'Oh. Wow . . . Congrats, Matilda. That's really lovely news,' Emily managed, despite the overwhelming sensation of irrational anger that was forming inside her right now.

How dare she steal her announcement day? It was impossible for this to be intentional, but this was just so bloody typical.

THUNDER. STEALING. BITCH.

For the next hour or so, Emily sat listening to Matilda banging on about New Year's Eve . . . whisked me off to Rome . . . Trevi Fountain . . . champagne, pasta, five-star hotel . . .

All Emily could think about was how annoyingly smug Matilda's face looked.

When you dislike someone, it's just impossible to feel happy for them in the way you would someone whose face and voice you can stand to be in the presence of . . .

And if she flicked that giant diamond towards her one more time, pretending to have her hand weighed down from the weight of the rock, Emily may just totally lose her shit and beat her to death with the binding machine while the skinny-bees all looked on in horror . . .

Perhaps not.

Just then, Julie, the office receptionist, called down the office. 'Emily?'

'Yes, Julie?' Julie was wandering towards her, holding a ridiculously impressive bunch of roses and lilies. So enormous that Julie's entire head and torso was obstructed by them.

This was it, thought Emily, a little bit of thunder back in my direction. Thank you, Universe. Thank you, Paul. Emily couldn't help but feel a little smug herself as she smiled and stood up to help Julie.

Before Emily could get fully to her feet to begin her own gushing session, Julie poked her head out . . .

'Can you help me with the next bunch of these? They're all for Matilda, can you believe it? So beautiful! I honestly don't think I've ever been bought flowers like this in my life!'

Emily felt as though someone had suddenly let all the air out of her. She felt utterly deflated and like a total dick for her momentary misplaced smugness. She had no thunder. No fucking thunder at all. Fuck you, Universe. Fuck you, Paul.

What she had was an overwhelming desire to bring up her decaf latte in the unisex loos and go back to bed for the rest of the day.

She glanced at the clock. It was almost ten. She needed to get this done.

She walked over to Natalie's office and tapped on the open door.

'Hi, sweetie. How was your Christmas? How's the headaches? Hope they didn't spoil your break,' Natalie said.

'It was great – do you mind if I close the door? I only need a minute.'

'Sure. I'm due in the boardroom at ten, but I'm all yours until then. Shoot.'

'Well.' Emily closed the door and sat down opposite Natalie. She felt her adrenalin surge again and was trying very hard to not throw up in her own lap. 'I do know what was causing the headaches . . .'

Natalie smiled and continued looking at her, despite

Emily willing her to guess, purely so she wouldn't have to say it out loud first . . .

'Yes?' Natalie probed.

'Yes,' Emily replied. 'It's, erm, well. I'm having a baby.'

'THAT'S AMAZING NEWS!' Natalie jumped up and thrust her arms around Emily in what felt like an entirely honest hug.

Emily felt so relieved.

And slightly ridiculous for worrying so much when she knew Natalie would be nothing other than wonderful about it.

The two women chatted for a few moments before ten o'clock came and Emily headed back to her desk.

Thank fuck for that, Emily thought to herself. And promptly went and threw up in the middle cubicle, bypassing Brian on the way.

Chapter 18

BACK TO REALITY

Hey it's me.
I'm here.
Can we talk?

Liz just let the words hang there for a few minutes.

She cycled through a hundred angry responses in her head but knew there were no words that could adequately sum up how disgusting she thought he was.

She'd been back at work for a week. And had been very relieved to find out he had been on annual leave for the first part of January, so it had been easy to pretend she was okay so far . . .

But she wasn't okay.

She'd deleted every message, every voice note, every everything he'd tried to send her over the last few weeks. But she couldn't hide from him any longer. And knowing he was here in the same building as her right now, and that she'd have to face him soon, had brought back all her anger in a flash.

His nonchalant, unassuming message . . . Did he think he could just say sorry, and that was it? Or worse – did he actually think they were just going to kiss and make up? Carry on as they were now she knew his wife was about to have his child?

The idea that he thought she would ever let him touch her again made her feel physically sick.

But she knew if she was going to get on with her job and her life she needed to do this.

Liz took a deep breath and responded:

> **Liz**
> We clearly have a lot to talk about.
> I can meet at 4 p.m.
> Usual place.
>
> Okay.
> See you there. x

The kiss at the end of his message made her blood boil. But the more he did to make her hate him, the easier this will be . . . Liz thought. And hoped.

As she walked into the familiar bar, heading to that familiar dark corner, looking at the back of a familiar head, Liz felt her strength beginning to leave her.

She thought she had it all planned out. All the words, all the responses, how she'd storm out after saying her piece, feeling so triumphant and high on 'girl power' that if Geri Halliwell herself had been there she'd probably shit herself and give her a round of applause.

But as she'd walked towards the man she hated and

loved so much in equal measure, and saw his face for the first time in so long, she felt instantly wrecked.

She approached him silently. Stood next to him, unbuttoned her coat, and placed herself on the barstool to his side.

For a moment, neither spoke.

She couldn't find any words yet. And needed a moment to gather the courage to look him in the eyes.

'You look beautiful,' he said smoothly.

Liz felt instant anger.

'You look like shit,' she responded instantly, not yet facing him. 'But then, that's more than you deserve.'

'Okay. I know what I deserve, Lizzy,' he said with his head still hung down.

'Don't call me that,' Liz snapped back.

'Look. I just want you to know I never meant for you to find out that way,' he continued pathetically. 'I was going to leave her. Then she announced she was pregnant. And I just couldn't—'

'How gentlemanly of you.'

'I know you're not going to accept what I say.' He was speaking more firmly now. 'But for what it's worth, I do love you. And I never wanted to hurt you, Lizzy. I wish the situation was different. I don't even know if I want this. But—'

'But what? You want sympathy from me? You are so full of shit. I can't believe that I thought I'd come here and you'd say something worth me listening to. You make me sick.' Liz felt tears coming. She willed them away; she wouldn't let him see her cry.

She breathed purposefully for a moment. Then signalled Eyebrows the barmaid to bring her a couple of shots of tequila.

'I know I've fucked this all up. And I know it's asking a huge amount from you to not tell anyone. But I think for both of us, I think we need to move on from this. And pretend it never happened. I mean, unless you think you'd find it easier somewhere else? I have an old friend who's starting a new firm and looking for someone. I could put your name forward . . . I mean, if it's something you want?'

Liz listened to his words, feeling every single one of them stabbing into her. She couldn't believe what she was hearing. Was he actually trying to get rid of her?

Two tequilas arrived. Liz downed one, and turned to look at him.

Finally, she saw it. How pathetic he was. How desperate. In front of her was a lying, cheating, excuse of a man, who was trying so pitifully to manipulate his mistress into removing herself from his life so he could carry on his perfect guilt-free existence and never have to worry about her again,

'That won't be necessary,' Liz responded dryly, maintaining his gaze.

'Look. Just think about it, Lizzy. You don't have to make any decisions right now. Besides, Stanton's about to officially announce his retirement and we all know the partner role is mine. I'm not sure you really want me as your boss. Do you?'

'Now, why would you presume that I'm not going for

partner?' Liz tried hard to display no emotion, even though inside she felt as though she was on fire.

'Well . . .' he scoffed, seeming surprised at Liz's response. 'I don't know. I just never really thought of you as partner material, I guess. Look. We're getting off the point. This is about me and you. And what's best for us now we're going our separate ways. I just think you should think about it. That's all I'm saying.'

'There's nothing to think about,' Liz said. 'I love my job. I'm good at it. I'm as much in the running for partner as you, and perhaps if you feel so awkwardly about having shat on your own doorstep, you should take your friend's offer up yourself.'

Liz broke eye contact and did her second tequila, before gracefully descending from the barstool. She felt like she could finally see clearly. She had a plan now.

She stood up, and looked down at him. Feeling stronger again.

'I've actually got to get going now. Thanks for the chat. And the tequila. I'm glad that you've found someone who'll settle for you, in spite of your underwhelming personality, compulsive lying, below-average penis and under-par sexual technique. However, I'll be investing my energy in finding a man who's previously found the clitoris and doesn't think it's exciting to talk about craft beer. It's not. It makes you a dick. And you should know that once I've made partner, my first task will be to get rid of some of the dicks bringing the firm down and replace them with some rather excellent vaginas.'

And with that, Liz strode out with her head high and her strength fully restored.

Geri Halliwell might not have been there to see it, but an open-mouthed Eyebrows had . . . and by the looks of it she had, rather satisfyingly, very nearly shit herself.

Chapter 19

FANNY FOREST

Here's a little poem
All about maintaining
Your bits and your bobs
While you're growing a baby
Some let it hang out
Some keep it neat
Others couldn't give a shit
While they can't reach their feet
Somewhere in the lady-forest
Is your poor long-lost vagina
With the help of a professional
You can once again find her
Some just get the cream out
To frazzle those hairs
But it's a bit close for comfort
With your labia right there
Some get their other half
To give things a snip
Perhaps some bedtime tweezering
To tidy up each nip
However you do it
You'll soon have plenty to get through

Like producing a f@*king human
That's more than enough to do!

Emily was finally starting to feel better.

She'd made it to the second trimester and had almost stopped regurgitating most of what she was eating. She could even be in the same room as guacamole now. It was quite liberating. Plus she'd bought her first maternity jeans and banished all high-heeled shoes to the same place as her razor . . .

It had been over a week since she'd told work. Natalie had made the announcement in the management meeting after their chat, so the news had filtered down and everyone knew now . . . it was a huge relief. And everyone had been lovely. Even Matilda. (Although she was still a dick. Obviously.)

She felt like she could relax for the first time in months. She could spend her days collating images of tiny pink and blue clothes, and continually entering her details into the BabyCentre due-date calculator just to make sure nothing had changed. Which it never did, but it kicked the shit out of doing any actual real work . . .

She carried round the printout from her first scan in her wallet. She looked at it continually, it made it feel so real. She loved seeing her baby in there for the first time, floating around and doing little flips and somersaults. They had a date. Something to work to: 17 July.

For the first time, she felt like she was beginning to 'enjoy' it. Especially now she had stopped throwing up every morning and barely had to move from her desk as everyone just seemed to want to 'do stuff' for her . . .

She'd only been at work for an hour on a crappy, miserable Tuesday January morning and already three people had offered to make her a cup of tea, Lisa from HR had given her a special back support for her chair and one of the annoyingly thin work experience girls had offered to give her a shoulder massage.

Why hadn't she got knocked up before?

Yes. She was relaxing into it now. This next bit would be a breeze. Tonight she'd already planned an epic evening of researching NCT classes, signing up to antenatal Pilates and finally writing her first blog post.

Something she'd been waiting to do once she was reasonably certain she wouldn't throw up all over her laptop.

Emily removed her coat and shoes with a big tired sigh as she arrived home from work and plonked herself in her usual spot on the sofa.

She'd been willing the day to finish so she could get home and begin work on her blogging masterpiece. She'd been Pinteresting the shit out of this for weeks already. She was ready to create something beautiful . . . And, most importantly, start work towards getting a free iCandy pushchair. The real goal. The ultimate reward. Every pregnant woman's dream . . .

She fished her laptop out from down the side of the sofa and made herself comfy as she placed it on top of a cushion and opened it up.

She'd already created herself a blog page and titled it 'My Baby Journey'. Now all she needed to do was write something, and they'd come. (Hopefully.)

She began typing:

Prepping for Baby:
A Mummy-To-Be's List

Hello everyone . . .

She deleted it.

Ladies . . .

Deleted it.

Hey, Mammas . . .

Yuck. Not that.

Yo . . .

Oh God that was worse! DELETE.

Hi Mummies,

Yes. Okay . . . That's the one . . .

My name is Emily and I'm fourteen weeks pregnant with my first child.

Finding out I was pregnant has been one of the most beautiful and magical experiences of my life. I still can't quite believe this is really happening to me!

But I want to document all the amazing, beautiful, magical moments of my pregnancy and baby journey right here in my own little corner of the Internet.

I hope you enjoy reading it as much as I'm enjoying becoming a Mu

Emily had to stop quite suddenly there as she'd felt the extra-cheesy chicken burrito she'd eaten for lunch decide it actually preferred being on the outside of her body, quite urgently.

She made her way quickly to the downstairs loo and took up a familiar position.

Yep. Truly magical . . . she thought to herself as she finished emptying the contents of her stomach into the toilet and rose to her feet again.

As she began washing her hands and face over the sink she heard Paul come into the kitchen and place his keys on the side.

'Hey babe. You okay?' he called through the utility room to the slightly ajar cloakroom door.

Emily felt instantly tearful.

Paul made his way to the door and opened it, hearing her crying.

'Hey – what's wrong? Are you okay?' he asked gently, moving her curls to one side and rubbing the top of her back.

'I'm okay,' Emily managed through the sobs. 'It's just . . . It's just . . . I've thrown up so many times. I'm so bored of feeling like shit. And being sick. Every time I throw up it feels like I'm going to wretch our unborn baby up out of my nose. THROUGH MY NOSE, PAUL. A FOETUS THROUGH MY FUCKING NOSTRILS. I can't stop crying. Why can't I stop crying? I hate this. I hate being pregnant.'

'You don't hate being pregnant. You're doing so amazing. You are so brilliant at being pregnant you don't even realise it. Come here and give me a hug.'

Emily turned to face him, the tears rolling down her face as she tried to suck air into her lungs in little bursts between the sobs . . .

'I honestly don't think I can take any more of this. Every day I get a little bit fatter and can see a little bit less of my vagina. Do you know what that's like, Paul? Do you? The idea that in only a few weeks' time I won't be able to see my own fanny any more? I think my vagina actually hates me . . .' She let a little smile break through the tears as she dabbed her eyes. 'It must do. It's grown its own pubic defence forest so no penises can come near it ever again. That's what's happened, Paul. THAT'S WHAT'S HAPPENED.'

They both laughed.

'I saw your laptop as I walked in. I'm glad you've finally

started your blog. I reckon your vagina situation is prime material for it,' Paul said with a wink.

'Ha!' Emily responded. 'Hmmm . . . iCandy probably wouldn't be that impressed with that. Probably best to stick with the beautiful and magical vibe and keep clear of the fanny forest for now, I reckon.'

Chapter 20

AND THEN THERE WERE TWO . . .

It had been nearly four weeks since Molly had found out she was pregnant . . .

And she still hadn't told Tom. She was using 'Dry January' as an excuse for not hitting the vodka, and it was working well, but she felt beyond terrible for not telling him.

It was killing her.

But every time she thought she'd plucked up the courage to say something to him, she just couldn't do it. She knew it was a pathetic excuse, but she just didn't want to ruin everything. Or worse, lose him. The thought of him leaving her made her feel sick. Just thinking about it gave her heart palpitations.

It wasn't just Tom she was avoiding speaking to. She'd been fobbing Liz off with excuses since she'd done the tests on New Year's Day, but she couldn't do that any longer. She felt exhausted by the whole thing. If she didn't say something to somebody soon she was going to explode.

She'd finished her crappy admin job on a nearby business park for the day, and was walking back to her flat. She pulled her phone out of her coat pocket as she strode along the high street and decided it was time to open up to Liz and Emily.

Molly

Hey. Are you guys busy tonight?

Can you come over?

I really need to talk to you.

xxx

She tucked her phone in her pocket as she arrived home and made her way up to her front door. She already felt better just for sending the message. Once inside, she walked straight into her bedroom to change into something comfy. Her feet were killing her and she needed to get out of her bra immediately before it bonded with her ribcage.

Molly threw her phone on the bed as she pulled out a chunky knit jumper, some patterned leggings and a fresh pair of socks. At least, as fresh as socks got for Molly, that is . . .

She saw her phone light up as she quickly changed her clothes. She knew it wouldn't take her friends long to get back to her.

Liz

Hey you. Of course.

I won't be back until about 8, though?

Can come straight from the train . . .

Hope you're okay xxx

Emily

8 p.m. is cool for me.
Although I'll probably be asleep
by 9.30, just to warn you! lol
I'll eat and come round.
Are you okay?
Is it Tom?
Do you want me to bring anything?

Molly

I'm fine. Tom's fine.
Don't worry about bringing anything.
See you at 8.
Love you guys.
Thank you xxx

It was 7.57 p.m. and Molly heard the abrupt buzz of the entry phone.

She pressed the door release and held it until she heard expensive heels clip-clopping up the stairs.

Molly opened her front door and watched as Liz's perfect parting made its way up towards her.

As Liz reached the top, she looked at her friend with a gaze that needed no words: *'I know'*. Of course she knew. She'd known before Molly knew . . .

Liz hugged her. And swiftly made her way inside.

'Still living like you've just been burgled then . . .' Liz remarked, trying to bring a smile to her friend's face.

'A place for everything, and everything in its place.'

'And this?' Liz said, holding up a sock of dubious colour in between her fingertips that she'd removed from the arm of the sofa. 'Does this belong here? Right here?'

'Piss off. It's Tom's, I think . . .' Molly said, squinting at it.

'I'm intrigued to know how he managed to leave here only wearing one sock . . .' Liz said grinning.

'Well, he doesn't wear much while he's actually here, and that's all I'm really concerned about,' Molly smirked.

'Too much info, thanks!' Liz said, and perched herself neatly on Molly's sofa.

The entry buzzer sounded again.

Molly was relieved. She was glad Emily was here now. She could finally get this over and done with.

Emily climbed the stairs a little less gracefully than Liz had. She was breathing hard as she reached the top.

'Seriously. You have just confirmed why stairs are no longer my friend. And I'll be remaining on one level for the rest of my pregnancy,' Emily managed through strained breaths.

Molly sat her down next to Liz on the sofa to catch her breath.

She stood in front of her two friends feeling a little like she was being interviewed . . . Or was expected to break into interpretive dance or something . . . Their gazes were intense and full of anticipation.

'I'm just going to cut straight to it,' Molly said purposefully, not wanting to waste any time. 'So . . . It seems that you might not be the only one, Emily, who is, in fact . . .

Well. I mean. I don't know how this happened. But the thing is, I did the test. Well, a lot of tests actually, and, umm . . . Oh God, I don't know why it's so hard for me to just tell you this!

'Right.

'Here goes . . .

' . . . I'm pregnant.'

Molly spat the last sentence out and stared intently at her friends waiting for their reaction.

'WHAT?' Emily blurted out loudly after a short pause. Her mouth dropped open and her eyes were wide as she tried to digest what Molly had just told her.

'I know,' Molly said. 'It wasn't planned. I haven't told anyone yet. I don't know how to do this.'

'WHAT?' Emily said again, shaking her head a little. Still open-mouthed.

'So, when you say you haven't told anyone yet, you have told Tom though, right?' Liz said, her eyes on Molly as she came and sat down next to them.

'No,' Molly said sheepishly. She hated admitting it.

'Ohhhh . . . kay . . .' Liz said slowly. 'Well. Do you know how far along you are? Have you seen a doctor? Are you okay?'

'How are you not in shock?' Emily said to Liz.

'I kind of . . . knew,' Liz replied. 'I made her do a test at yours on New Year's Eve. I knew when I didn't hear from her that it must have been positive.'

Emily looked a little bewildered. This was a lot for her already scrambled-by-pregnancy mind to take in.

111

'I don't know what to do . . .' Molly finally said. 'I have no idea when my last period was. You're the first people I've said anything to. I just feel like this is totally the wrong time. I love Tom. It's not that. But we haven't even been together that long. It's only been eight months. And I don't even have a steady job. Or a car. And Emily said that prams cost a grand. And she keeps throwing up in bins. And I live above a fucking tattoo shop.'

'Look,' Liz said calmly. 'You're getting way ahead of yourself. You haven't even told Tom yet. He loves you. And you don't need to make any decisions about anything until you've spoken to him.'

'She's right.' Emily reached out and stroked Molly's forearm reassuringly. 'You're trying to tackle this by yourself and you don't have to. Okay. You didn't plan this. But it's happening. And you and Tom are going to work this out. Together. And be amazing parents. And we're going to have little babies at almost the same time. And that's actually quite awesome. In fact, it's brilliant timing if you think about it. Ooh. Do you want to see my Pinterest boards?'

'Emily!' Liz snapped.

'Sorry. Got carried away.' Emily pretended to zip her mouth closed and sank back into the sofa.

Molly smiled. 'You're right. I need to talk to him. I mean, I knew that, but I think I needed someone to say it to me out loud. You know what? I feel so much better just for telling you girls. I think this was the kick up the arse I needed! Thank you.'

'Hey – we haven't done anything. You just needed to talk.' Liz blew out a long breath. 'Wow. This is all such big stuff. Can we go back to thinking our biggest problem was what colour Body Shop lipstick to wear with our halterneck tops and how to skive off Games?'

'Well,' Emily said laughing. 'Firstly – Heather Shimmer. Every time. Obviously. And secondly . . . If I recall correctly, you spent most of school downing Southern Comfort in the girls' changing room and asking people for a high five . . . before slapping them round the face and calling it a "face five", then laughing and running away . . .'

'Oh yes!' Molly laughed. 'I'd forgotten about that!'

'I don't know what you're talking about.' Liz straightened up and tried to disguise her smile.

'Ha!' Molly exclaimed. 'And, don't forget it wasn't that long ago that I had to explain to you that quinoa wasn't actually pronounced "qui-no-a". Remember?'

The three friends fell about laughing, dabbing their eyes as little tears of joy squeezed out of them.

'So . . .' Emily said, getting her laughter under control finally and raising her eyebrows at Liz. 'It seems like you're the only one of the three of us without a human in your uterus now . . . I think you better hurry up and find yourself a fertile man. I'm pretty sure Tom's friend Dale with the face tattoos could provide you with some pretty potent sperm . . .'

Liz fired a sarcastic glare right back at her friend, 'If I want to jump on a bandwagon, I think I'd rather go gluten-free or buy a vegan cookbook.' She snorted. 'Given the choice, pumpernickel bread will always win against a human being tobogganing its way through my cervix. Thanks.'

Chapter 21

TIME TO TELL TOM

Being nervous, or stressed, or in fact giving any real-life shits about anything of any kind, was just not something Molly was used to.

It had been hard enough telling the girls about her little 'secret'. But now came the really hard bit.

Telling Tom.

And he was due to arrive at her flat in ten minutes.

Ten minutes.

Ten tiny, panicky minutes for her to work out exactly how she was going to explain to him that, instead of their usual Friday night 'naked Twister' party for two, she'd instead be informing him he was about to become a father . . .

She just couldn't get her brain to find the right words.

Or any words at all . . .

Molly jumped as the door buzzer interrupted her thoughts.

She opened her front door as she pressed the button on the entry phone. Tom's familiar face appeared at the bottom of her stairs and started climbing up towards her.

'Hey,' he said smoothly as his eyes caught hers.

He reached the top in no time and planted a long,

lingering kiss on Molly's lips then stepped inside her flat and began removing his coat and scarf.

'We need to talk,' Molly said quickly, almost taking herself by surprise.

'Okay,' Tom said casually. 'That sounds ominous. Should I keep my coat on?' He was smiling but Molly could tell he was sensing her discomfort.

'No. God no. Ummm . . . You might be here a while, actually.' Molly was keen to get to the point, although she still couldn't quite find the words to take her there.

'Phew. I thought I was for the chop!' Tom laughed.

Molly couldn't manage to laugh back. How could she? What was funny about this? She was about to ruin everything.

Tom sat himself down on her sofa and patted the space next to him, gently signalling for her to sit by him.

'What's up?' Tom pushed a wayward strand of hair off her forehead.

Inside all the words were screaming to get out of Molly's mouth. Why was it so hard to make them come out? She sat staring into his big dark eyes wanting so much to not have to say what she knew she was about to . . .

'I'm pregnant.'

The words suddenly flew out.

And just hung there.

There was no taking them back now. Molly held his gaze and watched helplessly as his eyes widened and he slumped back on the sofa covering his face with his palms.

He slowly let his hands slide down his face until he was peering through his open fingers.

He looked at her.

But still said nothing.

He removed his hands and Molly could see his mind was racing. She saw the panic and the disappointment pasted all over his face.

She instantly regretted telling him. She wanted to take it back. But she couldn't. She wasn't sure what to say next. But she had to say something. It was too uncomfortable.

'I don't really know how far along I am. Maybe eight weeks? I'm honestly not sure,' Molly said trying to invite a response.

Tom still hadn't said anything. Molly really needed him to.

'Can you say something, please? Anything?' she pressed.

Tom dragged both his hands through his rain-soaked hair and let out the breath he'd been holding.

'I . . . I don't know what to say, babes. This has come as a bit of a surprise. I . . . erm. I don't know. What are you going to do?' He eventually managed.

'If by "do", you mean am I going to get rid of it? Then no,' Molly replied, tersely. 'I won't do that. But I'm glad your first question about our unborn child has been whether or not I plan to terminate its life. Thanks for the support.'

She rose to her feet. She knew he was freaking out. And that he was saying all the wrong things because of

117

that. But she needed him to leave. Before he said something that made it even worse.

'I think you should go, Tom. It's obvious you need some time.' She couldn't look him in the eye.

Tom paused for a moment, then swiftly picked up his coat and scarf and walked out without a word. The door swung closed behind him and Molly listened as his feet clumped quickly and heavily down the stairs.

For a moment, she just stood there. Even though she'd asked him to go, she didn't think he actually would.

She thought he'd put up a fight. Protest that he loved her. Tell her that he'd do anything to support her. But he hadn't.

He'd just left.

He'd quite literally run away.

It was fucked.

Everything was fucked.

And she couldn't even get drunk to make herself feel better.

Chapter 22

DUVET DAY

Molly
Hey girls.
I'm not sure I can face Last Saturday
Club today . . .

Emily
First Rule of Last Saturday Club!

Molly
I KNOW.
I invented those pissing rules!
But I honestly can't face it.

Emily
Second Rule of Last Saturday Club!

Molly
Okay.
You need to piss off now.
It didn't go well with Tom . . .

Liz
Shit. What happened?

Molly

Not much.

I told him.

He left.

That was last night.

Haven't heard from him since.

Emily

Oh sweetie, that's awful.

Have you tried to get in touch with him?

Molly

No.

What's the point?

He knows where I am.

He knows how to get in touch.

I know when he's ready he will.

Liz

OMG.

What the fuck is he doing?

WHY. ARE. ALL. MEN. DICKS.

Molly

Not all men are dicks Liz.

Tom isn't a dick.

He's just acting like a dick.

Emily

So you mean . . .

after several months of non-dickish

behaviour he's now making up for it
by being a giant dick-faced shit-bag
of epic proportions.
????

Liz
I think we can all safely say
that I'm the expert
in giant dick-faced shit-bags and
I'm inclined to agree.
Stop being nice, Molly
he's seriously fucked this.

                              Molly
                          I know.
            I just don't have the energy
                  to be angry with him.

Emily
Are you a real pregnant woman?
If Paul had done that to me I would
hunt him down, have his balls sanded
and placed in a jar of TCP.
While I filmed it and used it to
spearhead a new YouTube channel
clearly titled
'WHEN MEN ARE DICKS.'
(Sorry.)
(Just venting.)

Molly

I just miss him.

I feel more sad than angry.

And like this is all my fault.

Liz

Don't you DARE say that.

This one is on him.

He's being a selfish shit.

A shitty selfish shitty shitty shit-head.

It's not like you did this alone?

His penis did this too.

You're carrying his baby.

In your body.

And he can't even be arsed to send you a text??

Emily

What she said.

Molly

Okay.

You make a good point.

But today I'm not moving.

I'm sitting under a duvet with ITVBe,

a yard of Jaffa Cakes and a

multipack of Dairylea Dunkers.

And everyone and everything else

can fuck off.

Emily

We totally understand.
And if you want us to come over later
just say the word.
And let us know if he gets in touch!
(And I now need Jaffa Cakes so
thanks for that.)

Liz
Yes don't worry about today.
Tell Tom he's a shit from us.

Molly
xxx

123

Chapter 23

#TEAMLIZ

Liz had been working late a lot recently.

She'd always worked hard and done whatever hours she needed to. But without 'him' in her life, she suddenly had a lot more time. And a lot more motivation. She thrived off being busy with work, and having no distractions of the 'dickhead variety' was keeping her clear and focussed.

It'd been several weeks since their 'chat', and it seemed like he had finally left her alone. The messages, phone calls and emails had stopped. The only time she saw his name was on group emails, and other than that it was proving pretty easy to pretend he no longer existed. Which was exactly as she wanted it.

It wasn't that hard to avoid each other at work. She'd walked past his closed office door a few times, and he'd probably walked past hers. And that was that.

But today his name sat looking back at her in a clear official typeface written on the line above hers on the roster for partner interviews. In just a few short hours, she'd be welcomed into the main boardroom to make her pitch. Have her shot. And prove to everyone, including herself, that she could really do this.

He would be in there right now, she thought. Confident, qualified, full of bullshit charm. Probably the more desirable candidate, probably the more obvious choice – but she wasn't going to let that bother her. He was still a dick. Albeit a charming dick.

She knew she was young; thirty was nothing in a legal land of pinstriped dinosaurs, and she'd only been with the firm for six years. She didn't lick the partners' arseholes in the way that 'he' did. But she was amazing at her job. She was ambitious. She'd climbed the ranks quickly and efficiently. And Stanton had helped her every step of the way. Right from the moment he'd hired her, he'd seen something in her. And she was going to prove to him that his instincts and guidance were rightly placed.

Yes. She was a 'risk', but you can't effect change without risk. She needed to play this just right. She needed to show them that if they just take a chance on her . . .

She revelled for a moment at the look on 'his' face if she were announced partner. It felt good. It tasted a little like revenge. She might even prepare a little happy dance, maybe she could even twerk . . .

Perhaps not.

Perhaps a quiet, tequila-based celebration would do . . .

Liz's heart thudded almost audibly through her neatly ironed shirt as she sat as upright as her back muscles would allow her to outside the door to the main boardroom.

She did well under pressure. She knew the adrenalin

125

pumping through her body would give her presentation the surge of energy it needed. She just wanted to get in there now.

Liz clutched tightly to her trusty black leather folder containing all her notes and figures. She blew each of her breaths away and watched intently as the second hand ticked round on the wall-clock opposite her.

She was ready for this. She'd tried to put any thoughts of 'him' out of her mind. She'd virtually erased him anyway. She wasn't doing this because of him; she was doing this because of herself.

After a few slow-passing minutes, Hayley, the partners' PA, appeared at the door and invited Liz in with a warm smile.

This is it . . . Liz thought. She stood up, straightened her jacket and walked into the large wood-filled room.

A panel of five men sat at the end of a long, highly polished table. The two partners, dressed in well-tailored suits with aged faces, flanked the group. Hoare looked serious and intense, whereas Stanton looked more like a chubby-faced Father Christmas in a pinstripe three-piece. His eyes always twinkled. Liz decided to focus on him as she presented.

Over the next couple of hours, Liz flawlessly presented her vision for the firm, her ideas, solutions, targets and objectives. The panel nodded along, raising eyebrows and gestured approval at key moments, while the partners occasionally whispered in Hayley's ear as she jotted things down efficiently in shorthand. They asked questions, questions she had all the answers for. It felt brilliant. She felt brilliant. She *was* brilliant.

As she came to the end of her presentation, Liz thanked the room and began putting notes and papers back into her trusty black leather folder.

She hugged it to her chest and smiled to her audience as she prepared to leave the room.

'One last thing,' came a small yet commanding voice from the end of the table. 'Not everyone is an arsehole, Liz. Sometimes you need to let people in a little. To get a little something back from people.'

Stanton's words were friendly but poignant. He had an amazing ability to make something sound light-hearted and incredibly important at the same time. And she knew he was trying to help her, but she wasn't entirely sure how.

Liz acknowledged his words with a forced smile and an understanding nod, but couldn't help but feel a little uncertain. She'd got to where she was by distancing herself from those around her, closing herself off from others, by – quite frankly – being a bit of a cold bitch. Were they saying she needed to thaw out if she wanted to get promoted?

'We think you're quite wonderful, Liz. You are very much the future of the firm. I . . . We are more than sure of it. But you lack one thing,' Stanton continued, as Liz remained glued to the spot.

'If you don't mind me saying, you are a bit of a loner. I don't mean that offensively. I'm sure you have friends

127

and family who would very much disagree with regard to your personal life. But at work, you are out for only yourself. And to lead and make decisions for others, you must be able to help others, and let them help you. Do you understand what I'm saying to you, Liz?'

Liz nodded but remained silent. She didn't agree, but she knew this wasn't the time to argue back. It was time to listen.

'I think, if we are to make a final decision about your future in this firm, you need to first prove yourself as a team player. And as such we will be assigning you your very own team.'

For fuck's sake, Liz thought, but managed to not let her mouth follow suit . . . a little lump appeared in her throat as Stanton's words began to sink in.

'Effective immediately, trainee solicitors Hannah Grey and Gerald Hooker will be assisting you with your work-load and will be under your management.'

Liz gulped. Loudly.

Stanton smiled at her. 'Embrace this, Liz. Warm up a little. Impart your knowledge and let them work with you . . .'

Liz let out a long breath. She stared purposefully down the room and took in each of the five faces staring back at her. There was only one response. She had no choice.

'Well, thank you. I can see you have clearly thought hard about this before today and I'm very happy to accept this opportunity.'

'Excellent,' Stanton replied. 'I'll have Hayley set it up. Some rejigging will be in order.'

'Yes. Rejigging,' Liz said, trying not to let her voice portray what a fucking awful idea she thought this was. 'Thank you again for your time, gentlemen.'

And with that she turned on her expensive heels and swiftly made her way out of the room.

As she walked back to her office she mulled over everything that had just happened.

So, did this mean she had pretty much got the job then? Not officially, but with a few months of pain working with her new 'team', the role was hers. Right?

Liz smiled broadly.

Useless, cheating, craft beer-drinking shithead: NIL.

Liz and her excellent, soon-to-be-team-playing vagina: ONE.

She'd done it.

She'd fucking done it.

And soon 'he' would know she'd done it. And that she was better than him – she'd just proven it.

In celebration, tonight she would drink enough alcohol to knock out a horse. On her own, it would seem, since both her best friends were very selfishly up the duff. But still. This felt amazing. It deserved alcohol.

So. My own team. Team Liz. Hmmm . . .

Liz suddenly felt uneasy again.

Hannah. Keen, young, smart, energetic, could absolutely benefit from some decent lipstick . . .

Gerald. Smart, professional, thirty-ish, handsome, kind face, smells amazing . . .

Liz paused as she felt her cheeks heat up a little.

She cringed a little at that time he caught her sniffing him . . .

Liz smiled.

Oh. Gerald . . .

Chapter 24

HE LOVES ME, HE LOVES ME NOT?

It was the thirteenth of February.

And Molly had just arrived home from another long boring day of temping in an office nearby.

She kicked off her shoes and sank into her couch. And for a moment just sat, motionless in her quiet surroundings.

She hadn't really admitted this herself yet, but she felt a bit lost . . .

Tomorrow was Valentine's Day.

And it had been almost three weeks since Molly had last seen or spoken to Tom. She was trying her best to just 'get on' with things. But if she was honest, she was struggling.

She'd gone from sad to angry to utterly depressed and devastated, and back to angry again. And now she wasn't even sure what she felt.

She'd not even had the time or energy to feel 'pregnant'; she didn't feel any different at all. She was beginning to wonder if she even was pregnant. Her body hadn't changed. Her face still looked the same width. If anything, she looked healthier. Her mind, however, was preoccupied with thoughts of Tom. Or the lack of him . . .

But today she couldn't stop thinking about him, because

tomorrow night would have been their first Valentine's Day together.

Not that Valentine's Day really held much meaning for her. Mostly it had been awkward teenage dates in Pizza Hut, with tacky teddies and cellophane-wrapped roses, before some mild groping in the front of a Vauxhall Nova in a badly lit car park . . . And those were the more glamorous ones.

In the last few years, she and Liz had arranged an annual 'anti-Valentine's' night out where they both got drunk, pulled faces at smug couples looking too loved-up, and talked about how empowered they felt without proper boyfriends in their life . . . Before crying into wanky cocktails served in jam jars and passing out in a loo somewhere.

Molly didn't care about big romantic gestures or expensive gifts, she never had. But having someone she actually loved to spend it with for the first time ever, the thought of it was amazing . . .

But this wasn't amazing.

This was shit.

Utterly shit.

She took her phone out of her handbag and unlocked it. She found Tom's name in her messages, dated from last month, and scrolled through the first few. The reminder of how things were a few weeks ago, how perfect they were, how they could barely go a few hours without texting each other . . . it made her feel so sad. And sorry for herself.

She had managed to resist the urge to contact him up until now. She wasn't sure if on top of everything she was already going through she needed the extra rejection.

But she didn't know how much longer she could stop herself. She was desperate to speak to him. Even if it was only a text. Perhaps it was time to try.

Molly

I miss you . . .
Please text me.
I love you.

She sighed after she'd sent it. Had it been the right thing to do? Perhaps she was making it too easy for him. But she was hoping this was her best chance of a reply.

Molly sat watching her phone for a few minutes.

Nothing came back.

It was like torture.

She was exhausted anyway. She'd just get into her PJs, make some dinner and get an early night.

Maybe he'd come back to her in the morning.

She got up and headed into the kitchen. How could she have so little food in her cupboards? And only food that required major culinary effort, which was totally beyond her right now.

She opened the fridge.

Some mayonnaise, some badly wrapped cheese, a cucumber that had made itself into its own soup in the veg drawer, something beige in a Tupperware that she was definitely not brave enough to investigate, and . . .

. . . pesto.

YES.

She allowed herself a little triumphant fist pump.

You can't go wrong with pesto pasta. Although there was always that moment where you wondered when you did actually first open it, was that furry bit mould or just the pesto? Would it matter so long as you put enough cheese over it?

Fuck it, thought Molly.

And cooked herself a lovely hot bowl of furry green pasta with extra cheese. For the baby, of course.

Chapter 25

BEING PREGNANT ON VALENTINE'S DAY . . . IS SHIT.

Emily 'went big' for Valentine's.

She and Paul always had.

That is to say, she had, and Paul was too scared not to, so he did too. Which was very sensible of him.

And now she was carrying his child around in her uterus, and had spent the last four months without wine while regurgitating all legumes and bread products, he'd better be putting some serious effort into tonight.

Emily had put some groundwork in. Obviously. To ensure Paul knew how vitally important it was that he made her feel special this evening . . . Which had mostly involved her surfing the Not on the Highstreet website and saying 'Ooh, That's nice . . .' loudly and showing him each time she saw something she liked, while he tried to pretend she wasn't there and played Clash of Clans on his iPad.

And in case he needed reminding, she'd been texting him the links to suitable gift and restaurant options for the past couple of weeks to ensure there'd be no disappointment.

Yes. Surely he would nail it tonight, Emily thought to herself as she pulled up outside her little cottage after work as she did every day, but this time, brimming with excitement and anticipation for the evening ahead . . .

She wondered what she might wear, or, more to the point, what would fit. She had quite an impressive stomach girth now. She 'looked' pregnant. Which she was enjoying because it seemed to distract from the size of her face . . .

Once she'd taken off her shoes and coat in the hallway, she headed straight up to her bedroom, where she pulled open the wardrobe doors and began perusing her options . . .

Now that she had an obvious 'bump', she was finding it was easier to look nice in clothes. No more sucking your stomach in and hoping your support tights would keep any escaping rolls at bay . . . No. Letting it all hang out was quite liberating. Or, at least, letting it gently escape over the top of specifically designed maternity clothing.

She'd even ordered some maternity dresses from Isabella Oliver which were still hanging in their plastic packaging, but she felt tonight was the night to forget the baggy tops, and show off her bump in style. Or at least lots of Lycra.

She took out a stretchy black body-con maternity dress and held it up to herself, turning sideways and stretching it over her bump.

She hadn't properly noticed before, but her bottom had also expanded, almost like a counterweight. She guessed that was the point anyway. And her boobs looked suddenly enormous . . . She was going to need to invest in new bras. This one was cutting into her chest, creating four separate breasts where there should only be two. Not a great look. But she certainly had enough breast to go around for both her and Paul now, so at least he'd be happy about that. Not that she'd let him touch them. Obviously. They were agony. Veins were starting to appear. And soon her areolas would be the size of plates . . . so for the moment, her boobs were for display purposes only.

Just then, her phone buzzed in her pocket. She pulled it out and smiled as she saw Paul's name:

Paul
Hey beautiful.
Just leaving
Tonight is all in hand . . . don't worry.
See you and bump shortly.

Emily's smile turned into a beaming grin.

She'd wear the dress. She'd wear heels, even if they killed her. (Which they quite possibly would.) She'd attempt a wired bra. And she'd shave her legs and fanny even if the laws of physics said that was no longer a possibility.

Paul opened the front door and struggled to get through it with the width of the enormous bunch of flowers he'd arrived home with.

Emily was ready and waiting on the sofa, and saw

immediately that the huge bunch of roses in his arms was not from the bargain bin at Tesco Express, picked up on the way home, and in fact were real proper florist ones, and began having a happy little sob to herself.

'Hey. That was not quite the reaction I was after . . .' he said, laughing, as he placed everything down on the coffee table and moved round in front of her.

'I know,' Emily said, fanning her face with her hands and trying desperately not to smudge the smoky-eyes make-up she'd worked so hard at. She'd even used a YouTube tutorial. There was no way she was crying all her hard work away.

Paul crouched down in front of her and planted a kiss on her cheek. Her lips were heavy with red lipstick, and he was a man who knew smudging his pregnant wife's make-up before a night out was a big no-no.

'You look stunning. These are for you. Both of you,' he said, gently rubbing her stomach.

'They're so beautiful,' Emily said, feeling her tears coming back. She really needed to get her hormones under control if she was going to wear this much mascara.

'Beautiful flowers for my beautiful wife,' Paul said, smiling at her. 'I'll put them in some water and nip upstairs to get changed. It won't take me long. Okay?'

Emily nodded and took a few deep breaths as he disappeared. She could already feel that tonight was going to be amazing . . .

Within minutes, Paul was back downstairs, looking handsomely casual in a smart shirt and straight jeans.

'Let's go.' He helped her to her feet a little less grace-fully than she'd hoped.

As she tottered to the door, she immediately began regretting stuffing her puffy toes into her four-inch heels . . . but she was going to do this. Her and her sugar-puff toes WERE GOING TO DO THIS.

Emily's face dropped as Paul turned into the car park of their local Indian restaurant.

Was it a joke? Or was this where he was taking her? Her. The bearer of his child. On Valentine's Day. For a chicken tikka masala and a garlic-twatting-naan-bread.

Paul parked in a space near the entrance and took the key out of the ignition.

'So,' he began, turning his head to face her. 'I know it's not Michelin-starred fine dining or anything fancy like we've done before, but I thought as you love nothing better than a curry and a cuddle in your PJs on Friday night these days, we'd have a chilled one. And I read curry's good for the baby. Or labour. Or pineapples . . . or some-thing. So. Tah da . . .'

Emily listened to his voice slowly begin to lose confi-dence as he watched her reaction, and began to quite quickly regret his decision for a 'chilled' anything . . .

She couldn't speak.

She felt like she might cry if she did.

Or get so angry she'd bludgeon him to death in the face with a Jimmy Choo. (Not that she'd be able to actu-ally bend down fully to get it off her foot, but still.)

She had nearly punctured a lung while attempting to de-forest her labia, and he was taking her out for poppadums and a pint of fucking Cobra.

Emily knew exactly how she felt was written all over her face.

'Come on,' said Paul. 'I've got gifts too . . .'

Emily couldn't give a shit about gifts right now. But she'd give him the chance to redeem himself. Perhaps he had splashed out on something really special instead. Yes. That was probably it. That better be it.

'Okay,' Emily eventually said huffily. 'But those gifts had better be bloody epic.'

Paul laughed, grabbed a bag off the back seat and jumped out of the driver's door. He quickly nipped around the car and opened her door for her. He'd get half a husband-point for that, thought Emily.

He guided her through the car park and let her enter the restaurant first. Emily was desperate to sit down. Her feet felt like they were in their own private leather prison.

She was grateful when they were seated quickly. And within stumbling distance of the loos.

Emily decided she was going to make the most of this. The food smelt delicious and the waiter had placed down two perfectly chilled glasses of prosecco with strawberries bubbling away in them.

She managed half a smile.

'See . . .' Paul said, smiling and looking relieved as he took a sip of his drink. 'Not so bad now, eh?'

'I guess,' Emily said curtly. She wasn't going to let him off just yet.

He reached down and picked up the large gift bag he'd brought in with him and held it out to her.

Emily managed the rest of the smile.

Perhaps there were diamonds lurking in there, a Prada bag, Louboutins, a trip to Paris . . .

She untied the bow and peered inside. Her face fell instantly.

'A dressing gown. And slippers. With faces,' she said with utter disdain. Throwing every dagger her eyes could muster in Paul's direction.

'Well, I just . . . I thought that's what you'd want now you're going to be a mum . . .' he stuttered, regretting the words as soon as he'd said them.

'Take me home.'

'Oh Em, come on,' Paul said.

'TAKE. ME. HOME.' she responded. Loudly.

People were starting to stare. Paul knew she meant it.

And with that, Emily had Paul remove her shoes, and order her a chicken tikka masala with a garlic naan to go before taking her home.

Angrily.

And wearing her new fox-faced slippers.

Chapter 26

COME BACK, TOM

Tom
Hey.

Molly saw the message come in . . .

. . . And froze. She forgot to breathe for a moment. She waited to see if there was more. She didn't want to respond too quickly. She didn't want him to think she had just been sat around checking her phone every few seconds for the past twenty-four hours, waiting for him to make contact.

Even though she had been . . . Obviously.

She'd just got home from work. She'd picked up a ready meal from Tesco on the way home to her flat, and had already resigned herself to the fact that a Tesco Finest lasagne for one in a microwaveable tub was her Valentine's Day evening dinner . . .

But she'd only made it as far as the sofa once she got in. She felt completely drained.

She stared at her phone in her lap, and considered carefully how to respond.

Molly
Hey . . .

It was a start, right?

She waited a few minutes, but nothing came back. It was infuriating. She'd make dinner and check again in a bit. She might lose her mind otherwise.

Before she could stand up. She felt her phone buzz again.

Tom
I need to talk to you.
Are you at home?
Can I come over?
I really need to see you.

Molly let the words sit there for a moment. She felt an odd mixture of anger and complete elation. She desperately wanted to see him. So much. But she felt so let down by him, and by how casual and presumptive his texts were.

She took a deep breath. She couldn't be arsed to play games.

Molly
I'm home.
Okay.
Come now.

She'd lost her appetite for lasagne.

And she didn't have to wait long.

Ten minutes later, the familiar sound of the entry buzzer filled the flat and Molly let him in.

She waited for him to climb the stairs. His face was expressionless. As was hers.

He didn't say anything as he made his way inside sheepishly.

She wasn't going to be the first to speak. She'd already decided that. It was his turn to talk.

She sat back down on the sofa and kept her eyes on him as he removed his jacket and sat down next to her.

'I don't know how to start,' he eventually said, his voice sounding small as his eyes became moist.

Molly still said nothing. She just looked at him. And tried to fight back her own tears.

'I know I've been a complete and total idiot.' His eyes fixed on hers. 'I just freaked out. I couldn't stop freaking out. And I kept telling myself that I needed to get my shit together and come and talk to you. But somehow I couldn't. And then suddenly it had been a week. And then a few weeks . . . And I still hadn't. And it was getting harder. And . . . I promise I am not telling you this because I want sympathy from you, I swear. I just want you to know that that isn't who I am. I am not that person. I just couldn't . . . get a grip.

'And then I went to Dale's and stayed with him because it seemed like a good idea. But he gave me completely terrible advice, got me drunk and tried to convince me to get a new tattoo so that I could "get over it", which is literally the last thing I could ever do. Because I don't ever want to get over you, Molly. I love you . . .

'And even though I hadn't planned to be a father right now, I know that I only ever want to be with you. And I can do this with you. I know I can. We can do this. The two of us. The three of us, if you'll just let me. I . . . I don't know what else to say.

'I'm just so so sorry I let you down.'

Molly breathed in and out for a moment. She still felt angry but she knew that he meant every single word he'd just said to her.

She'd forgiven him from the moment he'd walked in, that was the truth. But now that he'd opened up to her, she knew that everything was going to be okay.

'You really fucked up, Tom,' she said. 'I thought that was it. I thought I was never going to hear from you again. And I was going to end up as some scorned single mum on *Jeremy Kyle* in two years' time, forcing you to pay childcare, or take a polygraph or some bullshit. I was so angry . . . And so scared.' Molly paused. And felt her own tears begin to flow now. She'd waited so long to let them out that they wouldn't stop.

'I was so scared . . .' she managed to say again, through the sobs. 'If we do this you need to promise me that any time you ever feel like you're scared or freaking out that we'll work on it together. Both of us. I'm freaking out too, Tom. But I can't just run away. Can I?'

Tom was still staring at her intensely. He dropped his head down a little, and reached his hand towards hers. He gently interlocked his fingers with hers.

'I will never let you down again, Molly. I mean it. I fucked up. I know that. But we are going to be a family. And I will be there every step of the way. Every step. And way beyond the way. Whatever the way is . . . And even if you don't believe me right now, I will prove it to you. If you'll let me?'

Molly smiled. It felt like she'd been waiting for ever to hear him say that. She took a deep breath.

'I believe you,' Molly said. Squeezing his fingers with hers. 'It will take some time for me to completely trust you again Tom, but I believe you.'

Tom pulled his body closer to hers and put his other arm round her tightly.

'I know. Thank you. I love you, Molly.' He kissed the side of her head as he manoeuvred her body towards him.

'I love you too.' Molly's eyes welled up again, her tears a mixture of relief and happiness.

'Tolly is back,' Tom said, laughing a little.

Molly laughed too. It felt good to laugh. It had been a long time.

'Tolly is on its way to being back,' she said, correcting him.

'So, is it too soon for naked twister?'

'Yes, Tom. It is definitely too soon for naked Twister.'

Chapter 27

AFTER-WORK DRINKS . . .

It had been almost a fortnight since Liz had properly acquired her 'team'. And, despite her reservations, it was going quite well.

She'd worked shorter hours, been less stressed, taken proper lunch breaks, laughed more, even slept better – and had found that working with Hannah and Gerald had been the release she'd needed. They were both amazing. Gerald especially. He worked so hard, and not only that, he was so easy-going. It seemed like every time Liz got stressed about meeting a deadline on a case, or getting some paperwork in order, he was there. Diffusing her. It was a breath of fresh air.

It helped that he was ridiculously good-looking and charming too, not that Liz had any interest in men, IN ANY WAY AT ALL right now, but he had a kind smile and made her laugh. It made the day pass quicker. Even if his jokes were dreadful. They were actually so dreadful, that's what made them funny.

It had been a long time since Liz had had a 'friend' at work. She'd always steered clear of people. With 'him' it had seemed easier, but 'he' wasn't around any more. So what was the harm? Right?

'You seem different you know,' Gerald said, out of the blue.

It caught Liz a little off guard.

'I do?'

Gerald looked up and his sharp, blue eyes met hers.

'Yes. You seem . . . friendlier.' He smiled.

How was she supposed to respond to that?

'Well, I won't make partner unless I'm friendly,' Liz said, laughing a little.

'Ha. It's not just that, though. You're smiling more. You seem happier, or something. I mean it as a compliment.'

Liz nodded and looked back down at her work. He was right. She was happier. Without 'him', she had no secrets, no lies and no worries. All she had to do was be herself. Something she seemed to have forgotten how to be the last couple of years . . .

'And if it's not overstepping the mark, I think your hair looks really nice that way too.'

Liz's cheeks burned a little. She wasn't good at accepting compliments. She'd styled her hair more naturally today, left the natural waves in and pushed her fringe to one side.

'Thanks,' Liz managed, without lifting her head. Perhaps that way he wouldn't notice her luminous red face.

Just then Hannah returned with a tray of coffees. 'Here you go.' She placed the steaming cups down in front of her colleagues. Liz was grateful for the interruption.

'So,' Gerald began chirpily, 'as it's Friday, and we've managed to successfully complete an entire two weeks as a team, I propose a drink after work. A celebration. What do you say, ladies?'

'Ah, I can't,' Hannah responded quickly. 'I'm meeting my sister after work today. Sorry! You guys should still go, though. I'll come next time.'

Liz felt awkward. A drink with the team seemed like a great idea, but a drink with just her and Gerald . . . well, that seemed less of a good idea somehow. Although, did she want to spend another Friday night getting shit-faced with her cat and listening to Adele while crying? Probably not. It was just an innocent drink with a colleague. She needed to stop overanalysing everything all the time.

'Well,' Liz said looking at Gerald, 'we could just go for one, I suppose. If you like?' She'd said it now. It was out there. She couldn't take it back.

'Sure,' Gerald said casually. 'You can buy the drinks . . . boss.'

'You ready?' Gerald said poking his head around Liz's office door.

'Is it six already?' Liz glanced up at her clock and quickly shuffled a few things away as she closed her laptop.

'Indeed it is,' Gerald said smoothly. His broad, tall figure filled the doorway of her office.

Liz grabbed her coat and handbag and the two of them walked down the hall together.

'Is there anywhere you particularly want to go?' he said as he pressed the lift's call button.

'No,' Liz said. 'You choose. I'm good with wherever. Just not too far, if that's okay. It's just my shoes . . .'

'Ha. It's okay. I know a place nearby,' he replied, smiling as they entered the lift.

Liz was annoying herself. She needed to relax. Going for a drink was going to be painful if she could only talk in four-word sentences. Hopefully some alcohol would loosen her up.

They made work-based chit-chat as they headed out of the office and walked for a few minutes.

Liz hadn't paid too much attention to where they were going. It was drizzling. The pavements were busy. She'd mostly been hiding beneath her hood, sandwiched between long-coated commuters shuffling their way to tube stations to get home to their families.

When she did finally look up, she felt her whole body tense up immediately.

Out of all the bars he could have chosen, he'd chosen this one. The one that 'he' used to bring her to.

Liz felt sick.

She wanted to turn and run away, but how could she? Without explaining herself or looking like some kind of crazy lady.

'Everything okay?' Gerald asked.

'Fine,' she said.

And before she knew it, the two of them were walking in.

Okay. This isn't actually too bad, Liz said to herself as they headed to the bar. It looked different somehow, or perhaps it was that she'd never really looked around before. She'd always been too busy hiding herself away in dark corners.

There was no sign of Eyebrows behind the bar either. That was a small relief, Liz thought as they took a seat at a high table near the bar.

'Tequila?' Gerald said as they took their coats off.

'Absolutely,' Liz replied, and he headed off to fetch their drinks.

Unexpectedly, Liz started to feel quite liberated. Perhaps this was the way to get rid of the last of her demons . . . Yes. She'd tequila away the last remnants of that dick-faced bastard. And that would be that. This was closure.

Besides, she had Gerald to look at now. Not that she'd be doing anything more than looking – she'd learnt the hard way that work-based relationships are NOT for her . . .

But still . . .

Why did he have to be so good-looking? And tall? And smell so nice? And he liked tequila . . . He was beginning to seem a little too good to be true . . .

'To us,' Gerald said as he got back to the table and held Liz's drink out to her.

Her cheeks burned again.

'To the team,' she replied, feeling suddenly awkward about correcting him. She took it and downed it in one.

'Another?' Gerald smiled.

'Why not? I'll get this one . . .' Liz replied.

151

Chapter 28

PINK OR BLUE

Pink or Blue?
Impending baby-joy
Will this expanding belly bump
Be a girl or a boy?

Will we be joining the scrotum squad?
The V-gang or the brigade of balls?
Fanny or Willy? We're feeling a bit silly . . .
As either way we don't mind at all.

Somehow it was March. Emily couldn't quite believe she'd made it to this point after spending the last twenty weeks with every day feeling like it had lasted a month . . . A crappy, pukey, swollen-ankled, restless-leg-syndromed, month.

But finally the day of her twenty-week scan was here, and she was desperate to find out the sex of their baby. Her mind was racing with happy excited thoughts as she drove down the main road towards Wycombe hospital.

She couldn't wait to know what they were having. She had a nursery to decorate. Clothes, blankets and accessories to buy. A pram to customise. How could she do that without knowing if she had a pink or a blue womb tenant floating around in there . . .?

Her blog hadn't exactly rocketed her to stardom. She had checked the stats constantly, hoping that her 'Breakfasts for the Second Trimester', or 'Stretch Mark Cream Essentials' posts might have suddenly caught the eye of a celeb or a magazine, or something . . . but so far she was averaging about eight views a day. And two of those were definitely her mum, and at least five of the others were her continually checking if her blog was 'still there'.

She knew she hadn't really 'tried' that hard yet though. It was time to engage her PR brain and start writing some more engaging material. What she needed was a hook, and a 'gender reveal' could be just the thing, right?

But did she have enough of an audience who actually gave a shit? And more importantly, would iCandy give a shit?

She decided to clear her mind of blog thoughts. She was almost at the hospital where her mum and Paul would be meeting her for the scan.

Her mum had dropped more than a few unsubtle hints about Emily not *involving her enough in the unborn journey of her first grandchild*, which was probably true if she was honest with herself.

It was just that she'd been so preoccupied with feeling like shit, and feeling so sorry for herself these last few months that her life had mostly been about just struggling through. And spending her evenings in a pit on the sofa while getting on first-name terms with her local Deliveroo driver.

So she'd invited her mum to the scan.

She knew that'd earn her some serious daughter points. And that would obviously mean lunch and a shopping trip afterwards, so frankly it was win-win for both of them.

Emily drove her little car into the main hospital car park and began scanning the lines of cars hoping for a gap . . .

She got lucky with a parking space as someone pulled out just in front of her. Hospital parking was dog eat dog. And considering she was already ten minutes late, and five months pregnant with a spasming pelvis and desperately in need of her forty-seventh wee of the day . . . she was NOT in the mood to be messed with.

She parked. Badly. And huffed and puffed her way out of the car. Her Fiat 500 seemed to be shrinking with every week that passed, not the ideal environment for someone with the girth of a barrel.

She jogged as quickly as her swollen ankles would let her, and quickly made her way to the lifts and up to the antenatal wing.

As she continued to puff her way down the corridor, she spotted the familiar shapes of her husband and her mum in the distance.

Their faces lit up as she waddled towards them, breathing hard. And sweating. A lot.

Her mum started crying.

She cried every time she saw her. Not a sad cry, a happy

little sob at seeing her daughter pregnant with her first grandchild.

It was sweet.

But Emily couldn't help but find it a little irritating . . .

Because she found everything a little irritating at the moment. Regardless of whether it was or not.

Especially when she could feel sweat pouring from both under-boob areas and currently had the lung capacity of a toddler.

She paused to catch her breath, quickly kissed them both, and the three of them headed into the waiting room.

Emily looked around as she sat down, clutching her pregnancy notes. It was odd seeing so many pregnant people in one place. She didn't know why but it was freaking her out a bit today. It felt like a stark reminder that she was only halfway through. Things were about to get a lot harder. And a lot bigger if the lady sat four seats away from her was anything to go by . . .

She'd checked her app this morning and it had said the baby was the length of a banana right now. A banana. Which didn't quite explain why she was already the size of a small planet . . .

'Emily Wells?' came the call from a small, dark-haired midwife from the other end of the room.

Paul stood up quickly and signalled they were coming, before helping his pregnant wife and still-sobbing mother-in-law to their feet.

The three of them headed into the room, and Emily got herself clumsily on to the bed.

The sonographer got quickly to work, and after a few moments turned the screen around so they could see a fully formed baby wriggling around.

Emily's mum burst into tears again. Of course.

But even Paul and Emily had damp eyes after seeing how much the baby had grown since the first scan. It was a proper little person now. It was beautiful.

There were a lot of measurements and checks. Emily lay patiently as the sonographer did her job, even though it was making her feel paranoid. And she just wanted to 'know' now . . .

After what seemed like an age, the sonographer had finally got everything she needed and turned to face Emily, smiling. 'Everything looks great. And now the important question. Do you want to know?'

'Yes. Absolutely. Please,' Emily said keenly, as Paul smiled and nodded in agreement next to her.

The sonographer moved the ultrasound scanner round Emily's belly until a clear shot 'up and underneath' the baby came into view, making it very obvious exactly what they were having.

Emily's mum began crying even louder.

Emily stared at the screen for a moment, frowning a little. She had been completely convinced she was having a girl.

'I'm sorry. I don't understand. Why does my baby girl have a penis?'

And with that Emily had a sudden, slightly hysterical, weep to herself, as she realised she'd been wrong. She wasn't having a little girl. She was going to be a mummy to a baby boy.

And while that was completely wonderful, and her tears quickly turned into happy, snotty, joyful sobs, she couldn't help but feel a little devastated about having to delete all her pink and purple nursery themes from her Pinterest boards.

Chapter 29

ALL TOGETHER NOW

The last few weeks had been amazing.

Tom had been there a hundred per cent. More than a hundred per cent. Perhaps he was making up for his brief period of lost time, but he was now embracing fatherhood completely. A little too completely, in places . . . especially after Molly woke last Saturday morning to discover he'd removed all trace of anything containing 'chemicals' from her flat. There was now a bottle of vinegar and a pot of bicarbonate of soda where the bleach used to be next to the toilet. He'd also substituted all the cow's milk for almond milk in the fridge after stating it had too many 'hormones', and insisted she eat raw organic spinach in at least one meal a day.

Molly didn't care. She loved him even more for it. She knew it came from a good place. Although she wasn't that sure about cleaning the loo with something she normally put on chips, and even she was going to have to draw a line at only drinking milk that came from nuts.

They'd gone to the first scan together, which had been both terrifying and wonderful. They'd seen their baby. They'd cried and hugged and asked questions. Well, mostly

Tom had asked questions. He'd clearly been reading up. A LOT. In fact, he'd made notes. But it showed he really cared. Molly liked that. It felt something like perfect.

Molly had watched as a tiny, partly formed person swam around inside her on the monitor while she'd not felt so much as a twitch. It was surreal. And she couldn't wait to fast forward a few weeks and be able to feel her baby inside her . . .

Tom held her hand the entire time and beamed with happiness as they found out she was further along than they thought. Nearly fourteen weeks pregnant.

Fourteen whole weeks. It was bizarre hearing someone say it. Especially as she still didn't 'feel' pregnant, or look pregnant, just a slight protruding tummy, but she'd had bigger 'bumps' from double helpings of roast dinner on a Sunday at her dad's.

She'd watched Emily puke and sweat and swear (a lot) her way through pregnancy and not known it would be so different for her . . . She was loving every moment. She was glowing. While Emily was avoiding stairs. And pastels. And avocados.

They also had a date, a real date. On the twenty-third of August she would be having a baby. An actual real-life human baby.

And she could not stop staring at the scan photo. It sounded so ridiculous to say it, because she knew that women everywhere had babies every day, but now it was happening to her it felt something like a miracle. It really did.

The weeks leading up to this seemed a distant memory now. Tom was back. Really back. In every sense. And Molly decided it was time to show her friends he was properly back. It meant a lot to her that they trusted him again too.

She'd organise a meal for them all at hers. That way the girls could see first-hand how committed he was . . .

She'd cook. It would be brilliant. She decided she'd waste no time on organising it . . .

Molly
Right, ladies.
I've decided to host a
dinner party on Saturday.
Obviously, it's not going
to be posh or anything . . .
But there'll be something edible.
(hopefully)
And it's a party.
(mostly)
Although I still can't cook.
And neither can Tom . . .
Two of us are pregnant
and will probably go to bed
before nine . . .
And I don't have enough chairs.
But other than that . . .
It'll be AWESOME.
Come from 8?

Emily
How can we refuse
when you put it like that . . . ☺
I had a date with my PJs
and a tub of Ben & Jerry's,
but I guess I love you enough
to dump them . . . lol

Molly
You know you love it!

Emily
So is everything cool with you guys?
Is Tom back for good?
I'm still angry at him . . .

Molly
Yes. It's not been easy.
He knows he fucked up.
But we are honestly cool.
Better than cool . . .
He's trying so hard to make it right.
You'll see that on Saturday.
He's impossible to stay angry at, I
assure you!

Emily
Okay.
It's nice to hear you are happy again.
I was so worried about you xx
Can't wait to see you Saturday.

161

I'll bring a bottle.
(Of Shloer. Obvs.)

Molly
Thank you.
(Fucking Shloer.)

Emily
LOL xxx

Molly
Liz?

Molly knew Liz was probably just working late or something. But she was sure she'd be there.

It was all working out.

Now . . . to scour the Internet in search of a recipe that required no cooking skills, no real effort, and used only the food she had in the kitchen which amounted to cheese, some now very dubiously furry pesto and a bag of Bombay mix left over from Christmas.

Chapter 30

DINNER DATE

Liz had been stuck in a meeting for most of the afternoon and early evening.

She felt her head begin to bobble around of its own accord on her shoulders, as her brain lost its ability to soak up any more information and her body succumbed to weariness. Luckily, the meeting was wrapping up. She was more than ready to head home.

She yawned into her hand as she strolled back to her office and began shutting down for the day.

She pulled her phone out of her handbag and scrolled through the messages between Molly and Emily, smiling at the exchanges between her friends.

She was still angry at Tom too, but keen to see her friend happy. So she'd go on Saturday, of course. It wasn't like she had anything else to do.

She thought on it for a moment as her laptop shut down. She really was so bored of attending everything on her own. Why was she always the only single one? Why did everyone else in the world seem to be loved up, knocked up and generally just a lot more 'up' than her? Surely it was her time to be 'up' there with them now . . .?

'Hey. I'll see you tomorrow. Have a good evening,' said

a kind, familiar voice walking past her open office door. Gerald paused for a moment seeing the frown on Liz's face as she looked down at her phone. 'Is everything okay?'

'Oh yeah, sorry. It's fine.' Liz dropped her phone in her bag. 'It's just my friend. She's having this dinner party thing on Saturday, and she wants me to come and . . . well . . . you know when you just don't feel like being that "single person" at the dinner party any more? She always tries to set me up with someone terrible and I don't think I can be arsed with it any longer if I'm honest. The last one had tattoos on his face.'

Gerald laughed, and then paused, looking like he wanted to say something, but wasn't sure if he should.

'Well,' he said eventually, 'if it would save you from being chatted up by another face-tattooed suitor, I could always come with you as your plus-one. Just as friends, of course. I mean, I'm not doing anything so it's no trouble.'

Liz froze. Her cheeks burned hotter than ever before. She had not expected that. Was he just being nice? Or did he feel sorry for her? Oh God, he was pitying her, wasn't he. This was devastating. DEVASTATING.

'Umm. Well . . . I . . . I could never ask you to do that. My friend's cooking is awful. She'd probably poison you.' It was the best Liz could come up with. Her cheeks were starting to die down a little at least.

'Hey. What's a party without a bit of food poisoning among friends?' Gerald joked. 'But seriously. You'd be doing me a favour. I still don't know that many people round here and the weekends are getting pretty boring . . .'

Liz looked at him. He seemed totally genuine. What was the harm? They were colleagues. They were a similar age, they got on well . . . and they could easily become friends . . . so long as it was 'just friends'.

'Okay,' Liz said. 'If a night of bad food, poor entertainment and the company of my two pregnant best friends is your idea of fun on a Saturday night then you are more than welcome . . .'

'Great. You've totally sold it to me. Just let me know when and where you want me . . .'

'I'll text you.' She wondered for a moment if this was a terrible idea. And quite how she'd convince her two best friends that the highly attractive, six-foot-three blond man she'd brought with her to a dinner party was of no romantic interest to her whatsoever . . .

Chapter 31

CANAPÉS

It was Saturday night.

And Molly had, unsurprisingly, left everything to the last minute.

It was 7.34 p.m., and she was drying her hair with one hand and applying mascara with the other. Which in itself was quite impressive.

'Is that make-up vegan? I read somewhere that animal products in that kind of stuff can create really nasty reactions if it's over six months old,' Tom said loudly over the noise of the hairdryer. Molly took a deep breath and ignored him.

'No need to huff. I'm just looking after you. Both of you. You can't be too careful, you know? Plus, you do know your guests are due to arrive in less than thirty minutes, right?' Tom said, smiling at her from the bedroom doorway.

'Are you suggesting that I've not got this under control?'

'Absolutely not.' Tom raised his hands up to display his palms. 'It's just I don't see anything actually cooking, but hey, eating is overrated at dinner parties anyway. Absolutely not the main point.'

Molly rolled her eyes and willed her hair to dry quicker. She didn't need that kind of negativity in her life.

She'd decided on pasta. She'd chuck it in the pan for five minutes when people started looking hungry and until then she'd fill them up with slightly out-of-date Bombay mix and cubes of slightly crusty-edged Cheddar.

Excellent plan.

'So who is Liz's mystery man?'

'I honestly have no idea!' Molly said. 'But I am pretty intrigued. I thought we were on to a winner with Dale, to be honest . . .'

Tom smiled and sat down behind her, wrapping both his arms around her waist. He pushed her hair away from her neck on one side and kissed it.

Molly felt a thousand tiny sparks fly through her body.

'Not now, Tom,' she said, unconvincingly. 'I have pasta to cook. And cheese to cube. VEGAN cheese, obviously. So we do not have time. We are hosting a very sophisticated dinner party in twenty minutes.'

She reluctantly slipped out of his embrace and tried to distract herself with thoughts of chopping up pieces of Cheddar.

Tom sighed and smiled.

The buzzer rang through the flat.

'Bloody Liz! Always early!' Molly said, as she leapt up from the bed and buzzed her friend in.

Moments later Liz came through the front door. Looking a little nervous, which was unusual for her.

'Sorry I'm a bit early.' She was moving restlessly from one foot to the other, clutching a bottle of red wine. 'I brought alcohol. I think I need some.'

 167

Molly laughed, closing the door behind her as Liz headed immediately into her kitchen and sourced a glass and bottle opener, the way only best friends can in each other's homes. Having found what she needed, she then proceeded to pour herself an impressively full glass of red wine.

'So,' Liz said, looking around. 'Hate to sound picky, but I don't see any actual food here, Molly. Are we ordering in or just feasting on the electrifying atmosphere, perhaps?'

'Hilarious. It's all in hand, Lizzy-pants. Now tell me who this mystery man is before I explode. And no one wants to see a pregnant woman do that.'

'Well. He's no one really,' Liz replied, a little too defensively to be convincing. 'We work together. We're just friends. It's not like that. He offered to come in case you tried to set me up with another Dale.'

'There's nothing wrong with Dale. He's just an acquired taste,' Molly responded. 'And if you're just friends, why are you downing Shiraz and leaping about like you need a panic poo?'

'I'm not!' Liz said, downing a glass of Shiraz and suddenly feeling like she might actually need to use the facilities. 'Where's Tom?'

'He's in the bedroom waiting for his erection to go down,' Molly said.

Liz spat her drink out into her glass. 'Jesus, Molly!' she said, wiping the red wine from her chin. 'From anyone else I'd think that was a joke, but sadly, I know you.'

Both ladies laughed as Molly began getting pans out,

and put the Bombay mix into a bowl with absolutely no finesse whatsoever.

'I'm going to take the key and go wait for him outside,' Liz said, finishing her glass of wine. 'I don't want him walking in and being greeted with Tom's erection and some out-of-date Bombay mix straight off. I'd like to at least attempt to ease him in gently . . .'

Molly laughed as Liz put her coat over her shoulders before grabbing the key off the hook and heading quickly back down to the street.

Liz felt a bit sick. How had she got herself into this situation? Why did Gerald have to be so nice? Most people wouldn't be. They'd just give her a sympathetic look and let her get on with being set up with 'Dales' for the rest of her life . . .

She looked at her watch. It was a few minutes to eight. She knew he'd be punctual. She liked that he was a punctual person.

As she raised her head she saw a Gerald-shaped silhouette crossing the road in front of her.

She smiled. She honestly was glad he was here.

As he approached, she saw that he was smiling too. He looked casual but neat at the same time. She liked that he was neat.

'Well hello,' he said, approaching her.

There was an awkward moment where she almost shook his hand, and then she wondered if she should give him a kiss on the cheek, but then she didn't do anything . . . and the moment had passed.

169

'Hello,' Liz said, making sure she sounded casual. 'You found it then.'

'Your directions were very specific. And you are standing outside the door, so that was the main giveaway.'

Liz chuckled and turned to let them both inside. They climbed the stairs and got back into the warmth of Molly's flat.

Tom was there now. Erection-free, thankfully. He smiled at Liz and gave her a kiss on the cheek. He looked happy, Liz thought. Which was good. It was good to see him. And see him making her friend happy again.

'Tom, this is Gerald. We work together. Gerald, this is Tom, Molly's boyfriend,' Liz said, matter-of-factly.

The buzzer went again and Liz left the men chatting as she let Emily and Paul in.

Emily looked like she was sweating quite a lot by the time she reached the top step, but was clearly very happy to be back on a flat surface. She kissed Liz on the cheek and headed straight in. She was too puffed out to actually speak just yet . . .

They had a full set now. And it was so nice to be here with someone, someone whose company she actually enjoyed, Liz thought, as she rejoined Gerald and her friends chatting in the middle of the lounge.

She was so glad she'd invited him. He was getting on with everyone. He was so relaxed and such easy company. She felt silly for worrying. They really were just friends. A man and woman can work together and enjoy each other's company and be just friends. She didn't know why she'd wasted so much time thinking about it, to be honest.

Molly appeared from the kitchen with a tray in her hands.

'Canapés?' she announced triumphantly.

'By canapés, do you mean cubes of mild vegan Cheddar and some slightly bendy Bombay mix?' Liz said, inspecting the offering.

'Yes,' said Molly. 'Yes I do.'

Chapter 32

THOR AND THE PESTO PASTA

'So,' Emily said in Liz's ear as Gerald got up from the table and disappeared to the bathroom. 'Gerald?'

'Yes, Gerald,' Liz replied, deciding to play stupid until she was asked a specific question.

Emily nudged her in the arm playfully. 'Why have I never heard you mention him before? He's so nice. And tall. He looks like Thor. How do you get any work done? I'd just sit around staring at him, fantasising about how handy he might be with a hammer.'

'Because I'm a professional person, Emily,' Liz responded dryly. And trying quite hard not to fantasise about exactly that now her friend had suggested it.

'Is that why you've spent all night blushing, playing with your hair and laughing at his shit jokes, because you're so pro-fess-ion-al?' Emily asked, laughing a little.

Liz felt her cheeks heat up again. She was not at all comfortable with this line of questioning.

'Excuse me, ladies.' Gerald gently pushed past Liz's arm to get back into his seat. 'What have I missed?' he said, smiling and picking up his wine glass.

'I was just saying to Emily how lovely it was of you to come tonight,' Liz said quickly. 'As friends. It's nice to spend time with you outside of the office. As friends. I mean.'

'As friends,' Emily said, laughing at how unnecessarily awkward Liz was making it.

'And it's been lovely to meet all your friends. As friends,' Gerald said, chuckling and taking another sip of his wine.

As Liz racked her brain for a way to change the subject, the sound of a clinking glass silenced the room.

Tom stood tapping a knife gently against his wine glass as he rose confidently to his feet.

'Okay. I have your attention now,' Tom said, placing the glass back on the table. 'Thank you for coming. And thank you, Molly, for knocking up a diverse and eclectic feast of pesto pasta and cubed Cheddar, and thank you everyone else for eating it without complaint.

'I don't want to ruin the energy in the room but I just wanted to say, a few weeks ago, I almost made a huge mistake and, without dwelling on it, I was a total dick. Luckily, I happen to be the luckiest man in the world, and my beautiful Molly made me see that. Just by being the wonderful person she is.

'So, Molly. My Molly, I have something for you . . .'

And with that Tom reached in his pocket and placed a small shiny object down in front of Molly.

'It's a key,' he said, as Molly picked it up to inspect it.

'I can see that . . .'

'It's a key to my flat.'

Molly's mouth parted a little in surprise and she looked up at him.

'It doesn't make sense us being apart any more, I think if we're going to be parents in a few months' time, then we should live together. I want to look after you. And our baby. And I want us all together under one roof. What do you say, babes?'

Molly was a little choked.

'I, erm, well. I agree. I just, I mean, we could live here together, though, couldn't we? It doesn't have to be at yours . . .' She was speaking as she was thinking. This had taken her completely by surprise.

'Hey, I know you love this place, I love it too. But my place is bigger, quieter, has a bedroom we can turn into a nursery, and isn't above a tattoo shop that blasts out death metal for eight to ten hours a day . . .'

'Fair point,' Molly replied, as everyone laughed.

Tom was absolutely right. It didn't mean she wasn't slightly sad at the idea of leaving her little flat. She'd miss that ridiculously loud door buzzer that made everyone shit themselves every time it went off. She'd even miss the slightly strange smell at the top of the stairs and the random cat that would climb in her bathroom window and lick its testicles on her bath surround. But, she conceded, it wasn't the best place for a newborn.

'Okay. Let's do it,' Molly said.

Tom knelt down beside her, tipped her chin up with his hand and kissed her gently on the lips. He smiled as he pulled his head back slightly from hers. 'Tolly is officially back.'

Emily and Paul had left early; Emily had looked exhausted by 10 p.m., and there was probably only so much fizzy elderflower you could drink in one sitting.

The others had chatted for a while longer. And Liz had helped Molly clear up, but it was gone eleven now. And given their conversation when she first got there . . . she could sense Molly and Tom wanted some time to themselves. Plus, she'd had far too much red wine and could already feel the hangover looming . . .

'I think it might be time to call it a night,' Liz said to Gerald.

'I think you're right,' Gerald replied. 'It's getting pretty late. It's been a great night though. Your friends are brilliant. I haven't laughed so much in ages.'

'I'm so glad you had fun. Thanks so much for coming again,' Liz said, feeling a little woozy as the Shiraz pumped round her system. She collected his coat from the sofa and handed it to him.

'Honestly. Stop thanking me. It's been really fun,' he said, pulling his coat on.

'Okay. I'll stop it now. Let's just sneak out. I think they're a bit preoccupied . . .' Liz laughed, nodding her head towards the kitchen where Molly and Tom were fairly tongue-deep in a passionate kiss.

Liz opened the door, and they headed down the stairs and into the night air.

'I'm going to head down the high street and grab a cab from the rank,' Gerald said as the door closed behind them.

'Okay. I've got an Uber picking me up from here, so I guess I'll see you Monday?'

'Yep. See you Monday,' said Gerald, moving closer to her. Fixing his eyes on hers.

Then suddenly his face was inches away, his lips begging to touch hers . . . By the time her mind had processed what was going to happen, his lips were locked on hers.

Liz pulled herself back as immediately as her body allowed her to, unsteady from the amount of red wine she had drunk.

This was not what she wanted. This was a disaster. She didn't know what to do. What to say. What to feel . . .

Liz's Uber pulled up next to them.

Without speaking, she turned on her heels and scurried awkwardly into the back seat. Slamming the door shut behind her.

She racked her brain as the car pulled off, resisting any urge to look back at where she'd left him.

Had she done this? Had she somehow given him the wrong signals? She was sure she hadn't. This was the last thing she wanted.

FUCK.

Chapter 33

GIRL-CHAT

Liz
Shit.
Gerald tried to kiss me last night.
This is dreadful.
What was he thinking?
Oh God.
Do you think I gave him the
wrong idea?
Is this my fault?
Tell me I'm not an incredibly
terrible person
who deserves to be taken out to sea
and drowned.

Molly
Okay. You're not an incredibly terrible
person who deserves to be taken out
to sea and drowned.

Liz
Oh God.
I AM, AREN'T I.

Molly

No you're not.

Stop freaking out.

Look. What's the problem?

Perhaps what you need to

get over twat-face is to get

under Gerald?

Liz

That is literally the worst idea

you've ever had.

FACT.

Molly

lol

Well, he was probably just pissed

and misread the situation.

I think he might like you though . . .

Plus he's really hot.

I don't see the problem in a bit

of fun.

You take life way too serious lady!

Liz

I cannot believe you can't

see how FUCKED this all is?

I do not need another work-based

relationship thank you!

(Although I do agree

he's quite hot . . . lol)

Molly

See! You're coming round to it already!
Did you kiss him back?

Liz

No. Not really. I don't think so.
I can't remember.
I was so drunk.
But I definitely pulled away.
God, this is going to be so awkward
on Monday.

Molly

Look.
He made the first move.
He's probably bricking it right now.
He is a REALLY nice guy.
And he looks like fucking THOR.
I reckon he'll be in touch today.
He'll say sorry, blame it on
being drunk and the rest will
be history.
Or . . . confess his undying love, and
before the end of next week you'll be
fantasising about getting married,
making mini-Thors and buying a
house with a little white fence and a
fucking pug-dog.
100%

Emily

OH. MY. GOD.

I've just seen this!

Liz – you little Minx!

Totes agree with Molly though.

What is there to worry about?

It was only a kiss . . .

He's hot.

You're beautiful.

You're both super smart

lawyer people.

And HE'S HOT.

FUCKING SMART AND HOT.

PS: once you've seen it please tell us

in detail about his hammer.

☺

Liz

YOU ARE BOTH SO UNHELPFUL.

There will be no mini-Thors and

picket fence, thank you!

It was only a kiss.

Not even half a kiss.

Perhaps I'm over-reacting.

We're both adults, we'll just

agree we were pissed,

we'll never talk about it again,

and move on with our lives.

Okay. I'm starting to feel better now.

Emily
You know . . .
Your couple name is 'Giz'
There can be nothing wrong about that.

Molly
Pemily, Tolly and Giz.
This is one of the most amazing
moments of my life.

Liz
Okay. I'm laughing a lot at that!
But seriously. Please stop now.
It was just a drunken mistake . . .

Emily
Giz is real, Liz.
You just need to believe . . .
So long as it was only a kiss . . .
#sluttyLizzyisback

Liz
You cheeky bitch!
I'm not that sort of girl thanks.
YES. Only a kiss.

Molly
So how did you leave it last night?

Liz
Well. My Uber arrived.
Just after I'd pulled away from him

181

And I just got straight in it . . .
I didn't say goodbye or anything.
Do you think he'll think I'm a bitch?
I was just pissed.
I'm starting to panic again now!

Molly
No, he won't think you're a bitch.
I think he's probably just really
embarrassed.
Just wait and see if he contacts you
later.
It will be fine.
You'll see.

Liz
Okay.
Thanks for last night though, sweetie.
It was brilliant.
Sorry if I was a bit drunk.
I'm going to go cry into
some Alka-Seltzer
And try not to keep checking my
phone . . .

Emily
Yes, it was really fun.
Sorry I bailed early.
I feel like I'm breeding a rugby team
in here.

I'm being beaten up from
the vagina out.
It's hard work.
Big congrats on the move to Tom's.
You're right – you guys are solid again.
I no longer think he's a dick
I promise.

Liz
I second that.
Definitely no longer a dick.

Molly
Thanks ladies.
#TollyForever

Liz
#dick

Chapter 34

AWKWARD

Liz had practically run down the corridor on Monday morning to get to her office. She shut the door behind her and felt slight relief that she had made it to her desk without bumping into Gerald.

She'd checked her phone every four or five seconds for the past twenty-four hours, she'd not had a text, a message, a call, or anything from him.

She had expected him to get in touch. It was disappointing that he hadn't.

Perhaps he just didn't see it as a big deal? Maybe he couldn't even remember? They really had hammered the Shiraz . . .

Either way. She hated this feeling of awkwardness. She needed to speak to him. Clear the air. And get on with her day, her week, and her life.

It would help if she didn't feel so tired. She'd struggled to sleep, with tense thoughts whirring round her head about how she could 'will on' a mild disease or condition that would render her housebound for a few days, or perhaps the week. Or for ever. Just so she could delay facing him.

But she'd resigned herself to an exhausted, embarrassing Monday and had instead spent her morning commute rehearsing exactly how she was going to handle this without making a total idiot of herself . . .

First of all, she'd look fabulous, which was hard on four hours of broken sleep, but she'd brought 'strong fringe game' and applied the reddest of her red lipsticks. Then she'd nonchalantly play down what happened in conversation over coffee, pretend she could barely remember. That it was nothing more than a misplaced peck. And that was it. They never needed to talk about it again.

And she'd definitely not be inviting him to any other weird-cubed-vegan-cheese-and-pesto dinner parties above tattoo shops with her horny pregnant friend.

And she'd absolutely never be touching red wine again. Ever.

Which was all bollocks. Of course.

She knew she'd be shitfaced again on Shiraz by nine o'clock tonight, but this time with only Jasper the cat for company. Again.

Liz froze in her seat as a heavy set of knuckles rapped at her door.

'Just a moment.' She decided that pretending to be in the middle of something important was a good strategy.

'It's me. Can I come in?' said Gerald.

Liz felt her stomach do an awkward little flip. She started shuffling things a bit. She didn't really know why.

'Yes. Come in.' She straightened herself up and attempted to look relaxed, yet busy and important at the same time.

Gerald opened the door. He had a disconcerting smile on his face. He looked so handsome. And happy. It was off-putting. Liz was racking her brain for the words from her little speech. Which seemed to be absolutely nowhere right now.

'Hey,' he said casually as he shut the door behind him.

'Hey,' Liz said back, a little suspiciously.

'Did your friend Molly find my phone?' he said, still smiling. 'I know I had it when I arrived at hers. It must have dropped out of my pocket or something. Who knows . . . I think I may have drunk a bit too much. I had a bit of a fuzzy-red-wine head in the morning that's for sure.'

Liz let his words sink in for a few seconds. He'd lost his phone. He wasn't ignoring her; he just couldn't contact her. He wasn't a shit. She was glad he wasn't a shit.

'Err, no,' she finally managed. Smiling a little with the relief. 'Molly cleans her place about once a year so she might find it at some point over the summer if you're lucky.'

It was probably in the lounge somewhere, under a pile of something. Molly and Tom had more than likely had sex on top of it. They were quite possibly having sex on it right now. She wasn't sure if he'd ever want it back to be honest . . .

'Ha!' Gerald said, throwing his blond head back before taking a seat across the desk from her and softening his gaze. 'Yeah. Look. I know this is awkward. I'm sorry about the whole trying-to-kiss-you thing. I got a bit caught up in the moment, and all the wine . . . and . . . well. I'm sorry if you thought I was a bit of a dick. I'm actually not a dick at all. And I barely slept last night because I couldn't stop worrying that you thought I was. A bit of a dick, that is . . .' He paused and took a breath.

'Look. I know you probably think I only kissed you because I was drunk, but the truth is, it had nothing to do with the alcohol. I like you, Liz. I don't know how you feel about that, but I do. And I seem to find myself thinking about you a lot. I just . . . think you're pretty great.' He leaned in closer to her.

'I understand you might have reservations. I know we work together. And you're in line for this big promotion. But I honestly do really like you. And I . . . well, what I'm saying is . . . I'd like to get to know you. If you'll let me. What do you think?'

Liz froze momentarily in her chair, feeling a little shocked. It had been the last thing she was expecting. She didn't know what to say.

She just couldn't do this. She couldn't allow herself to do this. It wasn't that Gerald wasn't a great guy. He was. But she wasn't ready, and she just couldn't allow herself to get involved with someone from work again. But right now, she was struggling to find the words to tell him that.

'I think . . . I think that it's a really bad idea Gerald. I've just come out of something really complicated, and I just can't do that. Not now. Especially with someone at work. I can offer you friendship or nothing. I'm sorry.' She felt like she was kicking a puppy.

Gerald held her gaze, but his eyes saddened a little. He

looked crushed. He sighed and rose to his feet quickly, his lips pursed.

Liz didn't know what else to say. There wasn't anything else to say.

'Well, then I'll take friendship. Thanks for being honest with me, Liz. I really hope we can be friends instead,' Gerald said, sounding disappointed. 'I'll see you in the meeting room at eleven?'

Liz nodded. She felt dreadful. But hopefully the awkwardness would fade and they could be friends. She'd like that. That was all she ever wanted from him anyway.

She shook her thoughts out of her head. She needed to text Molly.

Liz
Hey it's me.
Did you find Gerald's phone at yours?
He says he left it there somewhere

. . .

Can you check and let me know.
Thanks xxx
(And depending on where you find it,
wipe any body fluids off
before handing it back . . . pls.)

Chapter 35

THE THIRD TRIMESTER
(THE REALLY TWATTY ONE)

Welcome my dear to the third trimester
Time to get angry and say NO to polyester
Man-made fabrics are not your friend, and
you no longer have control of your front or back end

Emily felt like every week of her first two trimesters had lasted her entire life. So clearly the third would be no different, especially as it was the longest, heaviest and apparently the 'twattiest' of the three . . .

But finally it was a rainy Wednesday in April. And she was twenty-four weeks pregnant now, so, with any luck, she had just sixteen weeks to go. She was on the home straight.

As much as she didn't want to wish it away, she just couldn't wait to not be pregnant any more. Less than four months now until there was no more weeing twelve times an hour, no more restless legs, no more giant feet, fingers and face, and no more only being able to view her fanny with the iPad on selfie mode. She couldn't wait. She was more than ready to have a waistline again.

She'd have an entire year. An entire year of maternity leave with her beautiful baby boy, where she'd float around cafes breastfeeding and drinking lattes and stuff. She'd do yoga and buggy-fit and baby-sensory the living shit out of her little guy. It'd be perfect. Maybe she'd redecorate the house, write a novel or take up sewing. Go vegan just for a change?

How much time can one tiny little human actually take up, right? she thought to herself.

Emily was fairly sure the baby would come early and would definitely be one of those ones that sleeps well from the beginning. She could sense it. She was sure people were just overexaggerating about the lack of sleep in the first year.

She was really struggling to concentrate at work now. She was there in body, but her spirit was generally off googling baby-groups, flicking through her Pinterest boards, or surfing the Internet feeling a little concerned that it was telling her the baby was already the size of an 'ear of corn', which was a strange analogy she thought, but not as concerning as week twenty-five, where it suddenly became a rutabaga (whatever the fuck that was) but appeared to have expanded significantly in girth. And it was making her and her vagina feel a bit queasy.

Now that she knew she had just ten and a half weeks, or seventy-two days (1,728 hours) before she left the world of PR behind for twelve whole months (or 8,760 hours, but who's counting . . .?), it was really quite hard to give a shit about luxury towelling.

Press releases that contained words like 'cotton density' and 'hook count' were a stretch too far. Literally, a stretch too far. She could barely reach her out-tray and had given up on attempting to strain for her stationery pot weeks ago. These were her perils now that she'd become fully spherical.

And Matilda was still a total dick.

Before finding out Emily was pregnant, Matilda was already a strong eight out of ten on the dick scale, but since she'd grasped that there might be a temporary promotion up for grabs, she'd suddenly become puke-inducingly nice. In an incredibly transparent dickish way. So she'd bumped herself right up to a full ten out of ten.

She kept telling Emily how wonderful she looked, offering to carry things for her, take meetings for her, kept ushering her home early, and spent most of the day fussing around her, bringing her drinks and continually feeding her.

Yes. Matilda had become her personal 'feeder'. And as much as she wanted to say no to the cakes, chocolate, biscuits and treats, Emily couldn't.

The baby wouldn't let her.

It had become quite dependent on the regular mid-afternoon Creme Eggs and a sharer-size packet of Frazzles it was being fed each day with a decaf latte.

Which 'could' be partially responsible for where her excessively sized bump, bottom and face were coming from. But probably not, Emily reassured herself . . .

Getting up had become an unattractive task. She'd begun making strange huffing noises every time she made it to her feet or sat down again. And the sweating . . .

well, the sweating was getting worse. And it wasn't even summer yet. Maybe she could ask Matilda to continuously fan her. She probably would . . .

This weekend, Emily and Paul had planned to decorate the nursery and begin getting ready properly before time got away from them. Emily had provided mood boards with her design ideas and planned to project-manage from a seated position. Paul hadn't looked too impressed, but she didn't care. He was the one who had done this to her. And he was going to make this nursery worthy of an MTV *Cribs* visit or she was going to lose her shit. She might even have a launch party. She hadn't decided yet. Maybe she'd start a Pinterest board for that . . .

She also couldn't stop ordering things. And neither could her mum, in between excessive bouts of hysterical crying. Every week another John Lewis or Mamas & Papas delivery would turn up at the door containing tiny clothes, lovely wooden toys and all other sorts of stuff that Emily had no idea if she needed yet or not.

Better safe than sorry, right?

Some days she'd go home early and start ironing tiny babygros, before laying them out on the bed in colour order and gently sobbing at how incredibly cute they all were.

But right now it was only 11.37 a.m. on a dreary wet Wednesday, and she had towelling to write about.

She'd just finish off the Frazzles and get going . . .

Just a few hours, and she could pack up, head home, take her bra off and spend her evening baby planning.

Perhaps she'd draft another blog post. She'd already started one about '*getting more dairy into your diet in the last few weeks . . .*' but right now she was considering a more accurate reflection of pregnancy might be . . . '*how to not lose your shit with the dickhead colleague who's after your job when you go on maternity leave and keeps feeding you bacon-flavoured maize snacks in an attempt to make you so fat you never come back . . .*'

That'd make her feel better.

Chapter 36

MOVE DAY

It was strange saying goodbye.

Molly had lived in her flat for over two years. It was the place she'd stayed longest at since moving out of her family home. And it was quite perfectly 'her'.

She looked around, taking it all in, as she moved a few empty boxes into the living room, ready to begin packing everything up.

It was small, a little scruffy, perhaps not entirely clean, full of trinkets, photos and slightly sad-looking tie-dyed throws, and utterly disorganised in a totally wonderful way. It made her smile.

She'd filled it with everything that made her happy. None of it matched. Some of it looked tired. But that didn't matter. She had surrounded herself with reminders of all the amazing experiences and wonderful people she'd had in her life. That was what mattered.

She'd given her month's notice straight after the dinner party. There was no point delaying. She was only going to get 'more pregnant'. And the three weeks since then had flown by.

She'd planned to move out slowly over the next week. They'd move everything across in Tom's car each evening, and she'd clean as she went. He only lived five minutes' drive away, and it seemed silly to leave it all until the weekend.

The empty boxes were littered around the place ready to be filled. And she'd had strict instructions from Tom not to lift anything heavy or dusty, of course. Which was quite hard in Molly's flat considering she couldn't remember ever having dusted. She didn't even own a duster. Besides, she was pregnant, not paralysed. And she felt like she wanted to do this on her own.

As she sat on the floor in her living room with the first empty box in front of her, she had a strange feeling of resistance. It wasn't that she wanted to stay; it was just hard leaving.

She thought back to all the decisions she'd made in her life that had got her to this point.

Two years ago, she'd arrived back from travelling with nothing but a backpack, a bad haircut and some tie-dye fabric from Bali. She had no idea where she was going or what she'd do next. She didn't want to know. She just wanted to earn a bit of cash, and do it all again. No point staying still, she might have to grow up. And who ever wanted to do that?

Somehow a year passed. And then she met Tom.

Mutual friends had introduced them to each other at a gig at O'Neill's in Wycombe town centre. And that was that.

She didn't believe in love at first sight, but it was certainly lust. They'd got drunk and ended up fumbling about near the bins round the back of the pub. Probably not the ideal first-date story to share with the kids as they grew up . . .

But she didn't care.

They'd found each other. And fallen for each other. Even if it was next to a line of Biffas while she stood in a partially eaten Zinger Tower Burger meal . . .

She knew now why she loved him. He'd given her purpose. Even if it hadn't been obvious at first.

She thought she'd been at her happiest floating around Asia and the Far East meeting people from all walks of life – although they were predominantly nineteen-year-old private-school graduates spending their parents' money and growing their hair into dreadlocks – but that was in the past. It wasn't who she was any more.

What she needed to do was to say goodbye to all of that. And start being happy she had done it, rather than sad because she wasn't still doing it.

'This' was her, now.

She was going to be a mum.

And Tom was going to be a dad.

Molly was starting to realise, as she carefully put photos of her up mountains and on exotic beaches into cardboard boxes, that even though this hadn't been planned, it was perfect.

She didn't need anything more than this.

And with that, she got to her feet and decided it was time for the throws to go in the bin. She couldn't remember if she'd ever washed them in the entire two years they'd been there. They certainly felt a bit crispy round the edges, and they were faded and full of holes.

As she pulled them off the sofa, something fell out of the folds and on to the floor with a thud.

A phone.

Gerald's phone.

Oh wow . . . so it was here . . . she thought to herself, smiling as she picked it up.

She'd text Liz and let her know.

And make sure she gave it a good wipe before giving it back.

Chapter 37

HAPPY . . .

It had been a long time since she had actually been 'happy', Liz thought as she sat in a familiar bar at a well-lit high table, waiting for Gerald and Hannah to arrive for drinks on an early Friday evening after work.

Life was good. Work was great. And things had returned to somewhere close to normal between her and Gerald after their chat, which was a huge relief. The awkwardness seemed to have evaporated. It was like the whole thing never happened. They were back to chatting, enjoying each other's company as friends, and she was back to laughing at his shit jokes. That had to be a good sign.

She was getting back to her old self. Enjoying her own company. She was even considering the idea that she might actually be able to date again soon, but she'd certainly be casting her net a lot wider than the office and Molly's pool of face-tattooed band members. Besides, she wasn't after a relationship. She certainly didn't 'need' a man in her life, but it would be nice to feel good again. Go out, meet new people, not sit around at home on a weekend like some crazy-but-nicely-fringed-cat-lady crying into a Wagamamas for one . . .

She snapped out of her thoughts at the sound of her phone vibrating on the table in front of her . . .

> **Gerald**
> I'm literally just leaving!
> Hannah's just finishing up too
> so won't be long.
> Get them in and I'll be there in 10 ;)

Liz picked up the cocktail menu. It was Friday, after all, and she was in a cocktail kind of mood.

She headed over to the bar and ordered two whisky sours on a tab.

Eyebrows served her. She looked Liz straight in the eye but didn't seem to recognise her, undoubtedly because she served hundreds of people every week, and to her, Liz was probably just another city-type in a designer suit looking to get shitfaced after work on a Friday.

But Liz hoped it was because she looked so different to how she did all those dark months ago.

She'd put on a little weight, in a good way. She looked healthier. She had her appetite back and was eating properly again. She was sleeping better. She now spent her spare time with her friends, or work colleagues, rather than hammering the treadmill at the gym trying to run away from how shit her life was before going home to down a bottle of Pinot Grigio for dinner . . .

Her face had filled out; the extra fat had softened her angular features a little and plumped out her gaunt cheeks

199

and eye bags. She was styling her hair differently, less severely, and even experimenting with lipsticks other than her trademark red.

But most of all, she was smiling. All the time. Her eyes were smiling too. She didn't look drained and tired any more. Everything in her life was coming together and she was getting back to being herself again.

So she was sure that was why Eyebrows couldn't see that she was that same sad-faced bitter old cow who sat at the end of her bar week after week downing martinis and trying to save her from men by converting her to lesbianism. She was certain of it.

The drinks arrived. Liz carried them back to the table and decided to waste a few moments messaging her friends:

Liz
Hey, ladies.
I'm about to drink cocktails
until I'm dead.
What are you two crazy
preggo cats up to?

Emily
Please shut up!
I could murder a cocktail.
I'm on my seventy-fifth cup of
Raspberry Leaf Tea.
Which tastes like hot,
red, diluted arse.

And I'm about to get Paul
to give me a pedicure.
I haven't been able to get
down there properly since February.
SO it's ALL GLAMOUR here . . .

Liz
Wow.
That's true love.
I would never touch
someone else's feet.

Molly
If you think that's love . . .
Wait until she asks him to do her fanny.

Emily
LOL
(I'm laughing. But this is going
to happen soon . . .
It's bad down there.)

Molly
Like 70s porn-star bad? Or worse?

Emily
If I could see it. I'd tell you.

Molly
I think Tom quite likes that look . . .
I think he's looking forward to
mine reaching its full potential tbh!

Liz
Right!
This conversation has gone to
a weird pube-related place.

Emily
Hey – you asked . . .

Liz
I'm pretty sure I didn't actually . . .
I've gotta go now anyway Gerald will
be here any second.

Molly
Ah yes . . . Gerald.
Still pretending you don't fancy him
then . . .

Liz
Yes.
Mainly because I don't?

Emily
You're just lying to yourself . . .

Molly
LIES. LIES. LIES.

Liz
As mature as this is.
I'm just going to go now.
Have fun tonight you hairy sober
bitches.

Just as Liz typed the last sentence, Gerald took up a seat next to her as he stripped his slightly damp coat off.

'This for me?' he said, winking at her as he lifted one of the cocktails to his lips and took a long sip.

'Indeed it is. I chucked a load of Rohypnol in that one,' Liz said.

Gerald laughed, and ran his fingers through his thick blond hair as he took another sip of his drink. Liz liked how easy this was. She liked spending time with him. And that they could flirt a little without it meaning anything. Anything at all, right?

Chapter 38

SCAN SATURDAY

It had become harder and harder to stick to Last Saturday Club since Christmas. It seemed like everyone had so much in their lives (and uteruses) now. It just wasn't anyone's priority at the moment.

But Emily was going to make sure this one happened. She'd sent a series of passive-aggressive messages to her two friends throughout the week so they knew that no one was allowed to miss this one. It was the last Saturday in April, and they'd not managed to do one this year yet. There was no excuse.

Liz could take a break from work. Molly was now living with her ridiculously horny boyfriend, so tearing herself away for a few hours to look all glowy and comfortable and barely pregnant shouldn't be that hard, and Emily was determined to get there in spite of only being able to wear flip-flops on her puffy, badly pedicured feet and having now developed a full blown 'waddle' to match her giant face and arse.

Emily had managed to waddle herself the entire way from Sainsbury's car park to Wagamamas, panting like she'd just escaped from prison. She knew that Molly had had her twenty-week scan yesterday, and she was desperate to find out what she was having. She was almost as excited about that as she was about finding out the sex of her own child . . .

Much to her irritation, Molly had refused to divulge any information over text, phone, email or social media for the past twenty-four hours. It wasn't Molly's style; she was happy to keep things low-key, and just 'tell them all about it when she saw them'. As she kept saying. Repeatedly. Which was killing Emily. She hated not being told everything straight away. She was a 'sharer'. And could not understand it when other people weren't.

She and Liz had been waiting patiently at the table for Molly, who was now fifteen minutes late. Emily had chosen Wagamamas as the location, since she was now at that really special part in late pregnancy where you're unable to go more than an hour without eating something.

However, watching everyone else's food being brought out and having delicious smells continually wafted in her direction was like being subjected to some kind of noodle-based torture. Right now her two biggest fears were the word 'heatwave' and the idea that the UK might suddenly stop doing chicken yaki soba. Or Toblerones. It didn't bear thinking about . . .

A few moments later, Molly strolled in, with no acknowledgement that she was nearly twenty minutes late or of the agony her very-much-more-pregnant friend had suffered having people eating noodles around her for the duration.

'Ladies,' Molly said with a relaxed smile on her face.

205

Emily was finding it increasingly irritating how not-pregnant and non-waddle-y Molly looked. She was floating around in cheesecloth, looking all fucking dewy and serene with a delicate little bump, while Emily had back acne, a face like a blimp, and was wearing Paul's Havaianas.

'You're late. Let's order!' Emily said without hesitation. She'd been eyeing up the half-eaten udon guy next to her for the last few minutes. She was very close to snatching it and shovelling it into her face with her hands . . .

'I think that's heavily pregnant and angry speak for "Hello, how are you? You look wonderful, I'm a little peckish . . ."' Liz said, laughing.

'Ha. It's cool. You guys should have just ordered for me if you were hungry. I always have the same thing anyway! Ramen me up,' Molly said with a wink as she pulled her jacket off and sat down.

'Excellent,' Emily said snappily, sitting up straight and making *come-here-now-before-I-start-eating-my-menu-and-have-you-murdered* eyes at a young messy-bunned waitress.

Messy-bun headed straight over. And stood poised at the end of the table with her ordering tablet and pen.

'Right. I'll have a seventy-three, a thirty-eight and a fifty-four,' said Emily without flinching. 'Don't judge me. I'm heavily pregnant. And I'm registering a ten on the fat-angry scale now . . . It's like the Richter scale. But fat. And angry.'

Messy-bun didn't react. Emily didn't care.

'Hmmm . . . I'll just take a fifty-four and some miso soup please,' Liz said.

'And an eighty-nine for me, please,' Molly added. 'With a glass of tap water. Thanks.'

Messy-bun scuttled off as quickly as her badly laced Converse trainers could carry her.

'So! Tell us, then,' Emily said, glaring at Molly and squeezing her hands together in anticipation.

'Tell you what?' Molly replied innocently.

'YOUR SCAN. Tell us what you're having,' Emily said, louder.

'Oh right . . . Well. I don't know. We didn't find out,' Molly said calmly.

'WHAT?' Emily responded. 'How could you not find out? How will you know what to buy? How to decorate the nursery? How will you be able to prepare?'

'Emily!' Liz sensed her outburst may be primarily down to lack of noodles.

'I don't see why you need to know?' Molly said, shrugging her shoulders. 'It's a baby. I've got nearly four months before it's due anyway, and then I'm just thinking I'll get one of those basket things that goes next to your bed and grab a stroller off eBay. Loads of people have offered to give me babygros and stuff. So I just figured that's it.'

'Well, when you put it like that, I am slightly concerned at how I spent almost three grand in John Lewis last week . . .' Emily genuinely began to wonder if she could remember anything she'd bought so far.

'Hey, we're just different.' Molly touched Emily's arm

reassuringly. 'Me and Tom . . . we just don't have that kind of money, and even if we did we wouldn't spend it on the same stuff you guys do. We're just not made that way. I think so long as the baby is happy, warm, fed and loved . . . what else does it need?'

'That's a lovely way to think about it,' Liz said, smiling at her friend. 'My sister bought so much crap for her first one, and barely used any of it. Some of it never even made it out of the box. She reckons she spent most of her maternity leave trying to sell it all again on Facebook to people offering her a fraction of what she asked for, continually calling her "hun" and asking if she could deliver things. To Kent. From Hampshire. Her second baby spends most of its time in hand-me-down babygros, bouncing in the Jumperoo and eating dirt. And she seems totally fine.'

The friends laughed. Emily thought on her friend's words for a moment. She was right. All the shopping she'd been doing, perhaps it was more for her than the baby. She had a room full of stuff and no idea what most of it was or did. Ah well. It had been fun buying it all so who cares? Right now all she knew was that she really needed those noodles now . . .

'I know you're right,' Emily said eventually, smiling. 'But I do still need that iCandy. I actually do NEED that.'

The three friends laughed again as Messy-bun began placing steaming plates of yummy things down in front of them. Most of it in front of Emily, of course.

'Ooh, maybe after this we can go have a look at it in

the shop? Take it for a little spin around the highchair section and see what new colour packs they have coming out for summer?' Emily added, stuffing dumplings in her face without pausing in between.

'Um. Sure . . .' Liz said hesitantly.

'Count me in!' Molly said as genuinely as she could manage. It was pretty much her idea of hell, but Emily would love it. And taking your heavily pregnant friend buggy-shopping while they're wearing their husband's flip-flops and eating a Toblerone like a chicken leg is just what real friends do for each other . . .

Chapter 39

NCT

> There are things they try to tell you in NCT,
> Like how you're now committed
> to a life of puke, poo and wee . . .
> But you're not ready to hear that,
> you're more interested in the day,
> That a tiny real-life human comes
> flying right out of your Va-jay-jay.

There is something strangely unsettling about being surrounded almost entirely by pregnant women in a confined space, Emily thought as she surveyed the room, ignoring the perspiration that was forming on her top lip and soaking into the band of her maternity bra.

It was a warm Tuesday evening in early May, and Emily and Paul had taken their seats at their first-ever NCT class. They'd pressed the white name badges on to their chests, and picked a couple of chairs nearer the back of the room, where they could easily escape if this was too scary, or if she passed out from the heat . . .

This was the first session of a six-week course. Emily knew the baby was going to come out of her womb one way or another, even if she was trying not to think about that bit too much right now, so she'd booked their place a few weeks ago, knowing she was going to have to face reality sooner or later . . .

And where better to face it than the sixth-form common room of the girls' high school at the top of the hill.

Paul looked like he was really looking forward to it. (He didn't.) Which was slightly annoying Emily. (A lot.) But she also felt weirdly apprehensive as the room filled up with very pregnant ladies and their very unenthusiastic-looking partners and husbands.

The last couple took their seats and the room gently simmered down. Seven couples sat in a horseshoe formation around a friendly-faced lady in her forties called Tracey. Who sat smiling and facing the group, ready with a flip chart, some knitted boobs and a prosthetic pelvis complete with rubber vagina . . .

'Welcome everybody,' Tracey began, as all eyes fixed on her. 'Please take a couple of minutes to grab a glass of water and a biscuit. Or five, if you're anything like me. And if anyone needs the loo or needs some fresh air at any point, please feel free to step out.'

A few of the men headed up to fetch refreshments for themselves and their pregnant other halves, Paul included. Following a not-so-subtle nudge from Emily.

Emily took a look at the people around her. Seven couples couldn't look more different to each other if they tried, she thought. Other than the fact that all seven women were heavily pregnant, there were bumps, boobs and bottoms of every shape and size . . .

The couple on the far right were tall, lean and athletic-looking – Julia and her partner Charlie towered above the group with their long, slim figures. Julia's bump was round and neat, and at least half the size of Emily's. She didn't look uncomfortable in the slightest. From the back, you wouldn't even know she was pregnant. Whereas Emily looked like she was storing an extra baby in each arse cheek.

A little further round sat Ian and his very uncomfortable-looking wife Sophie. Her bump was probably bigger than Emily's, which was no mean feat. She fanned herself continually and had given up on shoes. A sensible choice, thought Emily, following suit and flicking off her flip-flops. They sat quietly as another couple stood in front of them chatting . . . Emily couldn't see their names from behind, but the wife looked entirely comfortable standing up despite a very large bump, something that was beyond Emily by now. Perhaps it was because she was short, Emily thought to herself. Gravity is definitely on your side when you're closer to the ground . . .

The lady sat next to Emily on her left looked nice. She was pretty and very normal-looking, whatever normal looked like. Perhaps it was because she looked like she was enjoying sitting down while her husband fed her tea and biscuits. Something Emily could totally relate to, as Paul shoved another Jaffa Cake in her face.

Rachael was a similar age to Emily – around thirty, she guessed. A lot of the others seemed mid-thirties or older. Not that it mattered. Emily was trying not to look like she was looking, but noticed Rachael's bump was quite perfect. Not too big, not too small. Somewhere between Julia's little round football bump and Emily's whole-team clubhouse . . . It was amazing how being pregnant yourself made you suddenly become obsessed with everyone else's bump sizes and shapes. Emily hadn't even realised she was until right at that moment.

The room quietened down again as everyone made it back to their seats.

It reminded Emily a little of being back at school. They took it in turns to tell everyone their names and, if they knew it, the sex of their baby along with the expected due date, as Tracey and her knitted boobs wrote all the details down on her flipchart.

As the evening wore on, they covered lots of useful but daunting things about what to pack in your hospital bag, types of pain relief and the various stages of labour. It was mostly terrifying, but fascinating at the same time . . .

Emily had already decided she wouldn't be needing pain relief. At most, she might suck on some of that gas-and-air stuff, but she'd already made the decision she was going to be good at labour. She was the kind of person who was 'good at things'. And while she hadn't been that great at being pregnant so far, she was going to make up for that by squeezing her baby out in record time, without any need for drugs, and with her hair freshly highlighted with a full face of make-up on. She'd make it look easy. Stylish, even. She had it all planned out.

Although, sitting here listening to Tracey, the reality of what would actually happen to her body during labour was beginning to sink in. Up until now, Emily had been too scared to think about it. It was far easier to keep buying tiny babygros and cute hats, and remain in denial about the half-metre-long human who would surf through her cervix in a couple of months' time . . .

Emily looked around the room, until her eyes landed on her husband. Paul looked terrified. But actually, everyone looked a bit terrified. It made her feel better.

Emily zoned back in on Tracey, just as she picked up her prosthetic vagina and a plastic baby.

'So, ladies and gents, this is where your baby's head will be sitting once they've become engaged,' Tracey said matter-of-factly.

Emily felt a wave of horror as Tracey began to guide the baby's head down through the pelvis. She had a lovely calm voice that made it all sound a breeze. It felt like a trap.

'Your cervix will fully dilate to around ten centimetres, usually at a rate of about a centimetre an hour, before you feel the overwhelming urge to push, and can use the power of your body to gently assist your baby out,' Tracey continued, pushing the baby's head further down and through the cervix, that was represented by a painfully taut elastic band. Emily felt the overwhelming urge to cross her legs.

Tracey was making it sound like popping open a tube of Pringles. Emily was starting to feel a bit queasy. One centimetre per hour? Was she drunk? That can't be right, surely? That's ten hours. And now she'd started thinking about it, she could murder some Pringles . . .

Just as she thought she might have to step out for a moment, the plastic baby's head suddenly flew off and landed in the biscuit tin after a slightly misaligned exit from the birth canal.

Everyone laughed. It relieved the tension, and they all started to relax after that.

Over the next hour or so, the group started to get to know each other, being split into smaller teams to chat and complete tasks. They took it in turns to scribble things down and shove the baby down the rubber fanny. Without decapitating it again.

It was strange talking so candidly in front of complete strangers about what was about to happen to your body. And your life. But it felt good.

Everyone seems really nice, Emily thought. And really normal. She wasn't sure why she'd worried so much. There were already a few couples she'd picked out as having good 'friend potential'.

Emily had spent a lot of the evening chatting to Rachael. Her and her husband Fergus lived just down the road from her and Paul. They even knew some of the same people. They'd probably been at some of the same drunken teenage parties.

Paul seemed more relaxed too. He'd hit it off with another dad when they discussed car-seat installation and rugby, so he was back in his element.

Emily felt so happy that she'd done it. Even if it was a little bit like being part of some kind of social experiment. Like an antenatal *Big Brother* house, but in a sixth-form common room, with lots of hormonal women downing Gaviscon and biscuits, and playing with a plastic fanny.

Chapter 40

SETTLING IN

Molly
Are you guys awake?

Emily
We are now . . .
I don't sleep longer than twelve
minutes on each side these
days anyway so
I wouldn't worry about waking me up!
What's up?

Liz
I'm awake.
Can't sleep.
Been lying here with my eyes closed
trying to remember if I put the
dishwasher on.
My life is so glamorous . . .
Everything okay?

Molly
I don't know really . . .
I feel a bit weird.

Emily
Weird how?
Do you mean the baby?

Liz
Are you okay?

Molly
No. The baby's totally fine.
Sorry I didn't mean anything like that.
I meant in myself . . .
Everyone keeps telling me
how lucky I am
to have moved into Tom's.
How much I should be enjoying it.
How wonderful it should be . . .
But I just feel a bit weird.
I've never lived with
a boyfriend before!
Am I just being an ungrateful twat?
It feels strange not having
my own space.
I miss my little flat . . .
Even though everyone thought it was
a total shithole, and if I'm
honest it was a bit of a
total shithole . . . but I liked it.
Because it was MY shithole.
But now I don't have a shithole
of my own.

I'm living in my boyfriend's
quite nice maisonette
And I never really thought of
myself as a
'quite nice maisonette' person.
I'm just being a twat, aren't I.
I feel like I'm being really selfish
but it's just how I feel.

Liz
I think that's really normal sweetie.
You don't need to feel bad.
It's a really big adjustment.
Just take some time.
Give it a few weeks and see how you
feel then . . .

Emily
Exactly.
You're pumped full of hormones too.
That's going to make
everything you feel
about 10 times stronger!
Trust me! I know this! Lol x

Liz
Have you spoken to Tom about it?

Molly
No.
I don't want to hurt his feelings.

219

He's being amazing.
Yesterday he ran me a bath
(one of those ones with proper
candles and bubbles and shit.),
massaged my feet, made me dinner,
and did all my washing.
He even ironed stuff . . .
I don't even iron stuff.
He is so sweet.
It's just he won't let me do anything.
And I do mean ANYTHING.
And he's turned into the food-police.
Yesterday he practically rugby tackled
a Mini-Babybel out of
my hand because
he hadn't checked the label to see if it
was unpasteurised, and
when I got home he
made me eat a bowl of
edamame beans.
I don't even know why.
I think he might be losing it . . .

Emily
Jeez . . .
Well he might be going a
bit (a lot) overboard
but he is trying to be sweet?
You've got a good one there xx

I'm crying right now!
How are you not crying!

Liz
I threw up in my mouth a little bit . . .
Sounds like he's trying really hard to
make you feel like it's your home.
Maybe you need to chat to him about
the bean-force-feeding though. That's
a little weird . . .
Seriously – don't worry.
Things will work out.
You can always chat to us, sweetie.

Molly
I know.
Thanks, girls.
Love you guys xxx

Chapter 41

BEING PREGNANT ON YOUR BIRTHDAY . . . IS SHIT.

Today was Emily's thirtieth birthday.

It was a Thursday. The sun was shining and the air was full of early summer heat.

Which would normally make her very happy. She loved having a late May birthday.

But this year was different. This year she was pregnant. Very pregnant.

And the sun felt like it was cooking her from the bra down. She didn't know how it was possible for one person to sweat this much, and no matter how much she fanned herself and tried to limit the waddling, she still couldn't stop the under-breast sweat patches that kept appearing.

Plus she was at work.

And Matilda was yet again being a total dick.

'So, as it's a big birthday, have you got any big plans? Hope that husband of yours is treating you?' Matilda said from across the desk.

From anyone else it would seem a perfectly sweet and innocent question, but Matilda had an uncanny ability to make everything sound like a competition or a mild threat. And Emily wasn't entirely sure if that last line wasn't also a dig at her husband . . .

'Birthdays at seven and a half months pregnant aren't really that much fun, to be honest,' Emily said dryly, trying not to sound irritated.

'Aww, don't say that. I've had pregnant friends who've rocked their birthdays. If you want to have fun, you will!' Matilda replied. Dickishly.

Emily took that not only as a criticism of her character, but also pity. Pity mixed with Matilda telling her she was not as good as being pregnant as her friends were. *Excellent. Happy fucking birthday to me.*

'I'm just happy to have a chilled one,' Emily replied, trying to cut the conversation dead, with her eyes fixed on her screen.

'Fair enough.' Matilda seemed satisfied with that answer for some reason . . .

Just then, a chorus of badly sung 'Happy Birthday' began to ring around the office as Emily looked up from her screen. She turned round in her chair to see Natalie walking towards her holding an enormous chocolate cake with a single lit candle in it.

Emily immediately welled up. Natalie placed the cake down carefully on the end of Emily's desk as the singing came to a welcome end. A spattered round of cheers and claps resonated around the office floor as Emily bent slightly forward (as far as her human-carrying uterus would allow her) and managed just enough puff to extinguish the candle.

'Thank you!' Emily managed in between snotty sobs as Natalie gave her a big hug while she remained in her chair.

223

'Happy birthday, sweetie!' Natalie said, passing her a card and a knife to cut into the cake.

Emily opened the card and felt the tears flow a little stronger now. She loved cards. She loved reading all the sweet messages people had written. Even those who hadn't spelt her name correctly, or hadn't actually ever met or spoken to her. But still. It was so sweet.

She also loved cake. And this birthday was getting a whole lot better now that she'd cut herself a slice of chocolate cake that would have sustained a family for a week.

Within moments, the office floor had returned to normality. Emily hadn't paid too much attention. She had cake now.

Matilda's comments did play on her mind for the rest of the day. Perhaps she *was* a bit of a fun-sponge at the moment. That didn't make it any less irritating that Matilda might be right; she'd certainly never let her know that.

It's just she was finding it hard turning thirty and not having a big party to look forward to, or an expensive romantic trip, or any idea what her body looked like from the waist down without the use of a mirror. She knew she was at risk of sounding like a spoilt brat, but she'd always gone 'big' on birthdays and she couldn't help but feel a little bit disappointed.

GOD, SHE HATED IT WHEN MATILDA WAS RIGHT.

Emily knew she was being an idiot. She knew this was a mix of hormones, exhaustion and generally being fed up with having no bladder or lung capacity . . .

Just a few more weeks, and this would be over . . .

She'd have her baby. And she'd no longer give a shit about missing out on getting drunk in Ibiza or a boozy weekend to Paris with Paul to celebrate leaving her twenties behind. Because she'd have her baby. She needed to focus on that.

She'd had over a decade of partying, holidaying and boozing her birthdays away. This one was different, but it didn't have to be 'bad' different.

No.

It would be great.

She just needed to think of something she could do that would mean celebrating, without going too far from home, that didn't rely on alcohol in order not to be shit . . .

She racked her brain for a moment as the sun streamed in through the window and forced her to squint . . . That was it.

She'd host a barbecue at home in the garden. Invite all her favourite people. Play her favourite songs. Make Paul do all the cooking. And eat the shit out of some slightly charcoal-ly sausages washed down with a virgin mojito recipe she'd seen on Pinterest.

If I want to have fun I will. I bloody well will. So fuck you, Matilda, Emily thought to herself as she started to feel a little happier and tore off another giant piece of chocolate cake using both her hands . . .

Yeah. Fuck you, Matilda.

*

As Emily walked (waddled) in through the front door she was quite relieved to be home. And reunited with her slippers. She felt a bit silly for being such a birthday Scrooge – she'd actually had a lovely day and been really spoilt by everyone at the office. As the day had gone on, and the messages, Facebook notifications and phone calls had come in, she'd slowly begun to cheer up.

She'd also lowered her gift expectations from Paul, realising she was being a bit of a dick. He'd joked all week about buying her a slow cooker, which she was now too pregnant to find funny. And had mostly cried uncontrollably every time he mentioned it.

But she'd stopped dreaming of being whisked off to romantic European cities and showered in designer handbags and shoes. It was stupid. They'd just spent several thousand pounds on 'stuff' for their baby. That was life now. Her earnings were about to drop down to the pitiful payments of maternity leave, just as their family expanded by 50 per cent. It was time to embrace being a parent, and the sacrifices that came with that. Although, if he bought her 'mum gifts' again she probably would violently beat him to death with them. Before using the joint account to buy herself some shoes.

Emily felt happily relaxed as she lowered herself on to the sofa and flicked the television on, waiting for Paul to arrive home.

He'd sent her sweet messages throughout the day that had made her feel special. She was really looking forward to him walking through the door. She'd even decided he'd get lucky tonight if he played his cards right. Not that she knew 'how' exactly that would happen. She hadn't personally seen it for a few months, but she was fairly sure her vagina was still there, so that was a good start. At least.

She didn't have to wait long. A few minutes later came the familiar sound of Paul turning his key in the lock. He walked in with a wide grin across his face and immediately bent down to kiss her and then her bump in turn.

'Happy birthday, my beautiful wife,' he said gently, with his face still close to hers.

'Thank you,' Emily said.

'And how was your day? Did work make a fuss of you?' Paul said as he stood back up and took his shoes off.

'Well. They gave me an enormous cake. I'd say that counts as a pretty good fuss. I think they thought I'd share it with everyone. I didn't. I'm nearly eight months pregnant and it's my thirtieth birthday. That chocolate bitch was ALL mine.'

Paul laughed. 'That's my girl!'

'So I've decided on a barbecue for the weekend,' Emily said. 'I messaged everybody earlier and most people can make it. I can't be arsed with a big night out. What's the point in watching everyone else getting drunk while I sit there sober, and cry about the area formally known as my waist? I'd rather wear a big hat, eat meat and get a tan.'

227

'Sounds great to me. Eating dead animals is one of my favourite things.' Paul sat down next to her. 'So. When do you want your present?'

Emily felt her smile widen. She really did love him.

'Now!' she said, knowing he already knew that.

Paul reached into his back pocket and pulled out a small deep-blue velvet box. It hadn't been anything like she was expecting. She felt equally nervous and excited now.

'This is not the usual sort of thing I'd get you,' he said, keeping the box in his hand. 'But I wanted to get you something different, because things are a bit different this year. And I love you so much. I hope you like it.'

Emily loved how in tune he was with her. She felt her vision blur a little as she took the box from him.

She placed it in her lap and inspected it for a moment. It was old. In a lovely way. The edges were worn away, and little patches were threadbare.

She used both hands to gently lift the little box open, and as the lid snapped up, it revealed a fine-chained silver locket. It looked battered and beautiful with age. There was a pretty yellow stone in its centre, surrounded by little diamonds. It was well polished but full of character and history.

She loved it.

'It was my great-grandma's,' Paul said. 'It's probably the only expensive piece of jewellery she ever owned, but it's a total one-off. That's a yellow diamond. It's really rare, apparently. I don't think she had any idea what it was worth. Chances are she found it, my mum reckons.

But I always thought it was so unusual. So my mum gave it to me, and told me one day I should give it to someone I loved . . .

'And I love you so much, Emily. And today feels like the right day for you to have it. And I can't imagine anything more amazing than putting a picture of our boy in there. So you can carry him close to your heart.'

Paul sat back and waited for her reaction. He wasn't the most romantic of men, and she could see the words were a little awkward and embarrassing for him to say. Emily knew that. But he had said them. And everything he'd just said was nothing short of perfect.

'I love it.' She let a few happy tears roll down her face. 'And I love you so much too.'

Paul hugged her and kissed her again.

Emily wiped her eyes with her palms and shook the last of her tears away.

'With this diamond, you are definitely getting lucky tonight,' she said, winking at him.

'Well, if I'd known all I had to give you was a one-of-a-kind antique yellow diamond, I would have chucked it at you months ago,' Paul said, laughing.

'Right now, anything above a slow cooker would get you laid to be fair,' Emily said, nudging him playfully.

He pulled himself in close to her and placed one hand on her stomach to feel the baby's little kicks and wriggles. Emily loved it when he did that.

This was strangely turning out to be the most unexpectedly wonderful birthday. She had everything she

229

needed right here: the man she loved, the son she couldn't wait to meet, an antique diamond necklace, and the prospect of a night on the sofa, with tacky reality TV and not a slow cooker in sight . . .

Perfect.

Chapter 42

'HIM'

It was so typical that just as everything in her life was going right, the Universe would serve Liz up a giant slice of dick pie.

She had been busy being happy, getting to know herself again. She'd relaxed. She'd forgotten all the deep, dark and outright shitty times she'd been through over the last couple of years. She hadn't needed to think about them, why would she? There was no reason to recall anything from that period of her life.

Until now.

The message she used to yearn for, pray for, the one that said 'I'm here' and let her steal a few hours away with 'him'; the moments that she thought made her happy. But she now knew had just made her so so sad.

But right there on her phone as she sat in one of the boardrooms at work with Hannah and Gerald opposite her, was that message. Just sitting there. Like a gateway back to all the shit . . .

It's me.
I know you don't owe me anything.

I just hate how we left things.
Can we meet?

'You okay?' Gerald said softly from across the table.

Liz realised she was frowning deeply. She immediately relaxed her face and let out a small cough to clear her throat and buy her a few seconds to decide how to reply.

'Yes. Sorry. It's nothing . . .' she managed. She was desperately trying to stop her mind dragging up those old memories and feelings.

She couldn't deal with this right now. She'd slip out for an early lunch in a bit. And deal with it then.

She couldn't make eye contact with anyone until she did. She was terrified Gerald or Hannah would ask her a question and she'd be forced to lie, and the one thing recent events had taught her is that she never wanted to lie to anyone, ever again.

The clock had finally hit midday.

'I'm just popping out,' Liz announced, avoiding anyone's eye. She skipped out of the room quickly before anyone could ask her where she was going.

She headed swiftly out of the office and to a cafe round the corner.

If she was going to do this, she needed coffee. And bacon.

She ordered a bacon sandwich and a latte and perched herself on a stool in the window.

She took a deep breath and pulled her phone out of her pocket.

Her mind was racing. Even though she sometimes saw 'him' at work; passed him in a corridor, shared the same lift, even sat near him during senior firm meetings . . . That was different. He was easy to ignore in those circumstances.

Right now her mind was screaming at her. Every part of her knew she needed to shut this down now. Meeting him served no purpose. She'd heard everything she'd needed to when they'd met a few months ago. She was happy now. Why would she even give him the opportunity to get back in and poison her life?

Yet there was this niggling thought at the back of her mind. What if he genuinely wanted to clear the air? Properly. He'd know by now she was on her way to being made partner . . . she'd be his boss. Technically. So perhaps finding a way to move on and be civil with each other was in her best interests. She didn't need all that crap rearing its head unexpectedly just as she was getting the most important promotion of her life. It was time to be a grown-up about all this.

Before she knew what she was doing, she was texting him.

Liz
Cafe on the corner by the cobbler's.
I'll be here for 20 minutes.
That's it.

233

She had no idea if this was the worst idea she'd ever had. But it was done. She'd hear him out. And that would be that.

She didn't have to wait long. She'd barely managed a mouthful of her sandwich when he walked through the door and took a seat on the stool next to her.

'Hello,' he said, a little too casually for Liz's liking.

'Hello.' She wished she hadn't still got half a mouthful of bacon in her face.

'Thanks for meeting me, Lizzy. I know you didn't have to. I really appreciate it.'

'It's okay,' Liz said, matter-of-factly. She wished he'd just get on with it, whatever 'it' was.

'You look amazing. Different. Have you changed your hair or something? It suits you,' he said, smiling as if they were old friends.

Liz wasn't going to be sucked in by his charm offensive. She'd been here before. She deliberately didn't respond.

'Okay,' he said quickly, sensing her disdain. 'There's no easy way to say this. She's leaving me, Lizzy.'

It felt like someone had suddenly punched all the air out of her body. She was using every bit of her strength not to react. She didn't want him to think for a moment that she cared. She would not allow him the privilege of knowing he still had any kind of effect on her.

'Why are you telling me this?' Liz said as coldly as she could manage.

'I don't know,' he said. 'I think because I knew this was what you always wanted. What we always wanted.'

'You think what I wanted was for your pregnant wife to leave you after finally realising what a dickbag you are, so that you could come crying and grovelling back to me?' Liz said with a sarcastic laugh, shaking her head. 'I think what's really happened here is that you've carried on cheating on her with some other poor woman you've fed a bunch of lies to, she's caught you, and now that you've been rejected by absolutely everyone you have left in your utterly pathetic life, you're trying your luck with me again.'

'It's not like that, Lizzy. She doesn't love me any more. Yes, there were others, but no one like you. You're the only woman I've ever really loved. Can't you see that, Lizzy? I'm lost without you. Lost.'

Liz started to see red.

'Others? So you've been sticking your penis all over town because you love me so much? Jesus. You are such a fucking idiot. Look. Go back home. Stick your dick back in your pants. And work things out with your wife. Who has just had your fucking baby. And deserves so much more than you could ever give her. Step up. Be a father. Be a real man. And stay the fuck away from me.'

Liz got down from the stool. She'd heard everything she needed to. And she didn't want to be there a second longer.

As she went to leave, he grabbed her. He forced his face roughly on to hers and tried to kiss her. Hard. Liz kept her lips pursed and pulled her face away, freeing herself from his grasp.

He put his head in his hands and sat motionless on the stool. He was crying. It was pathetic.

She couldn't believe that this was the man she had thought she loved. This snivelling wreck of a human. She used to long for his kisses. Cherish them. But now they meant less than nothing. They disgusted her.

Liz scurried back to the office without paying any attention to the journey. She made her way through the main door and reached the lift. She let out a little sigh of relief.

She knew he would leave her alone now. He'd be too embarrassed not to.

That would be it.

She walked quickly down the corridor and made her way back to the boardroom.

Gerald was sat where she left him. Still smiling. It was strangely comforting seeing his kind, unassuming face. She didn't know why. It just was.

She closed the door behind her, and placed her bag down on the end of the table, smiling back at him.

'Hannah's just left for her lunch break. I thought I'd crack on for a while until you got back. Everything okay?' he said.

'You know what, for the first time in a long time, everything is more than okay. It really, really is.' She meant every word. Then she had a sudden thought, and before she knew it the words fell straight out of her mouth. 'Do you want to come to a barbecue at the weekend?'

Chapter 43

THE BIRTHDAY BBQ

> Happy-Pregnant-Birthday to me,
> I'm hormonal, fat and teary.
> Don't touch me else I'll cut you,
> I have to leave now I need a wee.

Emily had spent most of the morning rearranging pots of coleslaw while eating it.

She wasn't sure why she'd made Paul buy quite so much. Did anyone ever eat coleslaw except when confronted with it at barbecues anyway . . .? Either way the baby wanted it, and what it wanted, it tended to get. So she continued spooning it into her face.

She already felt exhausted just from the party preparation; the party itself might just finish her off. But she was determined to have a good time. And to make sure everyone else had a good time. And that required bunting and putting things in pretty bowls. While eating coleslaw.

'Stop fussing, will you?' came Paul's voice from behind her. He stepped into their kitchen wearing a very bad Hawaiian shirt and some shorts, and planted an enthusiastic kiss on her cheek.

'It's only our friends, sweetie.' He lifted up a tray of barbecue tools to take them outside. 'I wouldn't worry too much about condiment presentation. They're coming to see you – and for the meat. Obviously.'

Emily smiled and stepped out into the garden after him.

The garden looked wonderful, like a miniature fete. Emily had instructed Paul to put out the deckchairs, wrap bunting around the fence posts, lay down some checked picnic blankets and stick some jugs of Pimm's on a table. And he'd done a brilliant job. Under her strict instruction and supervision. Naturally.

All they were missing was a few donkeys and a tombola, and they could probably charge people an entry fee.

Their garden wasn't a big space, but they had a decent-sized, sunny decked area at the top, and a little lawned section beneath where people could grab a seat shaded by a large patio umbrella. This was where all the food was laid out. And primarily where Emily would be remaining for the duration.

She thought it looked perfect.

Paul had set himself up a barbecue station on the deck, and used an old paddling pool they found in the shed when they moved to keep bottles of beer cold in some icy water.

'Very professional,' Emily said as she placed her cole-slaw down on the table.

'Just call me the barbecue grandmaster,' Paul said, tipping charcoal into the barbecue drum.

'No,' Emily responded flatly. Before a little smile crept on to her face.

She became aware she was heating up quite rapidly. There wasn't a cloud in the sky; perfect barbecue weather. There wasn't even a breeze, and a hot wavy sun was pouring light and heat into every inch of their back garden. Not so perfect when you're growing another human in your body, and feel like you might combust if sunlight hits your skin directly, but hey. She'd wear a big hat and stick her feet in the beer pool if she really needed to . . .

'Hey, hey, hey!' Molly made her way into the garden, emerging with Tom behind her from the little tunnel that ran next to her neighbours' house, between the terraces.

Molly didn't look hot. Or exhausted. Or like she had clown feet and a clicky pelvis. As usual, she looked her irritating, breezing-through-pregnancy self.

Emily huffed and gathered up the energy to waddle towards her friend to greet her.

'We're early!' Molly announced loudly as she reached Emily.

'Yes. I'm in shock. Is this the new Molly? Or is this like the only other time in your life you were early, when you accidentally read the wrong time on the invite?' Emily rolled her eyes and hugged her friend.

'Hey! I've been early before, thank you. I just decided I should make the effort for my best girl's big birthday. And also Tom made me,' Molly said, laughing.

'Well. Thank you, Tom.' Emily gave him a friendly hug

before he headed off up the garden to inspect Paul's barbecue station.

'So, I hear Gerald's coming today then?' Molly said raising her eyebrows and taking a seat in the shade as Emily joined her.

'Ooh I know!' Emily said. 'She keeps saying they're just friends, but I think she secretly likes him. Who wouldn't? He looks like a Ken doll on steroids for fuck's sake!'

'Ha! I know. She's just scared to get close to anyone again, I guess. It's stupid. They'd be great for each other. And he clearly likes her, else he wouldn't have tried to kiss her that night. She's just being stubborn. They should just get on with it. Have sex. And buy a town house. That's how real life works.'

'Molly! Although basically . . . yeah. Anyway. We'd better change the subject. They'll be here any second.' Emily knew they wouldn't have to wait long, given that Liz was the most punctual person in the known Universe.

'Right. On to more important things . . . Happy birthday party day! How's it all going? How are you feeling?' Molly said.

'Thanks sweetie. I'm okay. And by okay, I mean hot, fed up, and still unable to wear any footwear outside of Paul's flip-flops, but I've decided this is about as good as it's going to get while my baby is still on the inside of my body, so fuck it. Let's have a thirtieth birthday virgin mojito to that!'

'Oh honey – it's really not long now,' Molly said sympathetically. 'You relax and enjoy today. I'll spoon coleslaw, meat and cake into your mouth, and you just sit back and open presents. That'll make you feel better . . .'

'Well, when you put it like that . . .' That did sound pretty good, actually.

The side gate slowly swung open just down from them, and Liz appeared round the side of it. She looked immaculate as usual, and her trademark red lipstick was firmly in place.

'Afternoon, beautiful pregnant people,' Liz said smoothly as she walked towards them. Alone.

'Hello!' Emily was desperate to ask where Gerald was, but managed to restrain herself.

'Happy birthday again, my gorgeous friend.' Liz bent down and hugged Emily, before placing a small, beautifully wrapped gift and card in her lap.

'Where's Gerald? Lover's tiff?' Molly asked.

'Hilarious.' Liz rolled her eyes. 'He's parking the car. There's no space nearby so he dropped me off first. Is that okay with you? Or would you like me to Skype him in for this section so you know he's really here?'

Liz gave Molly a hug too as she sat down next to her friends.

Within a few seconds, Gerald came strolling through the gate and up the garden to greet them.

'Afternoon, ladies! Happy birthday, Emily!' Gerald said chirpily as he pecked Molly and Emily on the cheek, before heading up the garden to the barbecue station.

Liz watched Gerald as he headed up to join Paul and Tom. He seemed so comfortable chatting to her friends' other halves. It was sweet. He was sweet. And he really was handsome . . . But now, watching him laugh and chat like he'd known Paul and Tom for half his life, he suddenly seemed more attractive. Really attractive, actually . . .

Liz snapped herself out of it.

'So who else is coming?' she said quickly, distracting herself by reaching for a glass of Pimm's.

'Not too many people. Just a few girls from work. Mike and Sue from across the road, Matt and Helen are going to pop in later. You know. All the usual folk.' Emily began worrying that her coleslaw wouldn't go round everyone.

'Great,' Liz said, raising her freshly pencilled-in eyebrows. 'Sounds like a party to me . . .'

'What about all your rent-a-friends from that TCP thing you're doing?' Molly said.

'If you mean my "NCT" group,' Emily responded dryly, 'then no. I haven't invited anyone. I can't even remember everyone's names yet . . . and the only pregnant pal I need is you, you know that,' she added, winking at Molly.

'Well of course. Our wombs are in it together, babes. In it together . . . Ooh! Open our gifts before everyone starts arriving!' Molly said suddenly, reaching down into a carrier bag by her feet and pulling out a badly wrapped square parcel.

'Okay!' Emily tugged at the wrapping as it fell away.

Inside was a picture frame.

Emily clutched it in both hands and grinned as her eyes misted up.

It was a collage of their friendship. All three of them.

A sort of shitty-but-brilliant reminder of being young and stupid and completely free of responsibility. The funny nights out, the parties, the holidays, the clothing and make-up disasters. It was embarrassingly terrible and wonderful at the same time.

'Thank you.' Emily hugged Molly with moist eyes, as her friend smiled back at her.

'Thanks for that, Molly! I'm not sure how I'm going to top that . . .' Liz said, rolling her eyes exaggeratedly as Emily began unwrapping her gift.

Emily struggled to break in through Liz's impenetrable gift-wrap, but eventually got a finger into a corner seam and tore her way inside.

Inside was a black box, containing a delicate silver bangle. It was simple and stunning. Emily put it on instantly, admiring it on her wrist.

'It's so pretty. Thank you so much. I love it,' Emily gushed, feeling teary again. 'I love you guys so much. I'm so glad you're my best friends. I don't know what I'd do without you!'

'Don't get soppy on us now, will you,' Molly said, leaning in to hug her.

Emily took a deep breath, and smiled with hot, teary eyes at her friends.

It turned out being pregnant for your thirtieth birthday party wasn't that shit after all.

Chapter 44

TOLLY

For the first time in her entire twenty-seven weeks of pregnancy, today Molly actually 'felt' pregnant.

It was the first Sunday in June, and for the past forty-eight hours the UK had been suffering through a relentless freak heatwave.

Molly felt like she was finally getting a glimpse of what Emily had been going through the last few weeks and even months now. The heat was utterly debilitating. Even her trustee airy kaftan was failing her as she sat in Tom's flat, sweating into the sofa with her legs spread unattractively apart, holding her hair up to keep it off the back of her neck. She'd never felt more glamorous . . .

Tom, and inevitably the rest of High Wycombe's wider population, had gone out to scour the land (mostly Argos) in search of a free-standing room fan before his pregnant girlfriend melted into the upholstery.

Molly felt a surge of relief as she heard him come back through the door noisily, struggling with something heavy.

'I'm back! I've got one!' Tom called into the living room, sounding hot, exhausted and out of breath as he closed the door to his upper-floor home behind him.

'You're amazing,' Molly said, as he planted a sweaty-but-still-incredibly-pleasing kiss on her lips.

'Well. If you think that was amazing, you're possibly going to go into premature labour when you see this.' He pulled from behind his back a box of ice lollies. Organic, vegan ice lollies, of course.

Molly almost squealed as she snatched them from him, and moved the box across her forehead in an attempt to suck some of the heat out of her face.

There were moments he'd driven her mad with his constant fussing, food checking and fucking nut milk, but he really was wonderful. She loved every organic, vegan, bicarbonate-of-soda-cleaning inch of him.

Molly knew she'd struggled initially to settle into living at his place, but the last few weeks it felt like they'd finally reached a state of normality. 'His place' was slowly beginning to feel like 'their place'. And that was all she wanted. To be somewhere that felt like home.

Tom peeled his T-shirt off and began assembling a fan the size of a wind turbine in the corner of the living room.

Molly sat watching him. Wanting him. Lusting after him. Pregnancy seemed to have increased her sex drive even more; she couldn't get enough. Not that Tom had been complaining, he was more than happy to oblige.

She fancied him so much. His body. His tattoos. His dark, unkempt hair. If it wasn't for the fact that she was midway through a vegan lolly, the temperature of the sun, and that she was welded to the sofa via her own bodily fluids she'd have pounced on him, but the thought of it right now just made her sweat even more . . .

She slurped the last of her current lolly (she was making her way through the box at an impressive pace), and watched eagerly as Tom finished erecting his new fan-based mega-structure.

He plugged it in, turned it to its highest setting and sat next to Molly on the sofa. For a moment, the two of them sat motionless in the artificial breeze, letting it blast cool air over their bodies.

Molly felt like she could breathe again for the first time in two days.

After a few minutes, Tom turned his face to her and smiled.

'I've got a surprise for you . . .' he said. In a way that probably wasn't meant to sound as horny as Molly hoped it was . . .

'Okay . . .' Molly said slowly, maintaining eye contact and squinting at him a little suspiciously.

'Come with me,' he said, getting to his feet and reaching his hand down to help her up.

He pulled her up from the sofa, and she followed him down towards the bedroom, still holding his hand. Perhaps her horny suspicions were right . . .

He reached the spare-room door and turned to face her as he slowly turned the handle and pushed the door fully open. Molly stepped in.

She couldn't believe what he'd done. It was beautiful. All the photos, the memories, the random pictures and keepsakes she'd had packed up in cardboard boxes from her old flat, everything she had to remind her of her travels, he'd taken it all and made it into collages across three large picture frames. It must have taken him hours.

As she looked closer, Molly saw that in between her travelling pictures, were old pictures of Tom, and more recent ones of the two of them together too.

It was like a canvas of their lives from before they met right up to now.

'I wanted our baby to see all the wonderful things Mummy and Daddy did before we became a family, so they can see all the wonderful things they've got in store.' Tom gently rested his arm around Molly's waist as she studied the pictures.

She was transfixed. She couldn't tear her eyes away.

'I think this is the nicest thing anyone's ever done for me. Thank you so much,' Molly said eventually. Happiness was oozing out of her, although that was more than likely sweat, as she'd been away from the fan for a while now . . .

She suddenly noticed underneath the frames there was a little hand-carved wooden sign that read 'Baby Tolly.'

'Baby Tolly!' she said laughing. 'We better be careful, otherwise that'll stick!'

'I don't mind if it does. I quite like it,' Tom said gently pulling her around until she was facing him. He pulled her in a little closer and kissed her mouth slowly.

Molly felt as though she might burst.

'I love you. I'm so happy we're doing this. I can't wait to be a parent with you,' he said, looking at her intently.

'I love you too. I can't wait either,' Molly said before he kissed her again.

'Would it be weird if we had sex here?' she said, attempting a sexy smile and come-to-bed eyes.

'Yes, Molly. Yes, it would.'

Chapter 45

'JUST FRIENDS'

Fridays seemed to come round quicker every week.

Liz had grown to really look forward to drinks with her team. It had become quite a routine.

They'd laugh, talk a little business, drink cocktails, and pat themselves on the back for another week well done.

Sometimes it would be just her and Hannah, sometimes just Hannah and Gerald, and sometimes, like today, just her and Gerald . . .

Liz sat at a high table, looking at the back of his head as he ordered the drinks at the bar. She liked looking at him. As their friendship had grown, and they'd chatted and got to know each other more, she'd enjoyed being with him more and more.

They flirted.

It made her feel good.

She liked it.

But they were just friends, weren't they?

Just friends who worked together, flirted together, had lots in common, spent lots of time together outside of work, and had once almost sort of kissed a few months ago, right?

Something had changed a little between them recently.

She felt it in the way that he sometimes looked at her, and in the way that she felt when he did.

Did she have a crush on him? Was that all it was? A harmless urge based on the fact that he was the living incarnation of an Action Man doll? Most women probably would fancy him. Was that all it was?

She really didn't know, but what she did know was that she was too scared to find out. She'd already rejected him once. She could hardly turn round now and say, 'Hey, why don't you try sticking your tongue down my throat again so I can see if I like it this time?' No. That didn't seem like a good idea.

'Tequila?' Gerald placed a shot glass down in front of her, interrupting her thoughts.

'It's almost like you know me,' Liz said, smiling at him. She felt an unexpected little flutter in her stomach as he accidentally brushed her arm with his before sitting down opposite her.

'So hey, I wanted to ask you something,' Gerald said, before knocking his tequila back.

'Yes?' Liz said, feeling a little unsettled by his change in tone.

'It's nothing bad!' Gerald said, smiling broadly. 'I just wanted to ask if you fancied dinner out one night? Maybe in a couple of weekends' time? If you're not busy already, that is? I owe you a night out after you invited me to Emily's barbecue last weekend. I just wanted to say thank you. What do you say?'

Liz felt uncomfortable. Was he asking her out as a

friend? Was this a friend-date? Or was this a date-date? She studied his face for clues but he was giving nothing away.

'So is this a "just friends" thing or are you trying to ask me out?' she said, much more confidentially than she'd meant to.

Gerald looked slightly taken aback. She was trying not to let it show on her face, but she was beginning to feel tense. And a little stupid.

'Well,' he said. 'Which would you like it to be?'

FUCK.

She'd done exactly what she shouldn't have done. She'd let him know in that instant that there was something there. Something between them. That she felt it too. Something that she had been denying for a while now.

FUCK FUCK FUCK.

Liz was scared of what she might say next. Scared of letting him in. Scared of letting anyone in. Of being vulnerable again. Was she being an idiot? Why had she said something?

'Because I thought that you only wanted to be friends?' Gerald said, fixing his eyes on hers as the pause following his question became longer and longer.

'I . . . well . . . I did,' Liz managed. 'But . . . I think I might feel a little differently now?'

Gerald's expression slowly grew into a grin.

She felt relieved. Seeing him smile.

Gerald got down out of his seat and moved around the table towards her. Liz felt her heart start to pump a little faster as his body suddenly seemed very close to hers. And his face very close to her face. And his lips very close to her lips.

She knew this was her last opportunity to pull away. But she didn't want to. She wanted him to kiss her. Yearned for it even. She didn't know now why it had taken her so long to see that.

He leaned in and planted a soft, deep kiss on her lips. It sent a rush of spiky tingles through her body. It felt nothing like when he kissed her before. It felt right. It felt wonderful. She wanted to do it again . . .

I guess this means we're more than 'just friends' now, thought Liz.

Chapter 46

THE HOSPITAL BAG
AND THE 'PUSH PRESENT'

'A what?' Paul said again, screwing his face up. They were in the sanitary products aisle in Sainsbury's. Where he was trying very hard not to make eye contact with teenage girls buying tampons.

Emily narrowed her eyes.

'A push present, Paul,' she said huffily. 'It's not that hard a concept. I'm pushing out your baby and ruining the gateway to my womb for ever more, and you get to buy me an appropriately sized gift because of that fact. I don't see what you're not grasping . . .'

'Sounds like some kind of new-age bullshit you saw on the *Kardashians*, to be honest with you, babe. I don't think you're going to give a shit about anything other than our beautiful baby boy when you give birth. Isn't that gift enough?' Paul said, smiling as he finished the last sentence. Emily was so easy to wind up these days, most of the time he didn't even know he was doing it until she burst into tears in the middle of a sentence.

Emily felt a surge of annoyance. 'Don't get cute with me. My gift expectations will only increase and you will have only yourself to blame . . .'

'Okay. Look, I thought we were shopping for your hospital bag? I don't even know how we got into this conversation?' Paul said, shaking his head, aware that the teenage girls were beginning to look at them now . . .

'Fine,' Emily said, waddling off angrily down the aisle. Signalling that she was anything but . . .

Paul referred to the list again. It was the printout they'd been given in this week's NCT class of everything they might need in their hospital bag.

Emily had insisted they do the shopping for it together so she could write a blog post about how 'Being Inclusive Brings an Expectant Couple Closer Together . . .'

So far they'd been in the supermarket for an hour, and had only purchased bacon. Which they'd argued about for twenty minutes. And which wasn't on the list . . .

So it was going really well.

And now they were looking for maternity pads, breast pads, make-up removing pads, and several other kinds of pad-based product that Paul had never heard of before . . .

'Okay. Look. We'll talk about the push present later. Let's get this done before I collapse with exhaustion. I think I have all the pads. What's next?' Emily said, waddling back towards him with her arms full of variously sized packets.

'Says here you'll want some nightdresses, comfy clothes and slippers . . .'

'Okay – I'll grab those from Primark on the way back to the car. They're only going to get a load of gunk on them anyway.'

'Gunk?' Paul regretted the question, almost immediately.

'I think you'd better prepare yourself for plenty of gunk, darling. It's going to be quite a gunk-filled affair. A gunk-plosion, if you like. Gunk-alicious,' Emily said, laughing as Paul looked repulsed.

'I'll get the energy drinks and sweets. You grab the arnica, tea-tree oil, Gaviscon and poo pills,' Paul said, diverting the conversation away from gunk.

'Ha! Okay. Poo pills. I'm on it,' Emily said. Finally, they were getting somewhere.

Before Emily knew it, they'd filled a large trolley with everything on the list and more. It looked more like they were stocking up for a nuclear attack than having a baby, but they were prepped for all scenarios now. Including one where she needed to survive solely on Ribena and laxatives for a month, wearing waterproof mascara, nursing bras and flip-flops, and eating only Lucozade energy sweets . . .

Emily let out a little exhausted groan in the passenger seat as they pulled up outside the house, the car laden with carrier bags stuffed full of their hospital-bag hoard.

Who knew shopping could be so exhausting? She wasn't even sure she could muster the energy to get to the front door right now, but she did.

Paul struggled in behind her, adamant he'd manage

255

every carrier bag in one hit. Emily would have helped, but carrying anything over and above herself was impossible right now. In fact, carrying herself was impossible right now.

She only had five-ish weeks to go. Hopefully.

Five weeks.

That was nothing. She'd been on training courses that had lasted longer than that.

Paul dutifully carried all the bags into the dining room and placed them down, with a '*do we really need all this shit?*' look on his face.

Emily felt a little energy return. She was looking forward to this bit.

There were so few things she'd been able to control as far as this baby was concerned. She hadn't been able to stop her face expanding, her stretch marks appearing, her knees resembling handbags, her pelvis aching, her carpal-twatting-tunnel, or her legs becoming increasingly restless, but she could control this.

She could sit down, itemise, label, and neatly pack her hospital bag completely the way that she wanted it.

She could delicately roll up her son's first tiny outfit, with its matching tiny hat and blanket, ready to be the first thing that he wore on his body.

She knew this pregnancy had been so far from the Pinterest-perfect dream she'd imagined when she saw those two little stripes on a test all those months ago.

For starters – no one had told her about the discharge. Seriously. Where does it all come from?

Then add to that the utter exhaustion, and the crippling effect carrying her baby had had not only on her body, but her emotional and mental state . . . She felt robbed of the perfect pregnancy she had envisaged, lied to, even . . .

Why couldn't she have been the one to breeze through pregnancy looking toned and blooming, and eating quinoa?

Ah well, Emily said to herself as she carefully paired some tiny socks and scratch mitts, none of that would matter soon.

Bollocks to it all.

Bollocks to pregnancy.

Bollocks to her pregnancy app telling her the baby was the size of a honeydew melon right now, as she began to consider the size of its exit path . . .

And bollocks to quinoa.

Chapter 47

UNOFFICIAL

Liz felt uncharacteristically nervous as she sat in the waiting area outside Stanton's office.

She'd received the meeting request late yesterday afternoon, and even though she was sure he just wanted a 'chat', a progress report on how her team was doing, it was making her feel a little uncomfortable.

She was glad it was Friday. If this went badly, she had every intention of heading straight out to the nearest bar to cry into some tequila. Or several tequilas, if it went really badly . . .

She knew it was ridiculous but there was a little voice in the back of her head that kept saying . . . *What if this is about Gerald?*

And what if it was? She had nothing to be ashamed or embarrassed about, did she? They'd only kissed properly for the first time a week ago. They hadn't even been on a proper date yet. It was hardly serious. And besides, what went on in her personal life was her business, as long as it had no effect on her work. Or his, for that matter. They were two extremely professional, senior people working together. And enjoying each other's company out of work too. That was it.

Liz felt satisfied with her internal pep talk as Stanton's door opened and his friendly smile greeted her.

'Liz,' he said like they were old friends, which instantly relaxed her a little. 'Come in and take a seat. Please.'

Liz smiled, rose to her feet and walked into his office as he held the door open for her. She took a seat in front of his desk.

'So,' said a jolly Stanton as he sat down, 'I think you know why I've called you in?'

Liz felt that horrible pang of paranoia again. Perhaps he did know. Her palms were getting clammy.

'Well, not specifically,' Liz said.

'I think it's time for me to say "I told you so" . . .'

Shit. She didn't like the sound of that. What did he mean? Surely he wasn't talking about Gerald? Was he?

' . . . about your team? How well it's working out. I feel I get some gloating rights for that one, surely,' Stanton said, raising his eyebrows, as a slight smirk appeared across his face.

'Oh I see!' Liz said. Not meaning to sound quite so relieved. 'And well, yes. I suppose even I have to concede it's going very well. Both Hannah and Gerald are brilliant. They churn through work at an incredible speed. I feel we've been very productive together.'

'Indeed you have,' Stanton responded cheerily, thumbing through a few printouts, as if checking some final figures. 'I'm very impressed Liz. Not just with them. With you. You've fully embraced this. In just three months you seem to have gone through quite the transformation. It's like you've come to life, Liz. I really do mean that.'

Stanton seemed to want to say something further, but was weighing up whether or not to say it.

'You know . . .' he said, 'I can't say any of this officially yet. But I will be recommending that we begin working on a new partner agreement immediately. So I'd like to unofficially say, well done, Liz. Well done.'

Liz sat still as she let what she'd heard sink in.

Who gave a fuck if it was official or not? . . . she was about to be made a partner.

A PARTNER.

Yes. Yes, she was.

'Thank you so much,' Liz said, containing her overwhelming urge to fist pump. 'An unofficial thank you, that is.'

Stanton smiled and rose quickly to his feet holding his hand out. Liz stood up, grasped his hand and shook it strongly.

'You are unofficially welcome. Now, I won't keep you. I'm sure you have plenty to get on with,' he said.

Liz felt her smile widen. She released his hand and walked swiftly out of his office.

She couldn't wait to tell Gerald. And her friends. And everyone. In fact, she couldn't wait to scream it to anyone who would listen. Unofficial or not, this was quite possibly the best moment of her life. There was no way she was keeping this to herself.

Back in her office, Liz immediately got her phone out of her handbag, opening a chat window to Molly and Emily:

Liz

GUESS WHO MADE PARTNER!!!!

(Unofficially.)

(But I'll be having tequila

like it's official

I can assure you!)

Emily

That's AMAZING!

I'm so happy for you.

You so deserve this sweetie!

Have one for me!

Molly

OMG! You're a superstar!

So proud of you.

YOU. ROCK.

(Officially)

Liz

Thank you!

Keep it under your hats for now . . .

I won't make the proper announcement

until the paperwork's done but

EEEEEEEKKKKKK!

Emily

Have you told Gerald?

How's he going to feel dating the boss?

Lol x

261

Molly
Does that sort of make you a cougar?
(Unofficially)

Liz
No.
Thank you.
He's older than me!
I'm just way more amazing.
AND A PARTNER!!
Plus, we've not actually had
a date yet . . .
So I don't think you can call it 'dating'!
And no – I'm about to go tell him now
☺

Molly
You enjoy it babes.
We'll celebrate soon!
Love you xxx
So proud of you xxx

Emily
Me too xx
OFFICIALLY.

Liz
Xxx

Liz couldn't get the smile off her face. She fired off a quick message to Gerald:

Liz
Can you come to my office?
I have good news ;)

It didn't take long before a loud knock sounded on Liz's office door as Gerald let himself in.

'Hey,' he said, as he gently pushed the door closed behind him. 'Judging by the enormous grin spread across your face right now, I'm guessing it went completely terribly with Stanton . . .'

'Oh yes,' Liz replied. 'Utterly dreadful. So utterly dreadful, that you are now looking unofficially at this firm's new junior partner.'

'That's amazing!' Gerald said, leaping quite dramatically across the room before scooping her up out of her seat and hugging her.

It made her feel strangely nervous having physical contact with him at work. The door was closed and no one could see them, but the idea that someone could walk in at any moment made her feel uncomfortable. She didn't want to reject him, but she couldn't be intimate with him here. She slid gently out of his arms.

'I'm so proud of you, Liz. Let's go get drunk.'

'Yes,' Liz said, smiling again. 'Let's go do that.'

Chapter 48

LAST DAY OF WORK

Finally.

FINALLY.

It was Emily's last day of work for an entire year. AN ENTIRE YEAR.

She'd been working in tandem with her maternity-cover replacement all week, and was quite literally at the point where she had nothing left to do. In fact, her only thing to do was to give someone else her stuff to do, which was a disconcerting yet rather euphoric feeling.

Equally, she had no idea what she was going to 'do' for an entire twelve months without work after today. Obviously, she'd be mostly looking after her new baby, but surely that wouldn't take up all her time, right?

She didn't really know, as she'd never looked after a baby before, but how much work could it be? Her NCT teacher had made it out to be pretty overwhelming and life changing, but she was probably exaggerating, right? Seemed to Emily that babies mostly got fed, had their nappy changed and slept. That was it, yeah?

This could be her chance to really work on her blog, start getting more of a following. (At least more than just her close circle of friends and her mum would be nice . . .)

Maybe she'd start writing that book she'd always dreamed about. She'd tap it out on her iPad while she breastfed her son in cafes sipping on wanky-flavoured lattes. She'd probably have it written in six months. Maybe she could write two . . .

'How you feeling? Bet you can't wait to get that baby out now!' Matilda glanced towards Emily's stomach.

Emily considered how to answer that without committing GBH.

'Yes . . .' she said, managing a fake smile. 'I am definitely more than ready to meet him now.'

'Well, I hate to break it to you but first babies rarely come on time. Every one of my friends that's had a baby has been at least a week overdue! Just so you know,' Matilda replied with a stupid smug look on her stupid smug face.

FUCK OFF, MATILDA.

'Yes. I've heard that,' she mumbled.

'One of my friends was in labour for about three days with her first one. It was terrible! She vows she'll never have another. I guess they just find it way too comfortable in there!' Matilda said, laughing obnoxiously.

FUCK YOU.

'Ha,' Emily managed weakly. 'Sorry – if you don't mind, I really just need to finish this . . .'

Emily fixed her eyes on her screen and pretended to type.

'Oh sure,' Matilda continued. 'Well. I hope you're not worried about anything while you're gone . . . Charlotte seems really lovely. So experienced. I'm sure she'll do an amazing job. Maybe an even better job than you!'

FUCK YOU. FUCK YOU. FUCK YOU.

'Yes. I'm sure she will.' Emily was irritated at how irritated her voice sounded.

It was a strange feeling, though. She'd worked there for nearly four years and really liked her job. She loved the people she worked with, with the exception of McTwatty-Matilda-Dick-Nose. Of course.

She knew she needed to stop thinking of maternity leave as 'leaving', and think of it as more of a temporary career break. But it was difficult. It felt so wrong upping and leaving everything she'd worked towards over the past four years in the hands of someone she met a week ago.

What if Charlotte was rubbish? What if she messed up all her accounts while she was away so she walked back into a shitstorm? Or worse, what if Matilda was right and she really was amazing? More amazing than Emily? What if all the clients preferred her? What if Matilda and Charlotte teamed up and plotted to overthrow Emily, take over her job and all the good accounts, and steal her lovely new only-one-in-the-office lumber-support chair?

Okay, perhaps she was overreacting. A bit.

'Hey, sweetie!' came Natalie's friendly voice from behind her. 'Is now a good time? We've got a little something for you . . .'

'Absolutely!' Emily said, smiling. She had no problem taking a break from pretending to type things in order to receive lots of lovely gifts.

'Great. Everything's in the boardroom, if you don't mind waddling your way into there!' Natalie said, laughing and helping Emily up.

Emily took her hand and walked slowly through the office down to the boardroom. Walking hurt now. It was only the prospect of presents spurring her on, if she was honest.

She walked in behind Natalie and immediately burst into tears. Standard practice for a heavily pregnant woman at all emotional occasions these days . . .

In the middle of the table was a huge 'bouquet' made out of rolled-up babygros, tiny socks and hats . . . it looked gorgeous. Next to it was a couple of stunning bunches of flowers. And also some smaller gifts in little 'baby-boy' blue gift bags.

Emily couldn't believe how generous everyone had been. It was incredibly touching. She had full-blown snot-laced tears streaming down her face as she began hugging her colleagues and friends.

Even though she couldn't wait to get out of there and become a parent, a small part of her really didn't want to leave today. She really was going to miss everyone so much.

Even McTwatty-Matilda-Dick-Nose. Just a little bit.

Chapter 49

LAST LAST SATURDAY CLUB

Suddenly June was almost over.

It was crazy to think that this would be the last 'Last Saturday Club' where all three friends would see each other before at least one of them finally had their baby on the outside of their body . . .

Thankfully, it was a relatively cool cloudy day, and Molly was enjoying the short stroll into town. Despite being less than nine weeks away from her due date, she still hadn't felt the aches, pains and exhaustion that Emily had been suffering with practically from day one . . .

For her, the weeks and months had flown by. She was sure Emily would say the exact opposite, but it felt insane that within the next few weeks they would both become parents. Real-life, responsible, we-have-to-do-actual-adulting-now parents.

She spent the walk reflecting on how her and her two best friends' lives had changed so dramatically the last few months . . . It felt like they were all proper grown-ups now . . . how did that happen?

It didn't seem that long ago they were necking Diamond White at bus stops and spending their weekends playing spin-the-bottle at drunken teenage house parties . . . Now two of them were growing human beings inside them, and the other had just been made a partner at a London law firm. It was madness . . .

But a happy, brilliant madness.

Molly made her way down the high street with her head full of awkward teenage memories and before she knew it she'd turned the corner and was heading down towards O'Neill's pub. Which was their venue for today's meet-up . . . not because it offered hard-core day-drinking opportunities like the good old days, but because it had an outside area, did table service and had A LOT of toilets. Which was all any pregnant woman could ever wish for.

As she started to approach the pub, Molly spotted the back of Emily's golden-maned head. She observed her friends as she strolled towards them. They were chatting and giggling like naughty schoolgirls in a way that only friends who've known each other for ever could. It was sweet to watch.

'Afternoon, ladies,' Molly said as she reached them, placing her handbag down on the table and taking a seat next to Emily.

'Only fifteen minutes late today! Don't you go exhausting yourself now will you . . .' Liz said.

'Ha! You know what I'm like . . .' Molly said jokingly. 'How is everyone? How are you, Mrs-almost-ready-to-pop-in-three-weeks? . . . More than ready to have your child on the outside of your uterus by now, I'd imagine?'

'I'd say that's pretty accurate!' Emily said, laughing. 'I

have had enough of it all now. I swear, if this baby gets any bigger it'll burst out of me. I don't even know how the rest of my organs are fitting in there? Have you ever thought about that? Where your other organs are? We were talking about it in NCT—'

'Oooh. NCT,' both the other ladies said in unison before bursting into laughter.

'Yes. NCT,' Emily said dryly before carrying on. 'They were showing us where all the other *junk* is, and I can assure you, it ain't in the trunk any more . . . I think mine is mostly in my ribcage . . .'

'I just don't think about it,' Molly said matter-of-factly. 'I just kinda think, my baby is going to grow the same way and come out the same way regardless! Why torture yourself wondering where your stomach is?'

'Well, that's a fair point,' Emily said. 'I do find it all fascinating, though. I thought it would be terrifying, but the classes are great, and are helping to relax me. I think I'd be freaking out without it, to be honest! The people are really lovely too. I'm really glad we did NCT.'

'Oooh. NCT,' Liz and Molly said at the same time again, giggling to themselves childishly.

Emily was too sticky and exhausted to find it funny or give her friends the satisfaction of knowing they were annoying her.

'How are you feeling anyway?' Emily said, directing her question at Molly. She was keen for someone else to talk now.

'Fine. Honestly. I'm still fine. I struggled a bit when it

was really hot a few weeks ago, but I'm cool now. Literally. I'm actually enjoying it.'

Emily wanted to punch her. But she didn't. She was too exhausted for that too.

'What are you going to do about work?' Emily asked.

'Actually, I have been thinking a lot about this,' Molly said thoughtfully. 'And I think I'm going to temp for a few more weeks now, and then when the baby comes, I'm going to put a plan in action so I can get out of temping for good.'

'That's great! Good for you, sweetie,' Liz said triumphantly. She'd always wanted Molly to find her calling. She and Emily both had. Molly was way too smart to be stuck photocopying and filing for the rest of her life, she just needed to apply herself to something and she'd be amazing. She knew it. They all knew it.

'Yeah,' Molly continued, 'I think it's about time I did something a bit more permanent now that we're about to become a family. So I'm thinking about starting my own baby-friendly travel company. For people who want a back-packing-type experience, but in a safe environment with baby- or toddler-friendly amenities so they can take young children. I've still got loads of contacts. I reckon there's a market for baby-backpackers. I'll certainly be one of them!'

'That sounds perfect for you!' Emily said enthusiastically. 'If you do it right, that could absolutely be a brilliant business. I don't know why you haven't done something like that before!'

'I know,' Molly said, seeming a little embarrassed. 'I think I've just spent a long time drifting. This baby will be the best thing that ever happened to me. It already is.'

'I think you're right.' Liz smiled sincerely at her friend. 'And I agree with Emily – it sounds perfect. We'll support you every step of the way.'

'Anyway. Forget about my career goals. What about you? Miss Law Firm Partner,' Molly said, nudging Liz's arm across the table.

'I know!' Liz said excitedly. 'I still have to pinch myself. I don't think I'll believe it until I sign the contract and get bumped up to a nice big office. Which is obviously the entire reason I did it. My view is shit at the moment.'

'It's amazing. We will celebrate properly as soon as it's official and our babies aren't inside us sucking all our joy away by preventing us from drinking alcohol,' Emily said, daydreaming about copious amounts of wine.

'Ah yes . . . alcohol . . .' Molly said wistfully, before the three ladies laughed.

'And . . . Gerald?' Molly continued, raising an exaggerated eyebrow in Liz's direction. 'I mean, I don't want to say I told you so . . .'

Liz huffed a little but knew she needed to concede defeat on this one as a smile broke out on her face. 'Okay, okay . . . you guys may have been right, but don't get too excited. I haven't even let him take me out to dinner properly yet. I'm not sure I even want him to. I'm pretty happy just getting pissed in nice bars together to be honest!

So it's not exactly the romance of the century, people . . . it's just nice not being alone. He's a sweet guy.'

'Yeah, yeah,' Emily said, grinning from ear to ear.

'We'll see, Lizzy-tits. You keep telling yourself that. I reckon you've got a good one there,' Molly added, smiling at her friend.

'Well, anyway, I'm so proud of us all,' Liz said, reaching out both her hands to squeeze her friends' arms.

'Me too,' said Molly.

'Me too . . . too,' said Emily. 'But I'm going to have to end this moment prematurely as I cannot wait any longer to go for a wee . . .'

Chapter 50

#TEAMTHOR

Liz
Hey girls?
How are you both?
I need your advice . . .
I want to know if I'm being a dick . . .

Molly
You are.

Liz
Very funny . . .
I want to know if I'm being a dick
BECAUSE
The thing is I like Gerald.
And everything is
going fine . . .
But he texts me A LOT.
I mean – constantly.
Every day . . . several times . . .
Just to say 'hi' or say
something pointless . . .
I don't know . . .
I've never been with someone who

does that and I'm finding it a bit much

. . .

Is it me?

Emily
YES.

Molly
Yes.

Emily
He likes you, Liz.
And you like him so what's the
problem?
That's what nice boys do when they
like nice girls, you know . . .
I think you just don't know a good
thing when you've got it!

Molly
I agree.
He's a nice guy.
You need to let your guard down
and embrace it.
He's not a dick.
He's a keeper.
Don't push him away babes.
He looks like Thor FFS!

Liz
Really?
I think I might need to
have a word with him . . .
I feel like I spend half my time away
from him being updated about his life?
I'm not sure I give a shit
that much if he's
just had a shower, or is
about to watch
Grand-Twatting-Designs.
It's too much . . .
I think I'm too used to being on my
own!

Emily
That's probably exactly it x
I think he's just a very open person.
You're a bit of a cold fish . . . lol

Liz
Thanks.
Remind me not to come to you when I
need cheering up . . .

Molly
She's right though.
He probably needs to chill a bit.
You need to open up a bit.
But don't go fucking it up.
He's a good one.

Liz
Okay. Thanks, girlies.
I know you're right.
I do like him. I just want
things to slow down
a bit if I'm honest!
I think it's just now I've finally
got what I always wanted
I'm trying to find fault with it . . .
I'm basically complaining because
he's too perfect and isn't
treating me like shit.
I clearly need my head examined!

Molly
What a bastard.

Emily
Exactly.
#TeamThor
Right - I've gotta go
my toes may take some time . . .

Molly
#TeamThorForever
See you later, ladies xxx

Liz
xxx

Chapter 51

BABYMOON

Emily couldn't actually believe it was July.

In two weeks, she would be having a baby.

A real-life human baby.

It all seemed scarily close now, and scarily real.

She'd almost completed the longest pregnancy in the history of time, and it seemed hard to imagine not being pregnant any more. She wasn't sure if she could actually remember what it felt like not to have a constant wriggly rave going on in her uterus. It would be so strange when it stopped.

As horrible and weird as some of (most of) her pregnancy had been, the idea of not carrying her baby around inside her any more felt even weirder.

She was sure this was down to hormones again. She was trying not to focus on it.

Her and Paul were currently on their 'babymoon' at a posh spa hotel in Marlow. She'd insisted they do it after one of the other couples mentioned it at their last NCT class. Paul hadn't been quite as enthusiastic about it as Emily was, but she didn't care. He wasn't the one with a womb the size of a cabin-legal suitcase.

She needed this. One last night away before the baby

arrived, where she could get pampered and preened to her heart and vagina's content.

She knew it was pointless going too far afield. Their son could come at any moment. But Emily had already decided that it would not be this weekend . . .

She simply wasn't prepared to give birth until someone had de-forested her unborn baby's entrance point.

She was quite adamant about that.

She sighed deeply as she stood in front of the mirror in her hotel bedroom, wondering how exactly the 'size medium' white towelling robe they'd provided her with was going to cover any of her protruding bump for her journey down to the spa. Paul seemed thoroughly uninterested in her plight as he lay down on the bed playing with his phone . . .

'Paul!' Emily snapped irritably. 'My robe won't go round me! I look ridiculous! I may as well stroll down there in my pants with my fanny hanging out. What am I going to do?'

'Don't worry, sweetie. Does it matter if you have your swimming costume on underneath anyway? Just chill. Or use mine?'

Emily decided she would let Paul's suggestion to 'just chill' go without violently murdering him as wearing his robe was actually a sensible suggestion. She slipped hers off and grabbed the XL version meant for Paul out of the wardrobe.

It still didn't quite meet in the middle, but it was better. She had her pregnancy massage in ten minutes so it would have to do.

She couldn't wait. After her massage, she'd booked every treatment she could find. When she had her baby, she was going to look GOOD.

She needed a wax (she'd conceded that without one they might never actually find her vagina to pull the baby out), her eyebrows threaded, semi-permanent lashes, a spray tan, and a facial, ending with a gel manicure and pedicure, ready for that special moment when she'd able to see her feet again.

'You better get going. Do you want me to walk you down?' Paul said, glancing at his watch while Emily tied the oversized robe as best she could so as not to reveal too much . . .

'Don't worry. You head to the gym and I'll just meet you back here in a few hours,' Emily said, waddling her way towards the door.

'A few hours? I thought you were just having a massage?' Paul pulled a puzzled face.

'Paul,' Emily said with a straight face. 'Have you actually ever met me before? Clearly not! So, hi. My name is Emily. And I'm your emotionally unstable, heavily pregnant, high-maintenance wife. And we're at a spa. So I'll see you in about four hours. Bye.'

Emily. Felt. Amazing.

She looked amazing.

She didn't believe it was possible to look and feel this relaxed with only days left until she gave birth to another person. And all it took was four hours and twenty minutes of incredibly expensive spa treatments. Who knew?

Life felt pretty perfect right now.

She was happy, relaxed and revived. And as if that wasn't enough, she was now in a dressing gown eating tiny cakes and sandwiches in the late-afternoon sunshine.

She left her robe open and let the gentle heat of the sun fall on her smooth, post-massage skin. She didn't care who saw her now. Everything was as neat and hair-free as it was ever going to be.

Emily sat up a little and looked at Paul. She studied his face for a moment as he sat with his head tipped back letting the sunlight hit his face.

He looked tired.

She hadn't noticed it before. She'd been so busy being relentlessly exhausted and uncomfortable herself, she hadn't stopped and thought how all of this might be affecting him.

Emily began to feel a slight sense of guilt. He really had been wonderful these last few months. Even though at times she must have been a little hard to live with, and by 'a little hard', she really meant emotional, restless, demanding, argumentative and actually a bit of a knob sometimes, if she was really honest with herself. He'd not complained once.

He'd slept on the sofa when she was too uncomfortable in the bed; he'd cooked, cleaned, shopped, and allowed her free rein to buy whatever she thought they needed for the baby.

She'd had a hard pregnancy. No one was denying she'd had it tough . . . but there was no doubt some of that had been tough for Paul too . . .

'Paul,' Emily said gently.

He slowly opened his heavy eyes and turned to look at her. 'Yes sweetie? Do you need me to get your something?'

'No. I'm good. I don't need anything . . .' Emily said smiling, beginning to feel emotional. 'I just wanted you to know that you're amazing. You've been so amazing throughout all of this. And I know you're going to be an absolutely brilliant father. You already are . . .'

'Oh right,' Paul said, smiling back at her. He clearly hadn't expected that. She could see how much her un-expected words had meant to him. 'I'm just doing what any expectant dad would do. Gotta look after my little family . . .'

'I know I haven't been that easy to look after these last few weeks. Maybe even the last few months. I don't know . . . But I really appreciate how wonderful you've been. I know you probably didn't even want to come here today, but you did it for me. I know that. Thank you. For everything. I really do love you.'

'I love you too, sweetie,' Paul said, his face beaming with happiness and pride. 'Even if you are a massive pain in the arse and just spent £378 on getting your fanny waxed. I wouldn't have you any other way . . .'

Chapter 52

DON'T TELL GERALD

Liz had been spending more and more time with Gerald outside of work. She was not putting any kind of label on it just yet. But they were enjoying getting to know each other. And right now, that was enough for her.

She was aware things were a little one-sided on his part, but she had no interest in rushing into a relationship. She just wanted to have fun. And spend her Friday nights kissing him and getting drunk in posh bars. That bit worked for her.

Perhaps she wasn't very good at the whole 'dating' thing. It had been a long time. She didn't really remember how to do it. But she knew that Gerald seemed keen. Perhaps a little too keen. She was fairly sure he'd try and see her every night if she let him. Which she wouldn't. There had to be 'Gerald-Limitation'.

But tonight she'd decided to take her friends' advice and let her guard down a little, and cook for him at her flat. She loved to cook, she was good at it, and it was about time she did something nice for him . . .

A gentle tap at the door gently pulled her out of her thoughts.

He was perfectly on time. Like always.

Liz removed her cooking apron, and put on her heels. She'd made an effort for tonight. She was not going to answer the door in a Cath Kidston pinny and the comedy-cat-faced slippers her nieces had bought her for Christmas.

She felt a flutter of anticipation as she twisted the lock on the door and opened it to see him there, smartly dressed and looking more handsome than ever. He was clutching a bottle of something expensive-looking and an enormous bunch of red roses.

'Hey, you . . .' Liz said, pulling the door fully open so he could see all of her. She'd squeezed herself into an expensive tight red dress, thin black designer heels and scooped her hair sleekly to one side . . . she looked amazing. And she knew it.

'Wow,' Gerald said, looking her up and down. 'You look stunning. I feel underdressed now!'

He leaned forward and kissed her.

She pulled him inside, their lips still locked. The door swung closed behind them.

'That's enough of that,' she said, teasing him as she tore herself away. 'I have cooked up a masterpiece, and we are going to eat and enjoy every bit of it before any of that, thank you . . .'

'Duly noted. Eat and enjoy; "that" later,' Gerald responded, following her into the kitchen.

Liz poured him a large glug of red wine and started hunting for a vase.

'Thank you for the flowers. They are beautiful,' Liz

gushed, as he passed her the flowers and placed the champagne he'd brought with him down on the side.

'They're not a patch on you in that dress . . .' he replied.

Liz found herself giggling like a teenager as she arranged the roses in the vase. He made her feel so good about herself; she wasn't used to it. It made her blush every time.

'To tonight,' Gerald said, raising his glass.

'Tonight,' Liz replied, locating her wine glass on the kitchen side and raising it in return. 'Now – if you wouldn't mind putting this cutlery out and taking a seat at the table, I'll be out in a minute with our starters,' she continued, passing him some well-polished knives and forks.

Gerald took them and headed out of the kitchen.

Moments later, Liz joined him and put down two beautifully presented plates of homemade salmon mousse. She'd created little dots and circles of different sauces over the dishes. She'd seen it on *MasterChef* once . . .

'This looks amazing. You've clearly got some serious culinary skills, lady,' Gerald said.

'Well, I'm a lady, of many talents . . .' Liz said flirtatiously as they tucked in.

'It's delicious. Thank you,' Gerald said after devouring most of it in a few seconds. He cleared his throat as if preparing to say something important. 'So . . . look, I know this is going to sound a bit soppy. I just wanted to say that I know it's only been a few weeks, but I'm so happy, Liz. I hope you don't feel like things are moving

285

too fast. I know I text you a lot, I know I probably want things to move faster than you do, but if you feel like I'm pushing things, you just need to tell me . . . okay? I know you said you had just come out of a complicated relationship when we first started working together. I hope that's not the reason you are pulling back from me? Is it? I mean, is that definitely over?'

Liz hadn't expected that. She was taken aback at how straightforward he was being . . . but similarly she wanted to be honest with him. Perhaps it would be good to get it all out in the open now, so he knew everything. And so there were no nasty surprises down the line, especially if they all had to work in the same building.

'Erm,' Liz began, a little nervously, not quite sure what she was going to say. 'You don't need to worry about him. He's in the past. And so so far from my life now . . . he's dead to me. It's just unfortunate that . . .' Liz didn't seem to be able to stop herself talking. He wasn't pressing her but she just felt the need to be honest . . .

'Well . . . he was married. I suppose he still is. Although I wouldn't imagine for long. And I know you probably think I'm an utterly dreadful person but I suppose I'm that clichéd idiot who believed the guy who told her he was going to leave his wife for her. And obviously, he had no intention of doing that. So I ended it. Finally. After wasting a long time lying to myself . . .'

Liz couldn't quite believe she'd just said that. But it felt liberating. Like she could breathe again. It was out there now.

Gerald didn't react. Perhaps he was so disappointed with her he couldn't bring himself to say anything . . .

'I'll understand if you just want to go,' Liz said eventually. A little scared that he actually would.

'Why would I want to go?' Gerald said soothingly. 'That's not who you are any more. You ended it. You need to stop beating yourself up. You're a good person. A great person. Don't ever think you're not.'

His words were such a relief. But Liz could feel that he knew there was something she was leaving out. And she wanted him to know the whole truth. He needed to. She needed him to.

'And, the thing is . . . you know him,' she said, with her head hanging down. As she prepared herself to finally say his name.

Why the fuck was she telling him this? Why couldn't she keep her big mouth closed? This was going to end things before they'd even started. He'd hate her for sure. She'd just spent several hundred pounds on tiny pieces of French lace for absolutely no reason. Why couldn't she just shut up?

'It's, well, it's . . .'

'I know,' Gerald said, cutting her off. And lifting up her head gently so he could see her eyes.

'I know, Liz. I knew that day we all gathered in the boardroom for his surprise birthday party. I knew when I saw your heart break in two as his pregnant wife followed him into the room. And I knew as you stumbled out of the door, choking back tears. No one else might have

287

noticed. But I did. And I never judged you for it. I still don't. I never cared. People fuck up. People make mistakes. It's okay, Liz.'

Liz just sat looking at him as the words poured out of his mouth. She felt embarrassed, relieved and angry at the same time.

How could he have known and not said anything? But then, how could he have said anything up to now? It was her confession to make. Not his.

'Wow,' she said, letting a long breath out. 'So you knew my secret and you still wanted to be with me?'

'Of course I did. Of course I still do. I think I fell in love with you from the very first moment I saw you, Liz. You're so much more amazing than you give yourself credit for. I can't believe you don't already know that.' Her eyes welled up a little with tears of relief and surprise. 'You know that I love you, Liz. Don't you? I really do. I love you.'

'Thank you,' she said eventually, getting herself back under control. She hated the words the moment they left her lips, but she was nowhere close to telling him she loved him. It felt ridiculous. She'd only known him for a few months; they'd only been seeing each other for a few weeks. This was crazy.

She felt annoyed at him for even saying it.

He'd ruined everything.

Chapter 53

'THANK YOU . . .'

Liz
FUUUUUCCCKKKKK!
Gerald just told me he loves me.

Emily
Oh wow!
Erm . . . That was quick!

Liz
I said 'Thank You'.

Emily
Oh . . .
Ouch.
Did you say anything else?
Where is he now?

Liz
I couldn't.
I'm hiding in the kitchen!
He's still sat at the table.
It's so awkward!
I don't know what to doooooo!

Molly
Wow.
Just catching up . . .
Eeeeesh.
Can you just get drunk?

Liz
Yes.
Great plan.
I'll get wankered and just
see what happens . . .
nothing ever went wrong ever before
when someone did that . . .

Emily
I don't think you should leave it
too long to go back out there . . .
If you feel awkward, imagine how he
feels!

Molly
Yeah.
I mean you just took his heart,
ripped it out of his chest,
stamped on it, spat on it,
curled one off on top of it,
and handed it back to him . . .
I'm not sure alone time is
what he wants right now.

Liz

MOLLY YOU ARE NOT HELPING!

Emily

Sweetie, I think you just need
to be honest with him.
You still like him right?
It's not like you're dumping him.
You just need to explain that telling
someone you've been seeing for a
few weeks that you're in love with
them is a bit extreme . . .
And failing that get twatted
and see what happens like Molly said.
#ProbablyBeFine

Molly

Yeah.
Don't dump Thor! I like him!

Liz

Okay.
Fuck It.
I'm going back out.
Thanks girls.
#ProbablyBeFine.

Chapter 54

FALSE ALARM

Her baby wasn't due for another six weeks.

But today Molly felt strange . . .

The day had begun like any other Monday. She'd got out of bed as usual, sat and had breakfast with Tom, trying not to think about how horny she felt watching him eat his toast. He had laughed and told her to calm down before kissing her and heading off early for his Monday morning sales meeting . . .

Then she'd had a shower, blow-dried her hair and got dressed ready to head down and join the usual queue full of Lynxed-up monosyllabic teenagers at the temp agency . . .

But then she'd started to feel odd.

A strange wave of nausea had washed over her as she stepped out of the front door and turned the key behind her. It was unsettling. She was fighting the strong urge to be sick. Perhaps she just needed to get outside into the fresh air. That was probably it, she reasoned with herself, as she tentatively placed her foot on the first step of the staircase down to the main door.

But as she began making her way further down the stairs, a scary unfamiliar pain stabbed her deep in her abdomen.

Molly moaned loudly and grabbed hard on to the hand-rail to make sure she didn't fall. The colour drained completely from her knuckles as she gripped the rail intensely and tried to breathe through the agony in her stomach, which was forcing her to bend over double as far as her heavily pregnant body would allow.

She managed to turn herself around, and fight the pain long enough to make it back up the stairs and on to the landing outside the door.

Her hands were trembling, and tears of fear and agony were rolling down her face as she fumbled frantically in her bag with one hand searching for her phone. It only took her a few seconds to find it, but it felt like for ever.

The pain was intense and unbearable. She was struggling to breathe. The tears continued to flow as her moaning turned into little yelps she couldn't control.

She managed to get Tom's number up and began phoning him.

He answered the phone within a few moments. She could barely get the words out in between her yelps and screams of pain.

'Tom! Help! The baby!'

'Where are you?' Tom's response was straight and calm.

'Home!' Molly screamed.

'Right. I'm hanging up and ringing an ambulance. I'm on my way. Don't move. Try to keep calm. Everything is going to be fine. I love you.'

Molly felt some relief just knowing he was on his way and the ambulance would be here soon. She hoped. The pain was too much to handle. She didn't know how much more she could cope with.

She knew Tom had told her not to move but she needed to get inside. If she could just get to the sofa, perhaps she could make herself more comfortable and the pain would lessen.

She was terrified she'd fall down the stairs.

She needed to try and get herself back in the flat.

She dragged herself to her knees and managed to find her key in her bag. She still let out yelps as the excruciating pain continued to stab on the left side of her stomach.

She just needed to focus and do this.

She twisted the key in the lock and dragged herself on to her hands and knees through the doorway and into the living room. It took every bit of her strength to heave her tense, pregnant body on to the sofa.

She couldn't stop crying. And screaming. She was panicking. She knew this wasn't labour. She knew this wasn't right. All she could think about was that something was going wrong. She just needed to sit, breathe, and try to focus on something other than the pain . . .

Please hurry. Please hurry. Please hurry . . . she repeated over and over in her head. Trying to clear her mind of the panicky thoughts creeping in.

Moments later she heard Tom's voice. She was so relieved he was there. She heard his feet thud up the stairs quickly as he raced inside the flat.

'Fuck,' he said. 'Don't worry. The ambulance is here.

They're just pulling up. You're going to be okay. Just keep breathing.' He was trying to sound calm. Molly knew he was as scared as she was.

Molly was trying hard to believe him. She was so glad he was there now. Her tears were slowing a little, but the pain was still there.

She was going to be okay. She had to believe that.

She and the baby were going to be okay . . .

Chapter 55

EVERYTHING IS FINE

Molly
Girls I'm okay.
Sorry if I scared you.
I scared myself too if it's any
consolation!
xxx

Liz
You really did!
I'm so glad you're all right now.
What happened?
Are you back home yet?

Emily
I was terrified!
What happened??
Thank you for letting us
know you're okay.
So glad you and the baby are safe xx

Molly
I'm still here but should be
able to go home in a couple of days.

They just want to keep an eye on me,
but they think everything is fine now.
It's just a precaution.
I had a placental abruption.
Which sounds terrifying!
But luckily it was only a tiny tear
and everything is fine now.
I feel exhausted but okay.
The pain has gone.
It was so scary.
I thought something was really wrong.
It felt like I was being stabbed or
something – that's the only
way I can describe it!
So scary!!
Luckily Tom was only up the road
and got to me in minutes.
He was so amazing.
I was really freaking out.
Never felt pain like that in my life.
I'm just so thankful that
everything is okay
and that the ambulance got
here so fast.
Don't want to think about what might
have happened if they'd taken longer!

Emily
Gosh that sounds so awful

Promise me you are going to take it
easy now??

Molly

I don't think I can do anything
but take it easy!
I know I've been saying how easy
being pregnant has been
for me so far . . .
But I think this is my
wake-up call to slow down.
Doctor says bed-rest
from now anyway.
Tom is adamant I'm not
going back to work.
I think he's right . . .

Liz

He is right!
Just got to look after yourself now,
sweetie.
So relieved you're both okay xxx
Do you want me to bring you
anything?

Molly

I'm fine honestly.
Tom is taking a few days off work.
He'll take care of me so don't worry xx

Emily

I could bring you chocolate
and Closer magazine?
That's the kind of friend I am . . .

Molly

Ha.
I'm cool, honestly.
I just want to go home now xx
Maybe you can pop round
when I'm back.
I'll let you know xx
If you can make it up the stairs
without passing out that is!

Emily

Hey!
(but yes, that is a fair point)

Liz

Well if you're making jokes again
I know you're on the mend.
Please don't scare us again like that
lady!

Emily

No. Don't!
And can I just say . . .
Obviously, now that I know
you're all absolutely fine . . .
if you had had your baby

before me, there's a strong possibility
I never would have talked to you again.
And maybe murdered you . . .
Just saying . . .

Liz
lol

Molly
lol
(I know)
(it was my main concern, obviously)
Thank you, girls.
You've cheered me up ☺
I'm honestly okay now.
Keep the texts coming to keep me
entertained . . .
Going to be a boring few weeks!
Love you xx

Liz
xx

Emily
xxx

Chapter 56

DUE DAY

Come on, baby
Please hurry up
We just want to meet you
Your tenancy is up
If you could vacate the uterus
Your eviction needs to be now
Mummy just wants her body back
Before she turns into a total cow*
(*and murders daddy)

Emily was rapidly beginning to realise that the main thing about pregnancy is you can't control any of it.

Pregnancy will do what it likes, when it likes and it couldn't give a shit how you feel about it.

She had woken up on her due date, feeling much the same as the day before her due date. And the many many many days before that. Only more pissed off. Because she still wasn't in labour. She was now painfully aware that this baby was going to do what the hell it liked regardless. And if this went on much longer, all her fanny hair would start growing back.

She'd decided if she was going to get through each day, she was going to need to keep herself busy.

So far, she'd rearranged the shed, descaled the entire bathroom and had a complete clear-out of all the random crap they were hoarding in the cupboard under the stairs, which mostly consisted of two broken vacuum cleaners, several rusty saucepans and a set of Tupperware with no lids she'd never seen before, but she was beginning to feel a little better.

She was now moving her attention on to the kitchen. First stop, the spice, herb and sauce cupboard. Where she'd just found a jar of garam masala that pre-dated her university graduation . . .

Just then, her phone buzzed.

It was a notification from the WhatsApp group for all the NCT ladies in her class.

They'd set it up at the end of the last session so they could all stay in touch. Emily thought it would be great to have a few new mums she knew to attend baby-groups and things with. Molly wouldn't want to do all the same stuff as her anyway. In fact, she probably wouldn't want to do any of the same stuff as her. She'd made a weird sneer-y face and laughed when Emily suggested they start baby-signing and swimming classes from four weeks old. They were clearly going to be different sorts of parents . . .

Emily liked the idea of having a little network of mummy friends. That was one of the main reasons she did the NCT course in the first place. She liked the idea of a group of mums she could talk to, share information and worries with, and generally bitch about piles and giant areolas with. They'd all be winging it together, right? What's not to like?

Emily had dipped in and out of the group messages and chats but hadn't managed to meet up with the NCT mums yet. She'd missed a couple of meet-ups while she was still working and one when she was on her babymoon . . . And for the last week she'd been a bit too angry about her baby still being on the inside and making sure the shed was organised to go eat cake . . .

She was just so desperate not to be pregnant any more. She had things to be getting on with. Like alcohol and unpasteurised cheeses. She was finding it very inconvenient that he hadn't made an appearance yet.

Emily unlocked her phone to scroll through the latest chat . . .

For fuck's sake.

The first baby had been born.

Emily knew she should be happy.

But she wasn't.

She was insanely jealous.

She knew it was totally unreasonable to feel that way but she couldn't help it . . .

Some fucking bitch had stolen her due date.

STOLEN. IT.

That message was supposed to be from her!

HEEERRRRRRR.

She was supposed to be the one sending out pictures

of her in a hospital bed clutching a tiny scrunched-up newborn, still covered in pieces of womb, announcing its name and time of birth and telling everyone her fanny was fine.

BUT SHE WASN'T.

SHE WAS CLEARING OUT EXPIRED SPICES FROM HER KITCHEN CUPBOARD AND CRYING.

She couldn't look any more.

This was not helping her.

Her baby was still very much on the inside.

Fuck it.

The cupboard could wait.

She was off for a mid-afternoon nap with an entire pineapple, some out-of-date curry powder, four litres of raspberry leaf tea and a quick message to Paul to let him know his penis would very much be on duty tonight, because one way or another . . .

. . . she would GET THIS BABY OUT.

Chapter 57

HOME

It felt so good to be home.

Molly had spent the last few days in Stoke Mandeville hospital, surviving primarily on toast, sweets and cups of vaguely beige lukewarm tea . . .

She'd finally made it back to Tom's flat and couldn't wait to eat real food again and have a lovely strong cup of Yorkshire tea. Decaf. Of course.

Tom had been more than amazing. Luckily, his boss had been totally understanding and had pretty much insisted he take the week off, which was good because Molly was not sure how she would have survived without him there. She hated hospitals. The horrible beds, the smell, the sounds, the fucking terrible tea . . .

He'd spent every available visiting hour by her side. Bringing her fresh fruit, bags of nuts and seeds from the wholefoods store, and more of those vegan lollies she'd become quite addicted to. If she was honest she could murder a Curly Wurly, a bag of Frazzles and a glass of wine but she knew he was just trying to look out for her. They watched movies together on the iPad and both felt so grateful and relieved everything was okay. The alternative had been too scary to contemplate . . .

He'd dozed off in the chair next to her bed every so often and Molly had sat and watched him sleep. Feeling so thankful for him. Loving him. Loving that he loved her.

But now she was back at home, on a comfortable sofa, where everything smelt and sounded so wonderfully normal, with a decent cup of tea. She felt even more grateful for him and everything else they had . . .

'I'm making us a Thai curry tonight, babes . . .' Tom called out as he made his way back into the lounge from the kitchen. 'I bought all the stuff yesterday. Plenty of veg. Plenty of protein. It'll help build your strength back up.'

'Thank you,' Molly said with a small voice from her horizontal position. She still felt weak. 'I'll be back to myself in a couple of days. I'm glad it's the weekend so you're here. I know you can't just keep taking days off . . .'

'Don't worry about that. I'll take as many days off as you need me to. The important thing is that you sit on your arse and let me run around after you. Okay?' Tom said authoritatively.

Molly liked it when he told her off a little bit. It made her feel safe, and secure, and usually a little bit horny. Obviously.

Tom made his way back into the lounge and sat down next to her, looking at her face as if checking her over.

'Well. Judging by that cheeky little twinkle in your eye I'd say you're starting to be on the mend already,' Tom said, stroking his fingers through his dark hair and winking at her.

He jumped up from the sofa and headed back out to the kitchen again. He'd barely sat still since they'd got back. He was busy looking after her.

And he was right. She was feeling a little better. Probably just for being home again. But she couldn't deny that she didn't want to be on her own at all at the moment.

The doctors had told her they had no idea why it had happened. And Molly reasoned that if she didn't know why it happened, then there was no real way of preventing it, so it was possible it could happen again. And that scared her a little.

She didn't like the feeling. She'd never really had anything in her life to be scared about before . . . Even when her mum died, she'd used all her energy being there for her dad. She didn't have time to be scared for herself, so she buried those feelings, and stayed strong for him.

But this was different. It had made her realise how much she needed Tom. How much she needed him to love her. And be there for her . . .

She'd never had to rely on anyone but herself before, but now she had him.

She really did have him.

'Here's some water,' Tom said, returning with a fresh glass. 'I spoke to your dad earlier, by the way. He's going to pop round tomorrow, if that's okay with you? I said I'd let him know if you weren't up to it . . .'

'That's fine,' Molly said, smiling and feeling tired. 'It'll be good to see him. I think he just wants to make sure

 307

I'm okay. He hasn't seen your flat yet either. It'll be nice for him to see me here.'

'Hey. It might be my flat, but it's *our home*. Ours. The three of us. Okay?' Tom said, placing the glass down beside her and smiling at her.

'Okay,' Molly said. She knew he meant it. Her eyes were getting heavy now.

Time to close them for a little while. She knew she'd feel a little better again when she woke up.

Chapter 58

THE WRATH OF CLOVER

It had been an awkward couple of weeks . . .

Liz had tried repeatedly to explain to Gerald that she still wanted to be with him, but they needed to slow things down. A LOT.

She had no idea if he fully understood but he seemed to be relaxing things a little, and had at least stopped texting her every few hours to let her know he'd just had his hair cut, eaten a chicken sandwich and seen a cloud that reminded him of the shape of her nose. She just wasn't the sort of girl who needed to hear that sort of crap.

The thing was, when he wasn't pointing out weather systems that looked like her face, she really did like him. When he stopped trying so hard, he made her really happy . . .

She hadn't had a drunken tuna-pasta night in with Jasper the cat in ages . . . And she certainly didn't miss those. And neither did Jasper, by the looks of it, as he had decided he preferred Gerald's company to hers anyway these days . . .

But today she had a dilemma.

On Sunday, it was her family's annual summer meal.

Every year, her sister hosted a family meal in her big, countryside garden in Hampshire. And every year Liz would attend, on her own, while members of her extended family that she barely knew would make sympathetic faces at her and ask why she didn't have a boyfriend yet, while offering to set her up with their friend's son Colin who worked in finance and probably wore chinos.

But this year she had the option of taking Gerald, which would save her from Colin, but would suggest to Gerald things were a little more serious than they actually were between them, and given current events, that was the last thing she needed. She had to decide which one was less painful . . .

Fuck it. She thought to herself. Anything has got to be better than Colin and his chinos . . .

And with that she texted Gerald . . .

Liz had never done anything like this before . . . she'd never been with someone that she *could* do something like this with before.

Taking someone to meet her family was new and untrodden ground for her. And her sister Holly's excitement about meeting Gerald for the first time was making her feel even more nervous.

Gerald was looking forward to it; he looked forward to everything. He was completely relaxed. Which had the effect of making Liz feel even more uncomfortable.

He'd met her friends; she'd met his. That was fine. But this was . . . different. It made it feel like they were in a serious relationship, and they weren't. Liz didn't even know what they 'were' yet.

The idea of exposing him to the full brunt of her family all at once made Liz feel physically ill. What if they hated him? What if he hated them? What if they asked him awful questions, made bad jokes and showed him that weird picture of her in the bath aged eleven with the dog? They might put him off her for ever . . .

She wasn't sure she was ready for this yet.

What if someone referred to him as her 'boyfriend'? She hated that word. She was thirty, not fifteen. She was more than happy not to put any label on whatever it was her and Gerald 'were'. As far as she was concerned, they were Liz and Gerald. Or Gerald and Liz. That was it.

'Are you nearly ready?' Gerald asked.

'Nearly,' she said as she applied her red lipstick.

'You look lovely,' Gerald said, smiling from the doorway.

'Do we have to go?' Liz attempted an over-the-top sulky face.

'Yes!' Gerald said laughing. 'Come on. You'll have a great time once we're there. It's only a couple of nights. And I'm really looking forward to meeting everyone. You look perfect. Everything will be perfect. Plus I'm driving so you can just sit back and relax the whole way. So stop stalling!'

Liz knew he really was right. And she knew he genuinely was looking forward to it. He was that sort of person. A people person. She mostly preferred cats . . . And alcohol.

'Okay,' Liz said, huffing herself to her feet.

Gerald picked up her case and they began heading out of her flat.

'You don't have to worry, you know. There's nothing that could happen that would ever change how I feel about you. You know that, right?' he said, giving her a reassuring hug from behind as she locked the door.

'I know,' she said, smiling and trying not to think about the bath picture . . .

Liz had barely managed to set foot inside the door before she was accosted by a very excited Clover, assisted by a full set of Tombliboos.

'Arnee Lizzeeeeeee!' Clover screamed as she flung her chubby toddler arms around Liz's neck and gave her a very sweet but slightly painful hug.

'Who dat?' Clover said, with a stroppy finger point at Gerald as he made it through the door carrying the cases.

'This is Arnee Lizzee's friend Gerald,' Liz said, smiling. 'He's come to stay here too this weekend. If that's okay with you?'

'He's big,' Clover said, frowning at him and looking him up and down in a way only a two-year-old can.

'All the better for climbing on,' Gerald said, lowering his head towards her with a smile.

Clover beamed. The idea of her own personal six-foot-three, blond climbing frame for the weekend was a very pleasing thought. It was pretty much the ultimate toddler dream . . .

Liz's sister Holly appeared from the kitchen, flicking hair out of her face and grinning widely as she approached them.

'Come in, guys. Come in. How was your journey?' Holly attempted to peel Clover away from Liz.

'All fine,' Liz said, kicking her shoes off and following her sister into the lounge. 'No traffic, so took us no time at all . . .'

Gerald left the cases in the hall. He strolled in and sat down next to Liz on the sofa, putting his arm around Liz's shoulder comfortably.

'Sorry,' Liz said, suddenly sitting forward. 'I haven't actually introduced you properly yet, have I? Gerald, this is my sister Holly and my niece Clover. Holly, this is my, well, this is Gerald.'

Liz's cheeks stung a little.

'Hello, *my* Gerald,' Holly said with a little smile on her face.

'Hello Holly. And hello Clover,' Gerald said, smiling as Clover pretended to be shy. 'I've heard so much about you. It's lovely to put faces to the names. Thank you so much for including me in the invite.'

'You are so welcome,' Holly said, glancing at Liz. 'Liz has refused to tell me anything at all about you! So I'm very much looking forward to hearing all of it this weekend.'

Liz threw her sister a look, in the way that only sisters can.

'Ah well, there's not that much to tell!' Gerald said,

laughing. 'But I'm looking forward to getting to know you guys too.'

'Where's Dan and the baby?' Liz said, changing the subject.

'He's just putting Isla down for a nap,' Holly said, raising her eyes towards the ceiling. 'He'll be down in a minute. I'll go open some wine if you both fancy some?'

'Always,' Liz said, sitting back again and relaxing into Gerald's arm as Holly headed out to the kitchen to fetch their drinks.

'See,' Gerald said with his voice lowered. 'Everything is fine.'

And with that he kissed the side of her head and slipped his arm out from behind her, so he could sit on the floor with Clover.

Liz smiled.

Everything was fine.

Better than fine.

Especially now she could relax, and it was Gerald's turn to attend an exclusive tea party with Lego Batman, Great Big Hoo, a selection of dubiously styled dollies and the Tombliboos.

Chapter 59

THE L-WORD

Saying 'I love you'
Means lots of little things.
I love kissing you, and hugging you,
And holding hands walking on the beach.
It also means I trust you,
And need you to look after my heart.
And expect you to pretend you never notice
When I let out a little fart.

It was finally Sunday morning.

The day of the family meal, and the day Liz knew she could get back home to Bucks and return to normality.

She was in her sister's kitchen peeling and chopping things.

If she was honest she wasn't really just chopping things . . .

She was hiding.

She loved spending time with her sister and brother-in-law, she loved seeing so much of her nieces, but she found it a little . . . intense.

She was used to living alone, having her own space and not being forced to move around the living room via the medium of dance, as instructed by a passive-aggressive two-year-old . . .

So every so often she'd skulk off out of the way under the pretence of fetching something, unloading the dishwasher, or chopping something up – just to get five minutes without being made to answer a plastic phone to Igglepiggle, Tombliboo Unn, or baby Jesus.

She knew Gerald would be fine for a few moments without her. He'd been wonderful. She knew he would be. Everybody loved him; he was easy to love.

Clover was especially taken with him. And had turned him into her own personal piggyback chauffeur within minutes of their arrival.

But he didn't seem to mind. He was amazing with children. Liz was beginning to wonder if he actually had any faults . . .

'There you are,' came Gerald's voice as he strolled into the kitchen.

'Yeah. Sorry. I just needed a few minutes. Thought I'd get started on the mountain of potatoes that need prepping for the roast dinner.'

'Ah yes. Potatoes. Very important,' he said with a wink and picked up the peeler to join in the production line.

'Okay. You caught me. I just need a breather every so often is all . . . I'm not the same as you. You're amazing with kids. And everyone, actually. I'm better with . . . cats. And things that don't talk back to you.'

'Ha. We all need a break every so often. Don't feel bad.

Your family are amazing. The kids are so great. I can't wait to have all of that stuff myself.'

Liz wondered why he'd said that. It caught her a little off guard. So she didn't have a pre-prepared response . . . she didn't really know how to respond.

They'd only been seeing each other a couple of months, if that. She hadn't expected that they would be having the 'marriage, babies, dog and a picket fence' conversation just yet. She couldn't even bring herself to call him her boyfriend.

'Yes. They're great,' Liz finally managed. Perhaps he wasn't even looking for a response to the other thing. She was probably overreacting. Again.

'So, do you think you want children, a family and all that stuff, one day?' he said, calmly and comfortably, as if he was asking her if she fancied some toast . . .

'Um . . . well. I've not really thought about it that much,' Liz said.

'Really? How can you not have thought about it?' Gerald said. 'I think I've always known I wanted kids. I thought everyone just kind of *knew*?'

Liz didn't want to have this conversation. Not right here. Right now. While she was out of her comfort zone. Chopping up potatoes. But she couldn't ignore him . . .

'I just don't know yet,' Liz said. 'I guess I used to want to. But then my career started to take over my life and I didn't seem to have the time for anything else. And then everyone around me seemed to meet people, settle down, get married, and then they started getting pregnant, and

317

I suppose I just stopped thinking about it. Because I didn't know if it would ever happen to me. I didn't know if I'd ever meet someone that I thought I might be able to have all that with.'

She paused for a moment. Not knowing whether to carry on, or stop and risk offending him . . . She seemed to have a knack for doing that.

'Until I met you, that is.' She turned her face towards him to look him in the eye.

Liz felt her cheeks redden a little. She wasn't good at expressing emotion. But she knew she needed to start letting her guard down a little. Gerald deserved that. He'd just spent the last hour and a half being ridden around the garden by her two-year-old niece. The least she could do was let him know it wasn't all in vain . . .

Gerald pulled her in towards him before planting a deep, loving kiss on her lips.

'You make me really happy,' he said, looking intensely into her eyes.

'You make me really happy too.' She kissed him again.

Liz looked into his eyes. She didn't know if it was the moment, or how amazing he'd been with her family, but she felt the urge to say something she'd not said to anyone for a long time . . .

'And . . . I love you,' she said. She had an instant surge of emotion and relief as the words left her mouth.

Gerald's face lit up. She knew those words meant so much to him. It felt good but terrifying to say them. It felt like she meant them . . .

'I love you too,' he said, kissing her again.
She'd done it. She loved him.
And she'd told him.
She'd finally said the L-word.

Chapter 60

GIZ

Liz
Okay.
I got a bit caught up in a
moment and told
Gerald I love him . . .
I'm trying not to freak out.
I think I'm okay with it . . .
I think?
I actually really think I might love him?
Do you think it's too soon?
I just don't know . . . Arggghhhh!

Emily
Ha! Thanks for the update!
Wow. Well if you feel it, you feel it!
I honestly didn't expect that!
I thought you guys were slowing
things down?

Liz
I know!
I didn't expect it either.
I don't really know what came over

me . . . but I really like him. And it
felt right . . . I guess.
I don't regret it. I think that means I
meant it? Right?

Emily
Yes. I reckon so . . .
How did you do it?
Was it all cheesy and romantic?
A confession of love on an evening's
walk through the countryside?
Perhaps a stolen moment under the
shade of the trees in the morning . . .

Liz
Actually . . .
We were chopping potatoes.

Emily
Pahahaha
Well. I like that you kept it real.

Molly
Wow.
Awesome news Lizzy-tits.
You know that this officially
makes you guys 'Giz'.
Don't you . . .

Emily
LOL

Liz

I do not.

I fully reject it in fact.

We're fully grown adults . . .

We are Liz and Gerald and

that's that, thank you!

Molly

You can't reject it.

It's done.

Giz Giz Giz.

Emily

Giz Giz Giz Giz Giz Giz

Liz

You girls need hobbies.

Seriously.

This is very sad to watch . . .

Molly

Oh that's soooooo something

Giz would say.

Emily

Giz Giz Giz Giz Giz Giz

Liz

Whatever . . .

I don't care anyway.

I'm just letting you know I said it!

I think this makes us official? Doesn't it?

Who cares.
I LOVE HIM.
☺

Emily
Wow.
This is not the sort of obvious display
of affection we expect from you Lizzy!
I might just throw up!
Just joking – I'm really happy for you.
He's great.
You're really great together.
We all knew that anyway!
#Giz

Molly
Ha!
I'm so happy for you too sweetie.
He's defo a keeper.
Giz, Tolly and Pemily it is . . .
it's just like we always dreamed!

Emily
LOL

Liz
LOL.
Well I can tell you're feeling
much better Molly!
Glad to see your sense of
humour has fully returned.

Molly
Much better thank you.
And don't think changing the subject is
going to make us forget about Giz . . .
WE WILL NEVER FORGET!!
I'm considering making you a little
sign for your new desk ;)
#GizGizGiz

Liz
I'm going now.
Bye.

Emily
#Giz

Chapter 61

ONE WEEK OVERDUE . . .

Emily sat down with a loud, frustrated huff on her sofa.

It was a hot, sticky Saturday morning and she'd left Paul sleeping in bed while she sat in the living room feeling sorry for herself and eating an entire packet of sharer-size Doritos.

Being a week overdue, having consumed most of the south-east of England's pineapple stock, and currently measuring the circumference of a wheely bin was really not fun any more.

Emily was thoroughly fed up. She felt like she couldn't take it any longer . . . Especially as since her due date a week ago now, another two of the NCT mums had had their babies . . . TWO OF THEM.

She'd received their twatty little smug 'ooh they were early' messages and pictures and responded appropriately. Even though both times they'd sent her into a teary sulky strop. She knew she was just being an overly hormonal bitch. But she couldn't help it. She was beyond being reasonable.

She'd had two sweeps, was eating her own (now-impressive) body weight in vindaloo each night and frankly just couldn't face any more raspberry leaf tea. It only tasted of disappointment now . . .

She was also forcing Paul into angry sexual acts he looked fairly terrified to follow through with, but did so on pain of death. And because he'd probably had more than enough of his wife being pregnant right now too, their marriage couldn't take much more. He'd learnt quite early on that you do *not* say no to a heavily pregnant woman. Especially when it comes to sex. Or KFC.

Emily had also completely lost the ability to be polite to strangers commenting on how pregnant she was in the street. She didn't have the energy to be nice. Yesterday she actually growled at a lady in Sainsbury's car park for asking her if she 'should be driving while like that'.

And if one more person asked her in the supermarket if there was 'two of them in there', she was going to totally lose her shit, grab a French stick, beat them to death with it, before fashioning it into a hook which she would then use to get the baby out of her uterus right there herself in the home-baking aisle . . .

Not only that, but there was nothing left to clean or tidy in her house, she'd done everything. Every cupboard, every cubbyhole, every dark corner . . . she'd scrubbed, organised and decluttered every inch of their home. At this rate, she was going to need to start redecorating just to keep herself busy . . .

She'd also barely blogged recently. It wasn't a time thing, she had plenty of that right now. In fact, she was actively finding ways to fill her time. No. It was a motivation thing. The entire premise of her blog was to try and write helpful tips and advice for women in various stages of pregnancy, and share how beautiful the journey through pregnancy had been, but it didn't feel beautiful. Right now, it was anything but. It felt sweaty and shitty and full of acne. And it was starting to sound a bit like bollocks.

She didn't believe in it any more. It felt like a lie.

There she'd been writing tips about making pregnancy more manageable, involving your partner and eating to feel good when really she felt like crap regardless of how much kale she washed her Zinger Tower burger meal down with, and the only time she wasn't angry with Paul was when she was asleep. And even then it was touch and go . . .

Plus, she'd still not got her iCandy. She'd put her name on the waiting list for one of the new limited edition peach pushchairs, but apparently they'd 'underestimated demand'. And couldn't guarantee exactly when she'd receive it. The bastards.

She'd completely given up hope that she'd get a free one through her rather underwhelming pro-blogger status. She was averaging about four hits a day, which meant that even her mum had given up reading it now. So she'd just have to wait it out with all the other angry heavily pregnant women sweating in the queue at the customer services desk in John Lewis.

She reached forward, picked up her laptop and logged in.

Perhaps she just needed to be a bit more honest. Maybe she wasn't the only one who hadn't enjoyed pregnancy, who'd struggled and cried and been a total bitch to their husband. Perhaps there were others out there who sent their partners out to the KFC drive-thru at 2 a.m. on a Saturday night because they needed popcorn chicken RIGHT NOW before they hurt somebody . . .

Hmmm . . . Emily thought, pulling up her blog site and logging herself into the back end.

Before she knew it, she'd begun to write . . .

MONDAY 24 JULY

Hints to Husbands of Pregnant Wives . . .

Okay. Let's cut the shit.

My name is Emily. I'm over 40 weeks pregnant, and I'm an angry, hormonal mess . . .

I've spent the last nine months, somehow surviving the longest, hardest, angriest pregnancy in the history of the Universe, and I'm fed up pretending I'm okay. I'M NOT OKAY.

So here, in case anyone in the same position as me is reading this, is a little referral list for the man in your life. Just because I'm angry and felt like writing it down.

Here's my 'Hints to Husbands of Pregnant

Wives' for you to laugh (and probably cry/sweat/ eat chocolate) along to:

1. If she can't see her vagina, neither can you. STAY AWAY BABY-MAKING-PENIS-OF-WOMB- DOOM.
2. If she's horny . . . (in which case, you'd better stop looking terrified and get on with it . . .) refusing a heavily pregnant woman in her hour of need WILL result in blood loss (yours).
3. Don't congratulate your balls. It's not funny.
4. No. You can't touch her breasts. Because it feels like a thousand tiny razors are slicing through her nipples. Do it again, and you will get cut.
5. When you're asked to rub her back, you better channel Hans the Swedish God of Hands and go to shitting town on those ligaments.
6. There can never be too much cake. Even when she says she doesn't want cake, you should ensure you have emergency cake. And carry Hobnobs about your person while out and about at all times.
7. Falling asleep before her is basically grounds for divorce.
8. Snoring will result in you being stabbed.
9. Your area of the sofa has been dramatically diminished. To the floor.
10. When she says yes, she means no. But if you then accept her no, she will be upset that you

no longer see her as a yes person. Which is the same as calling her fat. You bastard. Why are you struggling to grasp this??

11. Failing that, any time you can't think what to say; run her a bath. With candles. And bubbles. And magic fanny-mending fairies.

12. Last resort. Punch yourself in the face. It'll make her feel better.

13. When you signed the marriage certificate, you signed away your right to even look like you've noticed her pregnancy farts.

14. The above also applies to leg shaving, or lack of . . .

15. You only get the end bits of the garlic French stick now. Just so you know.

16. You should be sympathy-sober, sympathy-fat and sympathy-doing-the-fucking-housework from now on.

17. Don't tell her she's glowing. Buy her a KFC Bargain Bucket for one and watch as she cries tears of joy into the secret recipe coating.

18. Whatever you do, if you value your skin (and penis) don't mention gin. Or Camembert.

19. And finally . . . Any man who reads this and comments 'poor bastard' in regards to my husband should be reminded that throughout the three-quarters-of-a-year of sheer hell I am enduring, which will culminate in a human battering ram thrusting its way out of my

already battle-weary uterus, his contribution
was to have sex. So, unless you've shat out a
marrow with a face and fingernails you can't
fucking comment.

Just saying.
Bye.
Love, Emily xx

Chapter 62

BABY TOLLY

Molly was bored.

She'd been on bed rest, or 'Tom's-sofa-rest', for a week now, and she was beginning to feel like she was slowly going insane. Insane in a slightly chapped leather DFS two-seater-sofa prison . . .

Tom was back at work. He had to be. She understood that. But without him, the days were incredibly dull . . .

The flat seemed smaller and smaller as the time went on. She'd felt like she'd been staring at the same patches on Tom's badly painted walls for seven straight days, mostly because she had.

She was actually bored of Netflix. Something she never thought was possible. But she couldn't take any more being propped up in front of the television on a maternity cushion eating vegan oatmeal biscuits.

The last couple of days, she'd preferred to go and sit in the nursery anyway. She'd take a book in with her, but would barely read it. She liked just sitting in there, staring at the photos on the walls, and daydreaming of how life would be once a tiny person occupied that cot. She'd sink into the old comfy office chair in the corner. The one that Tom had found at a car-boot sale and had put in there as a nursing seat for her when the baby arrived . . . It was a lovely battered old thing. Worn at the edges but deep and comfortable with high arms, a neck rest and a little foot stool to rest her legs on. She was beginning to look forward to sitting in here throughout the long days and nights rocking and feeding her baby. It felt like where she was meant to be . . .

Maybe this unexpected and boring fortnight had actually been the first time she'd really bonded with her unborn child? Molly thought to herself.

She'd not done that up until now.

She'd not stopped.

She'd not taken the time to feel pregnant.

She'd just kept doing all the things she'd always done – working, running around, and generally just carrying on with life – not really thinking of what was to come. Or what was happening to her changing body and baby as the weeks and months went on. For the most part, it had been easier to almost forget it was happening. Why spend your time thinking about something you can't control or affect?

But after the scare she had had a couple of weeks ago, things were different. They had to be. The thought of losing her baby had created a change in her.

She'd realised in that moment, as horrifying as it was, that she was completely in love and attached to her unborn baby in a way she'd never noticed, or comprehended before.

She might not have planned to have a baby, but she wanted it so much now. It had taken this to make her see that.

So perhaps this time on her own had been a blessing in disguise. She was falling in love with this tiny little person she'd never met, but could feel with every bit of herself . . . Literally, given the gentle jabs to the ribs she was currently receiving as she drifted in and out of sleep sinking back into the chair . . .

But she didn't mind them. They made her feel connected to her baby.

She loved it.

'Hello?' called Tom's voice.

Before Molly could come around enough to answer him, he appeared in the doorway of the spare room, tugging his tie loose from his neck.

'There you are . . .' he said, leaning on the doorframe and winking at her.

Molly yawned and stretched herself awake.

Tom looked amazing in a suit. It flattered his slim but muscular frame. Molly always loved the way he looked when he came home from work.

It was becoming increasingly frustrating for her being forced to rest when her boyfriend looked so sexy and professional at the beginning and end of every work day . . .

'How are you feeling today, babes?' He walked forward and planted a kiss on her forehead.

'A little better . . .' Molly said sleepily. 'Still tired. Still bored. But I'm okay . . . How was your day?'

'Fine. Busy.' Tom placed a hand on her bump. 'Would have much rather been here with you two, eating biscuits and watching box sets!'

'Ah well . . . It's not all it's cracked up to be,' Molly said. 'I think I actually have a flapjack hangover.'

'Ha! I'm not sure that's even a thing, but hey. What do you fancy for dinner tonight?'

'You . . .' Molly said.

'Well, we both know that's not allowed. It's frustrating for me too, but we've got to look after you. Both of you,' Tom said with a little wink, still stroking her tummy.

'I'm feeling much better though,' Molly said winking back at him and letting a little smile creep on to her face.

'Molly. No,' Tom admonished, but was smiling too.

'I mean, this chair's very supportive,' Molly persisted, attempting to transition her voice from sleepy to sexy without him noticing. 'I'm just saying that I'm sure you can be gentle with me. The baby won't mind. It'll be fine . . .'

'MOLLY. NO!'

Chapter 63

THE DAY OF THE BLOG

Emily hadn't looked at her phone all afternoon. She'd mostly been at Homebase, heaving herself uncomfortably around the garden-centre section buying herbs for a new feature 'living-herb wall' she'd seen on Pinterest.

Paul had thought it was an utterly ridiculous idea for an overdue pregnant woman to begin herb gardening in thirty degrees of high-summer heat, but he didn't have the energy to argue with her as he left for work. She had her very-angry-don't-argue-with-me face on. He knew better than to challenge that.

She'd hoped it might take her mind off of being pregnant temporarily, or perhaps some particularly energetic basil potting might bring on labour . . .

IT HADN'T.

And it was now nearly 2 p.m. and all she'd really managed to do was to make a big composty, herby mess with a trowel, and sweat uncontrollably. And as her sweat had inevitably mixed with the soil, she'd also accidentally 'camo-ed up'. Which wasn't a great look, for anyone. Let alone a woman who'd been carrying a baby for nearly forty-one weeks and was about to spontaneously combust in the July sun . . .

She needed to get inside and out of the searing heat before she baked from the outside in.

She needed shade, a cold shower and several icy drinks. (And also for her fucking baby to be on the outside of her body. Obviously.)

Emily headed inside and began fanning herself with a magazine as she took a perch one of the dining-room chairs. She breathed deeply for a few moments as her body temperature began to descend a little from that of the earth's core . . . She looked at her phone for the first time since this morning, and immediately saw a few slightly strange messages from Molly.

Molly
OMG Have you seen your blog?
Why aren't you responding?
Are you having a baby?
You're not allowed to do that without
telling me . . .
I can't take it when you don't respond!
I'm bored and can't leave the flat!!
STOP.
IGNORING.
ME.

Emily
Sorry, been potting herbs.
Or at least pretending to pot herbs
while making a big mess with a

bag of soil for Paul to clear up . . .

Don't ask.

Not having a baby right now,

unfortunately . . .

Beginning to wonder if I will

EVER have this baby!!

What are you talking about?

What's going on with my blog?

What's happened?

Molly

Okay. Herbs . . . soil . . . sounds
great . . .

Ahhh! Come on little man!

Go have a look on your laptop . . .

YOU'RE FAMOUS!!!!

Emily made a puzzled face at her phone as she dragged
herself up on to her feet again and wandered into the
lounge.

She sat down on the sofa, opened up her laptop and
logged in. She was trying hard to be patient as it connected
to the Wi-Fi so she could log into her blog's back end.
But she didn't really 'do' patient.

What was Molly on about? Everything had been fine
on her blog this morning. She'd posted that new blog post
but hey, no one had read any of the others (except her
about seventy-five times) so why would this one be any
different right? Unless . . .

Finally. It was ready. She quickly entered her blog password and pulled up her stats page.

For a moment, she just stared at the screen. Was this right? Was this some kind of joke?? Since 10 a.m. this morning when she posted her latest blog post, she'd had over 100,000 views. This was crazy! What was going on?

She logged into her blog's Facebook page and took a moment to take in what was happening. The post she wrote earlier had gone viral, over 5,000 shares and counting. Emily watched as the likes and comments were happening right there continuously before her eyes. She felt a weird mix of excitement and anxiety. She'd wanted a bigger following but this was madness. She'd never expected thousands of people to read something she wrote during an angry, overdue baby-rant after breakfast. This was nuts . . .

Plus she had messages. Lots of messages. There were so many! Who could they all be from?

She began scrolling through, responding to the lovely words from mums who were pregnant or just had babies who were thanking her for being so real, so honest, so funny . . .

It was so touching. And bizarre.

She continued scrolling through the emails and notifications until she saw something she had been quietly hoping for . . . waiting for . . . wishing for . . .

'YES!' Emily shouted out loud. Unable to contain herself and her happy fist-pumping pregnant squeals.

It was just like she dreamed. Was this real? Yes. Yes, it was . . .

THIS WAS REALLY HAPPENING.

A message. Right there.

From the iCandy publicity team . . .

Chapter 64

PERFECT

Right now, life was perfect.

Liz had never been happier.

She'd just stepped out of a late-morning Friday meeting with the current partners, where she'd been told her official partner offer should be ready to sign within the next fortnight.

She felt epic. Better than epic. She felt like an actual real-life unicorn.

She'd done it.

She'd worked so hard; she'd done everything they'd asked of her and SHE'D DONE IT.

Liz had never been more proud of herself. As a lawyer, as a thirty-year-old, as a woman . . . she felt like she might be the actual grand supreme ruler of all the thirty-year-old lawyer-vaginas.

This would mean the role would become hers effective from the end of September, just in time for her thirty-first birthday.

There was no way she wasn't celebrating this.

She practically skipped back down the hallway back to her office. She couldn't contain her joy. She could see people looking at her oddly as she bounced down the corridor with a giant grin on her face like a toddler who'd just been told they never had to wear shoes or a hat ever again . . .

But she didn't care any more.

Let them stare.

She was brilliant.

And everyone could know it. In a fortnight they all would anyway.

Liz left the door open as she grabbed her phone out of her bag. It was time she got over her weird dinner-date phobia with Gerald. And what better time to do it than tonight. When she had something to really celebrate. She smiled and immediately opened a chat window to Gerald.

Liz
Let's go out tonight!
Somewhere posh.
My treat.
I am CELEBRATING.
Paperwork is on its way.
As of September I AM OFFICIALLY
PARTNER.
So let's go get twatted.

Gerald
Amazing.
I'm so proud of you!
I had already anticipated it, so I
decided to book somewhere nice

for tonight anyway.
I know. I'm pretty awesome.
Perfect, some might say.
I can't help it . . .
Plus I'm treating you.
No arguments.
You deserve it.

Liz
Ha! Okay xx
Even better!
I can't wait to get dressed up.
And totally twatted.
(in a posh way that is . . .)
#poshtwatted

Gerald
Ha! Posh twatted is my thing.
I'll pick you up at 8 p.m.?
Love you xx

Liz
Perfect. Can't wait!
Love you too xxx

Liz couldn't keep the grin off her face as she put her phone away and began to think about the evening ahead of her . . .

She had no idea where Gerald was taking her but she liked that she didn't know . . . she wasn't usually one for surprises but this one felt good. A little bit of extra excitement on a day she didn't think could get any better. She was going to leave work right now and make herself look incredible.

The sort of incredible that might mean they never make it to the restaurant once Gerald had seen her . . . She felt a little flutter of excitement in her stomach as she imagined him kissing her passionately, unable to contain himself . . .

She needed to focus.

She'd do her hair slightly to one side, the way he preferred it. She'd put a little more make-up on than normal, and create dark, smoky eyes to complement her trademark red lips.

Plus she had the perfect dress for tonight — classic, figure-hugging, and just short enough to be sexy without being overly slutty . . .

Yes.

It was going to be perfect.

Sexy-but-not-too-slutty perfect.

Chapter 65

TWO. WEEKS. OVERDUE.

There comes a time in every woman's pregnancy where she reaches breaking point, and today was it.

Emily was almost two weeks past her due date.

TWO. WEEKS.

Two additional weeks of pregnancy hell.

It just wasn't fair.

She was beginning to resign herself to needing some kind of medical help to get things started. She just couldn't take another day of it. Even her midwife was beginning to look a little concerned as Emily continued to waddle through the surgery door with her child still very firmly inside her body at each appointment, despite her desperation and spicy-fruit-based efforts . . .

She knew her next practical option was induction, but it didn't sit well with her. She could hear her NCT teacher Tracey's voice ringing in her ears: the cycle of intervention, unnaturally bringing on labour . . . It had been enough to keep her from doing it so far, but she was very close to saying 'fuck it'.

Another twenty-four hours and she'd be more than ready. She'd be hooking herself up to an induction drip quicker than you can say curried-pineapple-sex-life . . .

She was also becoming worried that if the baby stayed in there any longer it would be the size of a toddler by the time it evacuated itself. She kept having unsettling dreams about her vagina spitting out a two-stone, fully clothed two-year-old playing with a toy train or something. Hopefully, that was unlikely . . .

It was exasperating.

Emily felt utterly drained.

She'd been trying to keep herself busy at home for most of the morning but there just wasn't anything left to keep busy with any more. She decided there was nothing for it; she needed to get out of the house and go for a walk. She had to. Paul wouldn't be back from work for hours yet, and being at home just irritated her, and made her want to re-iron and reorder all the babygros again. Maybe knit something. Eat another Toblerone. She really needed to get out.

Emily summoned the energy to get herself upright and feel her way into some flip-flops. She was wearing the one remaining maternity smock she owned that hadn't become skintight. The last thing she needed right now was any kind of restriction.

She heaved herself out of her front door and down the garden path. It was downhill to the main road at least, where she'd cross over to the park. She was already dreading the walk back up the hill on the way home, but had decided to ignore that . . .

She kept her eyes down as she walked uncomfortably along the roadside. She couldn't be bothered to make eye contact with anyone. For the last few weeks, anyone she passed in the street tended to look at her like she had an extra head. And if one more stranger remarked that 'she couldn't have long to go' she might set them on fire.

She was almost there. It was warm but there was a light wind coming off the river that ran along the side of the park. Emily was very thankful for the breeze. She sucked the air in quickly, her lungs working hard, mainly due to their reduced capacity now they had to share her ribcage with quite a lot of womb.

Emily quickly began to feel quite exhausted. She headed for a bench in the dappled shade of a large oak tree. She'd rest there and pluck up the energy to walk back home again in a bit. Perhaps this walk wasn't such a great idea, after all.

As she hobbled her way slowly towards the bench, she became suddenly aware that her entire stomach was tightening up quite intensely. It didn't hurt. It just felt . . . incredibly tight and rigid. In fact it was rock solid.

Emily's heart rate quickened with a surge of excitement and nerves. Was this it? Was this finally labour? Or was that just wishful thinking? She was hesitant to allow herself to believe this was really happening, yet . . .

Her stomach was tightening more now. It felt like the entire front of her body was in spasm.

She could still walk. She turned around and began walking back home. She pumped her legs as fast as her

347

strained body would allow and fished around in her bag to find her phone. She needed to get back to the house. Now.

And somehow make it up that hill. That bastard hill. It might actually be easier to give birth to her baby right there at the bottom than attempt getting back up that bastard hill. Why had she done this to herself?

She found her phone and fired a message to Paul as she awkwardly made her way back to the main road. People were staring at her a lot now. She was trying not to let herself lose focus.

Emily
I think it's starting.
I'm walking back from the park.
I've got to get up that fucking hill!
Please come home now.
I need you. Please hurry!
I'm really scared.

Paul
Don't worry, I'm on my way.
Relax and get yourself home.
I'll be there as fast as I can.

Emily
I love you xxx

Paul
Love you too xx

Emily had crossed the main road now, she was struggling for breath and could feel her heart beat thumping through every vein in her body. But she was determined to get home. She'd made it to the bottom of her road. And the start of the hill.

She honestly had no idea how she would make it to the top, but she had to. She felt teary and overwhelmed. She just wanted Paul there right now.

She used the walls of people's front gardens to steady herself as she climbed up. Walking up a 30 per cent gradient while in the early stages of labour was the equivalent of abseiling forwards up a rock face with your uterus on fire . . .

Somehow, Emily made it. It seemed to take for ever. She was dripping with sweat and her heart was about to beat its way out of her ribcage, but she'd done it.

She let herself into her house. She had nothing left. She was completely exhausted.

The door closed behind her and she immediately headed into the lounge and positioned herself on her birth ball. She began rocking gently back and forth, up and down, concentrating on breathing in and out, slowly and deeply as her heart rate gradually began to drop. Paul would be here in a minute. She just needed to remain calm. She closed her eyes and sucked long, deep breaths in through her nose, and out through her mouth . . .

This is it, she thought to herself. This is finally it.

Hurry up, baby boy.

Hurry up, Paul.

Hopefully, she'd be better at giving birth than being pregnant. She'd been shit at that. This was her time to shine . . .

Labour seemed okay so far. She wasn't sure what the fuss was about. She was aceing it. It can't really get any worse, right?

Moments later, Paul was storming into the lounge looking urgent and concerned.

'Are you okay? Is this it?' He crouched down next to her as she continued to make little hip circles on her birthing ball.

'I don't know . . .' she said, becoming aware that the tensing sensation she'd felt so strongly at the park was no longer there. In fact, she was feeling rather normal again. As normal as a very-sweaty-angry-two-weeks-overdue pregnant lady can feel. 'I think it might have stopped . . .'

'Okay.' Paul said studying her face. 'It's clearly not going to be long, though. I think today is the day, sweetie. I can feel it. I'm going to pack the hospital bag in the car and get changed. Just let me know if it starts again.'

Emily admired his positivity, though she felt dejected right now . . . And she definitely needed that Toblerone . . .

Paul was right. Surely it couldn't be long . . .

It was 7.24 p.m.
Everything was normal.
Too normal.

Nothing was happening.

Especially in Emily's uterus.

It was as flaccid as it had been the previous seven thousand days she'd been heavily pregnant for . . .

Emily had abandoned the birthing ball and was now straddling a large tub of biscuits on the sofa, feeling very sorry for herself. Paul was trying not to make eye contact with her. She knew he was as disappointed as she was.

She had really thought today was going to be the day.

She'd texted everyone. Why had she done that? She now had to deal with a constant and intensely irritating stream of follow-up texts . . .

Molly
So what's happening?
Are you in labour then or what?

Emily
I don't know.
It's just sort of . . . stopped.
I hate my uterus right now.

Liz
Oh. Sorry, sweetie.
From what my sis has told me,
that's quite common . . .
I think when it really starts you'll
really know about it!

351

I'm just on my way out with Gerald
but let me know if anything starts up
again tonight!
Go eat some chocolate ;)

Emily
Will do.
Have a good night x
I've eaten an entire
Fox's biscuit selection in the last hour.
I don't even feel bad.
In fact.
I could do it again.
#sorrynotsorry

Molly
You deserve it!
You need to keep your strength up.
You're really just being sensible.

Emily
I'm so disappointed!
Why is this happening to me!
Or NOT happening to me!!
I feel like the Universe hates me.
I'm gonna have to go eat a
Toblerone now.
(Again)

Molly
lol

The Universe does not hate you.
That baby will be here really soon.
I know it. I can feel it.
Plus, once he's out, you'll be begging
to stuff him back up there!
Go get some rest while you can.
Xx

Emily

I hope you're right.
I'm gonna take myself to bed and
try not to think about how angry I am.

Molly

Good plan.
Let us know when it all kicks off!
It really won't be long now!
Xxx

Emily

I will.
Night, ladies.
Love from me and my rubbish uterus

xxx

Emily felt a little better chatting to her friends but she still just wanted to cry . . .

'I'm going to bed,' she said abruptly as she struggled to her feet. She was exhausted and she'd rather be asleep than sitting around getting irritated at Paul as he continually googled 'early labour signs' on his iPad. When she was in labour, she'd let him know about it pretty quickly. She didn't need him to google it. Dick.

'Okay, sweetie,' Paul said without looking up. 'I'll let you get off before I come up. Do you need anything?'

His question only irritated her further. She knew she was just tired and weary from everything that had happened today. She needed to get away from him now before she said something she'd regret.

'For a baby to fall out of my vagina?' she huffed at him as she shuffled out of the room. 'Otherwise. I'm cool. Thanks.'

Chapter 66

I DON'T

Liz had been to plenty of posh restaurants before.

She worked in the City; it went with the territory. She had spent many a night with colleagues and clients stuffing things in her face she couldn't pronounce in places she'd never go if she weren't paying with the company credit card. But this place, the place Gerald had just led her into, was something else . . .

As they walked through the foyer, Liz looked ahead through large glass doors into the main restaurant.

It was beautiful.

With its high ceilings, soft romantic lighting and polished black marble floor, it looked like something out of a Bond movie. There were beautiful sweeping drapes from floor to ceiling giving the room a dramatic gothic feel. The tables were well spaced and immaculately laid. It was all Liz could do to take it all in as she watched the waiters floating elegantly around the room like silent acrobats. This place was special. She was glad she'd dressed for the occasion. This wasn't the sort of place you rocked up to in Topshop jeans and 'that top you got off ASOS a couple of years ago' . . .

There'd even been a line of paparazzi at the door as

they'd walked in. Liz wondered if she had concentrated on making her face look sort of famous, if they would have thought she was someone important and papped her. Probably not . . .

She tried hard to not look out of her depth as they approached the restaurant doors, concentrating on not slipping in her high designer shoes. She clutched Gerald's forearm tightly, feeling quite amazing in her not-too-slutty black dress.

How on earth he'd got a reservation here she had no idea, but she was thankful he had. She felt like a film star.

They had been immediately greeted by the maître d' as they'd entered, and were now being marched efficiently through the restaurant and seated at their table in front of one of the beautiful draped windows.

The atmosphere bubbled away gently around them as they took their seats.

'This place is stunning,' Liz said, keeping her voice a little low. 'How the hell did you get us in here at short notice?'

'Well,' Gerald said, smirking a little, 'luckily I have friends in high places. And by high places, I mean I went to school with the guy who owns it. Otherwise they'd never let riff-raff like us through the door . . .' he said, whispering the last sentence and winking at her.

'Well, I'm very glad they did,' Liz said, beaming at him. He looked wonderful in the perfect soft lighting at their table.

'You deserve it. You're amazing. And you look stunning.

Tonight is all about you,' he said, picking up the menu and letting his eyes flick over the options.

Liz giggled like a schoolgirl as he complimented her, and felt her cheeks burn a little. Luckily the low lighting masked that.

She too picked up her menu. The food looked out of this world. Obviously, there were no prices next to anything, but she knew he'd want her to have exactly what she fancied, which right now was absolutely everything. With wine.

A few minutes later, a bottle of champagne was delivered and their orders taken.

Liz was still giggling. She felt completely spoilt. She wasn't used to being treated like this. She felt ridiculous for resisting going out on a 'proper date' with him for so long now . . . Why on earth hadn't they done this sooner? There was nothing not to like.

They sipped on their champagne before wine appeared, and then course after course of small, exquisite plates of food you were almost scared to cut into they looked so beautiful. Each one placed down by waiters you barely saw or heard. The food just kept appearing . . . It was wonderful.

Liz loved Gerald's company. He was so easy to spend time with. They had so much in common: they loved all the same things; they laughed at all the same things. It felt like she'd know him far longer than five months. It felt like he'd always been there. In a good way . . .

The evening had flown by; they hadn't got twatted at

all, not even posh-twatted – they'd spent so much time talking and laughing they still had half a bottle of wine left on the table. That never usually happened . . .

And it was amazing that, despite how small and delicate all the plates of food had been, they were both completely stuffed. Liz knew dessert was on its way, but she was wondering how she'd fit anything else in.

Just then, two small highly polished cloches were placed in front of them by invisible hands.

Liz watched Gerald's demeanour change. He looked a little uncomfortable, nervous, even. She didn't understand why. It was strange.

He got to his feet, his eyes fixed intensely on hers, and moved round the table towards her until he was next to her.

Why was he being so weird? What was he doing? Liz thought, continuing to watch him with a small puzzled frown on her face.

And then . . . he dropped down.

To one knee.

He removed the cloche lid from in front of her to reveal something small and shiny catching the light. A ring.

A diamond ring.

It had taken Liz until this moment to realise what was happening. Her heart started to thud in her chest, and her eyes refused to blink.

Was this really happening? This was madness. Was he really doing this?

'Liz,' he said, lifting the ring from the plate and

presenting it to her, 'I know this is fast, and I know this is probably the last thing you ever expected to happen this evening, but to me you are perfect. You are the most amazing thing in my life, and I can't imagine ever being without you. Liz. Will you make me the happiest man alive and become my wife?'

Liz was frozen to the spot. She knew she needed to say something soon but she couldn't get her brain or mouth to activate.

This was awkward. People were beginning to look up. And stare. And whisper . . .

Gerald's face was changing from nervous excitement to concern and panic.

'Gerald? What are you doing?' It was the only thing she could get to come out of her mouth.

'I love you. You love me. Let's get married! Why not?'

'Because . . . because . . .' Words failed her. What could she say that wouldn't crush him? She still wasn't sure if she ever wanted to get married, and she certainly hadn't given it any serious thought after knowing someone for less than six months . . . *six* months. This was insanity.

'Please sit down, Gerald. Please?' She put her head in her hands to shield her from the piercing eyes of the other diners and the waiting staff . . .

She wanted to shrivel up and die.

She couldn't look at him. She couldn't look at anything.

She was so angry at him. Why did he keep trying to push things on to the next step when they were happy where they were? Why had he ruined it?

She heard him get up and return to his seat opposite her. She still couldn't look at him. This was horrible.

'Can we just go, please?' she managed, her voice small.

'Okay. Liz. Okay,' he said, sounding defeated. 'Let's go . . .'

Chapter 67

I STILL DON'T

Liz
FUUUUCCCCKKKKK
I don't know what to do!!
This is insane!!
Gerald just proposed.
ACTUALLY. FUCKING. PROPOSED.
In the middle of a crowded restaurant.
I feel sick!
What am I supposed to do?

Emily
Okay.
Slow down.
WHAT??

Molly
Wow.
He's got some balls.
I'll give him that!
Where are you?
Are you still there?

Liz

NO.

I'm in a taxi.

He got a separate one . . .

I couldn't even look at him as I left.

He must hate me.

I really think I'm going to throw up!

Emily

I don't know what to say.

Of course he doesn't hate you.

He loves you . . .

That hasn't changed.

Was he okay as you left?

Liz

Not really.

He just didn't say anything.

I feel like I just ripped his heart out.

I don't know what to do.

This is horrible.

Molly

I think you need to leave it tonight

and contact him in the morning

to talk.

He's obviously going to be hurting

but you need to decide if you want

to come back from this . . .

If you even can?

Liz

OMG I'm actually freaking out.
Why has he done this??
Everything was perfect.
He's totally ruined it all.
I don't know if we can come back
from this??
How can we?

Emily

Take a deep breath.
Don't freak out.
Even though it's completely
insane that he's actually done this . . .
Maybe he did it because
everything was perfect?
I agree with Molly – you need
to sleep on it.
Everything will seem clearer
in the morning.
Hope you're okay.
Hope he's okay.

Liz

Okay. You're right.
I do need to sleep on it.
Even though I don't think I'll
actually get a wink of sleep!
I'll try and talk to him in the morning.
God, I can't believe this is happening.

Thanks, girls.
I'll let you know what happens.
Or doesn't happen!
xx

Chapter 68

GERALD DOES

Liz felt like she might throw up.

She was completely consumed with nerves. It was ridiculous.

She had a job where she fought court battles, argued cases, and spent her time butting heads with overbearing bullies, and sometimes outright horrible people, and yet, sitting here on her sofa, waiting for Gerald to arrive at her flat forty-eight hours after 'that' dinner date, was possibly the most nerve-racking, uncomfortable sensation she'd ever felt.

It didn't help that she'd barely slept the past two nights. Her mind hadn't let her.

Every time she'd temporarily forgotten what happened two nights ago, her brain would slap it back at the fore-front of her mind like a punch to the face.

She was happy he'd agreed to meet her, though. She wasn't sure he'd even text back.

But he had.

If he was still responding to her messages, then there was at least some hope he didn't hate her. She was so relieved about that. And that he was now on his way over.

Her flat had seemed like the best place to meet. The

last thing she needed after a humiliating public marriage proposal was a humiliating public dumping two days later.

She'd much rather have the bad news in her own home, where she could curl up in a ball with her cat and eat ice cream while crying into some wine for the rest of the day when he left.

She was trying desperately to relax. But she couldn't. And every minute that passed until he got here felt like an hour. An anxious, twitchy, sweaty-palmed hour . . .

Then. Finally. The doorbell sounded.

Liz felt her heart leap up into her throat, and her stomach begin to do continuous nervous flips as she rose to her feet and opened the door.

Gerald stood across from her looking far from his usual dapper self. He looked tired and broken.

He'd clearly had no sleep either. His usually perfect face was stubbly and ragged. His clothes were scruffy. His hair was unkempt and his eyes looked deeply set and troubled.

Liz flung her arms around his neck tightly and planted her face deep into his shoulder as tears immediately began to pour from her eyes and soaked into his T-shirt.

'Hey,' Gerald said soothingly. 'Let's get inside.'

Liz couldn't quite bring herself to let go of him. She didn't want to. What if this was the last time she ever got to hug him? She felt him gently lift her up and walk them both inside the door.

The door swung closed behind them and she slowly

lifted her head. She knew it was him that should be crying, not her, but she couldn't stop herself. Perhaps it was a mix of guilt and the fear of losing him, but she couldn't stop it pouring from her.

She took a few deep breaths and steadied her emotions, finally letting her hands slip from around his neck and taking a small pace back.

'Let's sit down,' she said eventually, not sounding herself yet. 'Do you want anything? A drink?'

'I'm okay.' Gerald managed half a polite smile.

They sat on the sofa. There was a space between them. Liz hated this.

'I don't know how to start . . .' she said, looking down. She wasn't ready to look into his eyes just yet.

'Shall we start at the part where you rejected my marriage proposal?' Gerald replied tentatively.

'I . . . I don't know what to say.' Liz felt the tears trying to return. 'It took me by surprise. I just . . . How can I make you understand that I want to be with you, and I love you, but I'm just not ready for that yet? Or maybe ever, I don't know. Just not yet.'

'I'm trying to understand that, but it's hard,' Gerald said, frowning a little and touching her hand. 'I love you too, Liz. But we're different. Obviously. I don't see the point in messing around. We're not teenagers. I love you. I love us.'

'I get that, but what's the rush?' Liz persisted, managing to look at him now. 'I don't want to lose you either. The thought of being without you kills me. I've barely slept since. I was terrified this would be it. I can't be without you. You know that, right?'

'I don't know what you want from me, Liz,' Gerald responded, sounding a little exasperated now. 'I'm not in the habit of humiliating myself intentionally. I don't actually enjoy it. You say you're terrified to be without me, but you keep pushing me away. What is that all about? Romance, love, security . . . isn't that what a relationship is supposed to be about? I don't get why you reject all those things. You know, I'm one of the good guys. I won't ever let you down, Liz. I love you. You love me. We're both in our thirties, in great jobs and we're in love. What is it you're so scared of? Do you actually want me to treat you like shit? Like . . .'

'Like "him"?' Liz said, finishing his sentence. 'That's what you were going to say, wasn't it? I can't believe after everything we've been through you want to make this conversation about "him"? How dare you say that to me? Surely you have enough respect for me to know that he is nothing to me. Absolutely nothing. Or do you actually think that little of me—'

'What am I supposed to think, Liz!' Gerald shouted. It was the first time he'd ever raised his voice to her. She realised how upset he was.

'I don't know,' Liz said, throwing her hands up in the air. She was no longer angry, just sad. 'I don't know what to tell you. I am not ready to get married. But I know that I'm not ready to give up on us either. I do love you. That has not changed. I don't need a ring on my finger to say that. I just need you. And me. Together. And back like we were before all that stuff happened on Friday night. I don't want the big romantic gestures. I don't need diamonds and champagne and all that bollocks. I just need you. Just. You.'

Gerald let out a deep sigh.

They were going round in circles.

It was frustrating for both of them.

'Okay look,' he said after a long pause. 'I can't lose you. The ring is gone. Okay. I don't want to dwell on this. I just want us, too. That's all I've ever wanted. And if you're not ready for marriage yet and all that other stuff . . . I guess I just have to respect that. All I wanted to do was prove to you how much I love you. Like I've never loved anyone . . . That's all.'

'And I know that,' Liz said. She touched his face and locked her eyes with his. 'I already knew that. I'm not ready now, but I will be. At some point. And it will only ever be with you. You have to believe that. I just want to get back to where we were before all this. Just. Us.'

'Me too,' Gerald said, a hint of a smile on his lips.

Liz kissed him softly on his mouth and hugged him. She felt the fear and anxiety leaving her.

It was going to be okay.

They still loved each other.

Nothing else mattered right now.

They were going to make this work.

Liz and Gerald was going work.

Giz was going to work.

Chapter 69

TOLLY–GIZ–PEMILY

Liz
Hey girls?
How are you both?
Any uterus action?
Either one of you managed to get your
baby on the outside yet?

Emily
You know what . . .
I might actually beat you to
death with my uterus.
Does that count as action?

Molly
Nothing here either.
I'm still just sat on the sofa downing
nut milk in Tom's jogging bottoms . . .
#pureglam

Emily
Ahhhh . . . jogging bottoms.
The pregnant woman's best friend.
(Along with Toblerones)

(And actually going into fucking,
labour that is)

Liz
I don't know what you're
both waiting for . . .
Chop, chop!
(I'm joking.
Please don't murder me with
your vagina, Emily.) lol

Emily
Don't worry . . .
Neither me or my vagina
has the energy.
Plus.
I'm partway through a
Toblerone and clearly I
won't be putting that down for
anything . . .
So you're safe ☺

Molly
So now we've established
no one is in actual labour,
tell us how it went with Gerald?
What's going on with you guys?

Emily
OMG yes!

371

What's happened since the
#GizIsn'tGettingHitched incident

Molly
nice hashtag.

Emily
Thank you.
I've been working on it for a while.
does a bow

Liz
Whenever you guys are ready . . .

Molly
Okay. We're ready now.

Emily
Shoot.

Liz
Well . . . Amazingly . . .
I think everything is actually
going to be fine . . .
We had a really long chat.
Got everything out in the open.
I think he gets it now.
And I definitely don't think that
ring will be making an appearance
again for a LONG time!
Thank God!
We're taking things slow again.

Getting back to dating.
Enjoying each other's company.
I honestly think we're getting
back on track.
I really hope so!

Emily
Wow that's brilliant.
I'm so happy for you sweetie.
You had us worried there for a
moment.
I'm so glad you're working it out xx
You guys are so great together.
We love Gerald.
Everybody loves Gerald.

Molly
Me too!
I'm super happy for you too.
You guys are pretty perfect together ;)
Can't wait to see you both soon.

Liz
Thanks, ladies.
Like I said we're trying to slow things
down a bit, but I really do think we'll
be back on track in no
time xx

Molly
#Gizforever

373

Emily
Nice.

Liz
I'm so happy that hashtag isn't
even bothering me today!

Emily
Ha!
Chatting to you girls on here
always cheers me up, you know.
I don't know how I'd manage
without you funny ladies xx

Molly
Me too!
Even though I'm stuck in a
sofa-based prison, these messages
always make me laugh!

Emily
You know there's a company
that will actually make your WhatsApp
convos into a book for you now . . .

Molly
OMG. We should so do it!

Liz
Err . . . No.
We absolutely should not!
I want this shit hidden away

for the rest of my life, thanks!
Quite happy not to have the car-crash
that is my love-life in
hardback form anytime soon!
Or any printed copies of Emily's
late-night ramblings about when
she used to be able to see her fanny
. . .

Emily
It's true.
I did use to be able to.
*stares wistfully off into the distance

Molly
Bahaha
I think it would be hilarious!
Although now I start to think about it
. . .

Liz
Exactly.
What goes on WhatsApp should
stay on WhatsApp.

Emily
Fair play!
Have a good day, ladies.
I'm off to see if my fanny's still there
using Paul's shaving mirror.
I'll let you know if I find it.

Liz
Thanks for that.
Have a great day too! xx

Molly
I'll try . . .
But it's definitely getting better now
I know that #Giz #Tolly and #Pemily
are all on track!

Emily
Nice.
Xx

Chapter 70

THIS IS IT . . .

Emily woke suddenly to a gushing sensation.

Was she weeing herself?

No. Surely not. Please not.

FUCK.

It was her waters breaking.

All over her sheets. Why hadn't she put an old towel next to the bed like her NCT teacher told her to?

'Paul!' Emily cried as she managed to manoeuvre herself out of the wet patch.

'Shit!' Paul said, coming out of a deep sleep quickly. 'Is this it?'

'Yes! It hurts!' Emily screeched back at him. She was feeling a tensing sensation far more painful than her earlier experience. 'I think I'm having contractions. It really hurts!'

A few panicked tears began to run down her face as the contractions began to take hold of her body completely.

'Okay,' Paul said, reaching for his phone. 'We need to time them and call the hospital when you're ready.'

Emily nodded with a grimaced face. She could feel the pain dying away. But she knew it would be back soon.

A few minutes later, the next contraction hit. Emily

tried to remember everything they'd been taught. But it was hard to remember while you were a bit preoccupied by being in agony. She breathed deeply and screwed her face up. Knowing each contraction would be gone again in only a few seconds made it more bearable.

'They're still a good seven minutes apart, sweetie. We need to wait until they're only five minutes apart,' Paul said clearly and calmly.

In that moment, Emily realised she'd underestimated him. She'd thought he'd not listened at their classes, she thought he'd just sat around chatting to the husbands about rugby and fetching her biscuits, but he clearly had been listening. She loved that he had. It was making her feel like he was in control.

All she needed to do was breathe and pray it didn't go away again.

She didn't have any chocolate left.

Emily could hear Paul on the phone but was in too much pain to listen to what he was saying.

She didn't know how long she'd been in labour now . . . a few hours she guessed.

The start had been slow, and manageable. In between contractions, she'd been able to eat, drink, chat normally, and demand Paul went out to get her a KFC. It was surreal. But that had passed now. Things were more intense. She couldn't eat right now even if she wanted to, which she didn't. Her cervix was on fire. This was not a Zinger-Tower-Burger-moment.

'Okay. We need to go,' Paul said, leaning in to help her up from the sofa.

'Don't I need to talk to the midwife?' Emily said through clenched teeth. Wondering for a moment if she could take the rest of her popcorn chicken with her just in case . . .

'I think they could hear you in the background, sweetie. I think the whole street can hear you!' He lifted her to her feet and held her steady as they made it out of the front door.

Emily slowly got herself down the path and into the car with Paul's help. She felt an overwhelming rush of emotion. Part fear, part nerves, part relief . . . she didn't have time to think about it properly before the next contraction struck. Harder and faster than the last.

The car journey to the hospital was a blur. Moments of clarity mixed with moments of pain she'd never felt before. No matter how much she breathed, nothing made the pain any easier. She just had to wait for it to go away again each time.

She no longer wanted popcorn chicken. She wanted drugs. And for this to be over quickly.

It was all she could think about.

Fuck what her birth plan said. If this was going to get worse, she was going to need A LOT OF DRUGS.

Chapter 71

HELLO?

Molly
Hey sweetie?
Any baby yet? Lol
So my belly button just
popped completely out?
It looks weird . . .
Like a tiny alien . . .
Is that normal?
Has yours done that?
I'll send you a picture.
Also . . . I've been watching X-Men
. . .
What do you think about
the name Xavier?
Too much?
I also like Marley, although Tom said it
made him think about that film where
that dog dies, so I guess I'm not sure
about a name that makes everyone
think about a dead dog, although that
sort of makes me like it more . . .
Am I weird?

Why aren't you responding?
Are you trying to find your vagina with
your make-up mirror again?
Can you please get back
to me? I'm BORED!
Are you having a poo?
Seriously . . . are you having
a baby right now?
You better tell me, you bitch!
Hello?

Chapter 72

CINE-DATE

It was a strange experience going to the cinema in your thirties. Everyone looked so . . . young.

It was a sea of testosterone-pumped teenage boys, strange haircuts, acne, and thin girls wearing 'bra-lettes' and shorts that were actually shorter than their vaginas.

Liz hadn't realised that was possible up until now. But clearly it was. She was trying to keep her eyes raised above shoulder height. She wasn't really sure she needed an eyeful of any of that before she tucked into her popcorn. Thanks.

Liz wasn't sure about any of this to be honest . . .

She hadn't ever really been a cinema-kinda-girl, even when she was young enough to wear shorts that barely covered her labia she hadn't been into films, but she understood why Gerald had suggested it. A quiet night watching a film together kicked the shit out of another rejected marriage proposal any day. So she'd deal with the odd flash of teenage fanny for the sake of her relationship.

She and Gerald were getting back to basics.

Trying to make time to relax and enjoy each other again. She couldn't handle any more romantic bombshells

. . . and Gerald certainly wouldn't be sticking around for another heart-pummelling rejection . . .

So it was time to be a bit more open-minded. She'd even let him choose the film – some spy thing, he'd said – a decision she was regretting, judging by the fact the rest of the audience had all got a lift there with their mums, and the smell of cheap aftershave was quite overwhelming . . .

But she was glad it wasn't some tacky romantic comedy.

Liz had perched herself on a comfy seat at the side of the foyer while Gerald was fighting his way back through the scantily clad teenagers after spending several hundred pounds on some drinks and snacks for them both.

Liz's phone buzzed in her pocket.

It was Molly, trying to get hold of Emily . . .

'Who's that? Emily?' Gerald said as he approached her, laden down with popcorn. 'Is she having the baby?'

'No . . .' Liz said, pulling a face. 'Just Molly talking about her belly button and checking on Emily. She's not responding. She's probably asleep or in some kind of biscuit-based coma to be honest!'

'Wow. That baby really doesn't want to come out does it? Poor her,' Gerald responded sympathetically. 'I'm just going to nip to the loo. Will you stay here with these?' he said, popping the food and drinks down by her feet.

'Sure,' Liz said, smiling up at him as he planted a quick kiss on her forehead.

Her phone buzzed again. Probably Emily banging on about her fanny again, she thought, rolling her eyes.

It wasn't.

Liz froze.

It was someone she thought she'd never hear from again. It was 'him'.

She frowned at her phone screen for a second. Her chest tightened a little. His messages had always had an effect on her. She hated that.

Should she just delete it without reading? Surely she owed that to herself. And Gerald.

She took a deep breath.

Gerald would be back any second. She needed to decide what to do.

She swiped her phone open. She was going to read it. Delete it. And delete him. Something she should have done months ago. In fact, she didn't know why she hadn't already . . .

I thought you should know,
I've left the firm.
I hope you're happy.
This is what it's come to then?
You have it all and I have nothing.
She's left me now.
Said she couldn't take any more.
So you've got what you've always
wanted.
Like I said.
You've got it all now.
Hope you're fucking happy.

Liz went quickly through every emotion in an instant . . . Angry, sad, defensive, confused, back to rage again . . . but then she realised something was different.

As quick as she had felt them, the emotions left her.

She realised the grip he'd had on her for so long wasn't there any more.

This was her finally stopping giving a shit about him. Or his opinion of her. She didn't care. Why would she . . . ?

She was finally becoming free of him. He was dead to her. Gone. In every sense.

She could see that now.

Clearly he'd meant it sarcastically, but he was right. She had got it all. She was happy. Really happy.

A smile grew across Liz's face. Any hold he had ever had over her was gone now.

She deleted the message. And blocked his number.

She looked up and saw Gerald's handsome, kind face heading towards her through a cloud of wiry Lynx-scented teenagers.

'Okay. You got everything? Shall we go in?' he said, picking the popcorn up with one hand and helping her to her feet with the other.

'Yep. I've got everything,' Liz said, smiling a little more than the moment called for and snuggly linking her arm with his. 'Absolutely everything I could ever need . . .'

Chapter 73

OKAY. THIS REALLY IS IT NOW . . .

Despite squealing her way in agony down the long corridor to the birth unit as Paul helped her stay upright, Emily was still convinced the hospital would say she 'wasn't in labour enough' and send her home.

Which she soon realised was completely ridiculous when she saw the faces of the midwives on the front desk as she burst through the maternity-unit doors, wailing and trying to remember how to use her legs . . .

She and Paul were instantly shown to a birthing room, and her midwife appeared looking almost disturbingly calm and relaxed as she helped Emily on to the bed so she could 'check' her.

It was not a moment for being prudish.

No sooner had the midwife introduced herself, than she was at the foot of the bed testing how far Emily's cervix had opened with a blue-gloved hand.

'Okay there, lovey. You're in between seven and eight centimetres,' the midwife said gently. 'So a little way to go yet. I'll hook up your gas and air, and we'll see where you are in an hour. The pool's almost ready for you if you want to use it too.'

An hour? Was she fucking high? Was that a midwife joke?

She clearly wasn't joking. Emily's heart sank. Another hour . . . she couldn't do this for another hour. She wasn't even sure how she was going to get through the next contraction . . .

The midwife passed her the gas-and-air mouthpiece and she sucked for her life. It took the edge off, at least.

An hour had passed . . .

It had been the longest hour of Emily's life. She'd spent most of it in the water-bath, but no matter what position she got herself into, the pain from each contraction was utterly consuming. She sucked hard on her gas and air, praying for the moment it began to relent.

Paul kept hovering around her with Lucozade sweets and a Ribena carton . . .

'Have a sip, sweetie. Keep up your strength. Do you want me to massage your back?' he'd say every few moments.

Emily had never noticed how incredibly irritating his voice was before.

'Come near me again and I'll stab you with this fucking mouthpiece, I swear,' Emily snapped back at him, barely recognising her own voice.

He didn't say it again though . . .

A moment later the midwife appeared again, and so did the blue gloves . . .

Almost nine centimetres.

She was getting there.

THANK FUCK.

The midwife scuttled out again.

Paul began fiddling around with something in the hospital bag.

'What are you doing?' Emily said irritably. If she was going to push his baby out, the least he could do was pay attention.

'I've been looking for the right moment to give you this,' he said, holding up a large, slightly crumpled gift bag. 'I knew you'd think I'd forgotten about your push present, but I didn't. Here you go.'

Emily was nine centimetres dilated after carrying a baby two weeks over term in a giant bath of slightly womby water. Why on earth he thought this was the 'right moment', she didn't really know. Plus, if this wasn't epic, it was entirely likely to end with her dragging him into the water-bath with her and drowning him among the floating sections of wayward vagina. She hoped he realised that.

Paul walked towards her with the bag, holding it out in front of him.

Emily glared at him. She couldn't take it from him right now . . . she was a little preoccupied.

Luckily Paul quickly realised that and began pulling something out of the bag for her.

'What is that, Paul?' she snapped, breathing hard through pursed lips.

'It's Pee-pee-Teepees.' Paul said, laughing a little nervously.

'What the fuck is that, Paul?' Emily responded. She wasn't laughing.

'It's little paper teepee cones you put over a baby boy's willy when you're changing him so you don't get a mouth full of wee. This guy at work said he used them all the time. I thought it was funny . . .' Paul said.

Emily grabbed his arm and almost reached bone with her fingernails as she punctured them into his wrist.

As she managed to blow the last of the contraction away, her face relaxed again temporarily.

'There had better be something else in that fucking bag, Paul,' she said, staring straight through him, rather than at him.

'Ummm. Yes,' Paul said, as he attempted to loosen her grip on his forearm, aware he was now a bit scared of his own wife. 'There's also one of those contour kit thingys you were asking for, a pack of Hobnobs and a Camembert . . .' he continued.

There was a long pause.

'So what you're saying, Paul . . .' Emily raged, sucking deep painful breaths in as she spat her words at him.

'WHAT YOU'RE ACTUALLY FUCKING SAYING TO ME, IS THAT, AS I SIT HERE WITH MY CERVIX RIPPING ITSELF APART WHILE YOUR SON ATTEMPTS TO HEADBUTT HIS WAY OUT OF MY BODY VIA MY VAGINA, TO HELP ME FEEL A BIT FUCKING BETTER ABOUT THAT, YOU'VE BOUGHT ME A CONTOUR KIT, SOME INFANT WILLY CONES, A PACKET OF HOBNOBS AND SOME CHEESE!!'

'Umm . . . Yes?' Paul said quietly.

'IS IT RIPE?' Emily screamed.

'Umm . . . what?' replied Paul, confused.

'THE CAMEMBERT. IS IT RIPE?' Emily screeched again.

' . . .Yes?' Paul responded. Scared. But going with it.

'THEN OPEN IT AND PUT IT IN MY MOUTH,' Emily continued to shriek. 'JUST SPOON IT IN. NOW, PAUL. NOW. OPEN YOUR CHEESE AND SPOON IT INTO MY MOUTH, RIGHT NOW, MOTHERFUCKER, BEFORE I CUT YOU.'

'Okay . . .' said Paul. He began frantically unwrapping the cheese and the chocolate Hobnobs while fighting the urge to run away and cry a bit because she was completely terrifying him . . .

Before Emily had the chance to scream at him any further, she felt an intense and incredibly powerful urge to push.

'Paul! He's coming! Get the midwife!' she yelped, grabbing the sides of the bath with both hands as her legs tingled intensely under the pressure of her baby beginning to push his way out of her body.

Paul dropped what he was doing and pressed the call button frantically. The midwife was there in a split second. Emily concentrated hard on her instructions. She pushed, rested and breathed exactly as she was told . . .

Knowing she was just moments away from meeting her

boy, her son, for the first time, gave her strength. She could do this.

She would do this.

She just needed to stop thinking about cheese and needing a poo.

Chapter 74

WILLIAM

My baby's here!
You say with a cheer,
But try not to cough, sneeze or laugh . . .
You can barely move around,
You daren't make a sound,
In case your uterus falls out of your arse.

Your little chap has arrived,
Your vagina survived,
He's a stunner, you're in love, he's a beauty.
You're a bloody super-hero
Even if your labia can now be tied in a bow,
But can confirm it still managed its duty.

Emily's tears flowed uncontrollably. She was laying back on the bed, wrapped in towels, as the midwife presented her with her son neatly swaddled in a white hospital blanket.

She pulled him into her and sobbed at the sight of how tiny and beautiful he was. He was completely perfect. She couldn't believe he had been inside her only minutes ago. It felt like a miracle.

Paul was right next to her. He was crying too.

'Welcome to the world, William,' he said softly, kissing her and gently stroking his son's tiny head.

The pain, the anger, the memory of how incredibly shit the last nine months had been, were instantly gone.

None of it mattered right now.

None of it would ever matter ever again.

This was the most magical, amazing and rewarding moment she'd ever felt, despite the fact she'd pooed in the water-bath, had just had several stitches to re-form the entrance of her vagina, and the midwife was about to insert a suppository . . . It didn't matter.

She no longer cared about anything other than this tiny little boy she felt more love for than she thought was humanly possible.

She could murder a Hobnob, though.

Chapter 75

WILLY PIC

Emily
So . . .
You're BOTH AUNTIES!
William Arthur Wells was born
(fucking finally) at
9.15 a.m. this morning.
Weighing in at 7 lb,12 oz.
Which is almost slightly disappointing
considering how much
extra cooking he had!
But then my vagina was quite
happy he didn't pack on any extra girth.
Anyway. I'm waffling!
Here he is.
He's utterly perfect.
We are so in love xx

Molly
OMG Amazing!
Massive congrats to you and Paul!
(And your vagina. Nice one. Obvs.)
He kept us waiting but he is

totally gorgeous!
Worth the wait.
I'm so proud of you!
(and your fanny)

Liz
He is so beautiful.
Well done you.
You've made an awesome one
there, sweetie.
I already can't wait to meet him and
give him big cuddles!
Once you've washed all the bits of
fanny off him and all that.
No offence.

                    Emily
                      Pahaha
                  None taken.
Without the fanny clumps he's even
                more utterly scrummy.
                Can't wait for you both
                  to meet him either!

Molly
It just makes me want mine to
come out!
Imagine what it will be like introducing
them!
So crazy and amazing that we are

395

doing this at almost the same time.
He's so gorgeous, Emily.
Give him the biggest cuddle from me
and Tom.
Xxx

Liz
And me.
And Gerald too!
Are you allowed to go home now?
Hope it's not too long xx

Emily
Hopefully within the
next couple of hours.
I really want to get out of here now.
I need real food.
And my own bed!
Right, I'm off.
He's asking to be fed again.
Which is mostly all he's done
since he's been born . . .
Pretty much every hour at the moment.
My nipples are starting
to resemble pâté . . .

Molly
Nice.
Bashed-up vagina and pâté nipples.
Really can't fucking wait now!

Emily
It's worth it! Don't worry!
LOL xx
Love you.

Molly
I'll hold you to that!
Love you too.

Liz
Love you all.
xxx

Chapter 76

THIRD WHEEL

Liz felt so happy for Emily.

It was hard not to fall in love with the beautiful baby boy her best friend had just had. He was totally perfect, in every way. Emily had a little family now. She was a mum. An actual parent. It was scary and amazing and wonderful all at the same time . . . She was so proud of her.

But there was a little uncomfortable thought niggling at the back of her mind that she was trying to ignore . . .

She'd known for a long time that her two best friends would be becoming parents at almost the same time. But she'd never really *thought* about it properly. What it meant for their friendships, and the dynamic between them all. It hadn't occurred to her to. She'd been busy with her own life. Her job. Her promotion. Her own priorities. Her own . . . Gerald.

But now, it was suddenly dawning on her that the 'three of them' was very much becoming the 'two of them' . . . And her. She was worried she was about to become a bit of a third wheel . . .

She knew that Molly and Emily would never deliberately leave her out of anything, but how would they be able to help it? They were going through something so amazing and life-changing, how would she ever fully comprehend or understand it? She couldn't. She knew that now.

The two of them were about to take a year off work. At the same time. Just as her work and life was about to become exponentially busier. Her time would be in short supply, while they would inevitably spend most of the week together, massaging and baby-sensoring the shit out of their newborns, and having lattes and cakes and going on daytime pub visits, or whatever it was new mums did . . .

Liz suddenly felt a little bit . . . jealous.

She couldn't help it.

It felt horrible to admit it.

But it was there.

Rearing its ugly 'I'm the only one who hasn't got a baby' head.

It was uncomfortable feeling this way.

Liz hadn't given any serious thought to having children for a long time . . . She'd been so focussed on her career for so long . . . but since meeting Gerald, she was beginning to realise that she hadn't fully let go of it. She'd only suppressed it.

The last thing she needed right now was for Gerald to know she was thinking about anything to do with babies. She knew he'd jump to conclusions and get all excited and carried away. He'd probably start trying to impregnate her on the spot while simultaneously proposing to her . . .

But she couldn't talk to her best friends about it either.

They had bigger things to worry about. Emily had only just given birth to a human being, and Molly was days away from doing the same. The last thing they needed right now was to listen to her ridiculous baby-jealousy issues . . .

Besides. She didn't actually *want* a baby right now. She just wasn't quite so sure she absolutely didn't *ever* want one . . .

That was it.

Wasn't it?

Chapter 77

WHAT NOW?

Emily, Paul and William arrived home for the first time ever as a family of three.

It felt so strange travelling with a baby in the car for the first time.

Paul had barely accelerated over 20mph, and had taken every corner, hill and roundabout so gently and smoothly, it had put Emily more on edge than she already was.

But they'd made it now.

They were home.

They pulled up outside their pretty little terraced house, like they both had countless times before and readied themselves for the moment they brought their baby son into his home for the first time . . .

Emily remembered in NCT they'd spoken about this moment, when you arrive back at your house after leaving the hospital with this tiny little person you're completely terrified of somehow breaking if you handle or even look at them the wrong way, and you carry this tiny human being strapped snuggly into an infant car seat into your living room and just look at them and think . . . What now?

And that was exactly what Emily and Paul were experiencing right now.

They had put the car seat facing towards them in the middle of the lounge as they perched on the edge of the sofa, staring at their baby son, and wondering precisely that:

WHAT NOW?

Should they take him out? Let him sleep? Move him into the bouncer? Hold him? Feed him? Sing to him? Flip a fucking gold coin over a rainbow and do a little jig for him?

Fuck knows.

This was terrifying.

It had been a good few minutes now, and neither of them had said a word, or so much as moved . . .

'This is weird isn't it?' Paul said finally, turning to look at Emily.

She smiled. It was a relief to know that he was as lost as she was.

'Yes,' she said, laughing a little.

'Why don't you go have a nap while he sleeps? He'll only want a feed again soon. Didn't the midwife say you should rest while you can?' Paul soothed, touching her hand.

'I don't think I can right now. I feel . . . odd. I think I just want to sit and look at him. Is that normal? I just don't want him out of my sight right now. I don't know why . . .' she said, her eyes locked on William.

'Of course it's normal. This is the moment that every new parent feels. We're all winging it. There's no right or wrong, babes. You've already done some pretty amazing shit with your fanny today. You're a fucking superhero as far as I'm concerned.'

Emily laughed. But had to stop quite instantly as her stomach muscles tightening suddenly had an unwelcome effect on her stitches.

'Thank you. Well done me. And my fanny,' she said, smiling. It was only now that she realised how exhausted she was. And how much everything hurt.

'I'll put the kettle on. If you want to have a little nap down here on the sofa, that's cool with me too. I'll bring him out of the car seat and lay him in the Moses basket next to you if you like? You can have a little snooze together side by side?' Paul said, smiling at his wife.

'That sounds perfect,' Emily said, wincing a little as she tentatively hoisted herself up to move position and sat back into the sofa cushion.

Paul left the room to make their drinks.

Emily wasn't sure what to do with herself.

She was utterly exhausted but brimming with emotion at the same time. Perhaps she needed to get it out. She realised she felt the urge to write. She just felt so many overwhelming and completely unknown feelings. Perhaps putting it into words would help.

She didn't necessarily need to publish something on her blog, she just wanted to write the words down. This was for her. She wanted to record exactly how she felt right in this moment so she could look back and keep remembering. It was a mix of so many different things.

403

And she knew she'd forget otherwise, she was so tired. It felt like something she had to do.

She reached for the laptop and started it up.

And then she started to write . . .

D-Day

Today it happened.

Finally.

The day came.

The one we've been waiting for.

The day your daddy and I both knew instantly . . . that we'd never be able to look at my vagina the same way ever again . . .

To be fair, I hadn't seen it in a while anyway. And yes, I do blame him for that and A LOT of other things. I have a list. And top of that list is the fact that he bought me cheese as a gift for giving birth to you . . . Yes. Cheese. BLOODY CHEESE.

Anyway.

TODAY. You arrived.

And you are beautiful. And more loved than I think I will ever be able to find the words to really tell you.

But right now, I'm too scared to even lift you out of the car seat we brought you home from the hospital in, in case I break you. Because you're so tiny. And scrunched up. And I'm also really concerned I might pop a stitch or wee everywhere from the effort of bending forward . . .

But I just want you to know that despite what you've done to my body, my boobs, my pelvic floor, my fanny, and my ability to poo without being utterly terrified, Daddy and I will love you completely unconditionally. And show you as many wonderful things as we can. And shield you from as much of the shit stuff as possible . . .

So welcome to the world, my tiny 7lb, 12 bundle of perfection.

I'm going to drink quite a lot of wine tonight. You should know that. Because if you think about it, it's your fault, really . . .

I love you.

Mummy xxx

#DDay
#GinDay

Chapter 78

HOME BIRTH-DAY

It was 3 a.m. in the morning on Molly's thirtieth birthday.

She didn't know why, but she couldn't sleep. She felt . . . strange.

She lay on her side, facing Tom and just stared at him for a few moments. He looked wonderfully calm and handsome. He always did.

He was also very asleep. As most sensible people would be at 3.07 a.m. on a Wednesday morning . . .

He looked so peaceful that she couldn't bear to wake him. But something felt different, she just wasn't sure how or why yet. Perhaps she was just imagining it. She'd go for a wee and see how she felt after that. Yes. Excellent plan. She could always wee. She currently had the bladder the size of a Borrower's . . .

She rolled herself over and out of bed, and dragged herself to the bathroom.

Her body felt different; heavier, perhaps. The baby's weight seemed to have shifted down. It literally felt like it had wriggled into her pelvis and stuck its head right down between her thighs. It was very odd. Not painful. Just odd. And bloody uncomfortable.

She sat on the loo wondering what was going on. She

wasn't due for another two and a half weeks. Surely this shouldn't be happening yet? Should it? Perhaps she should have taken a fancy class about all this like Emily had instead of just googling stuff on her iPad and buying a hypnobirthing CD off eBay for a quid . . .

Molly decided she'd text her midwife and head back to bed to try and get a bit more sleep. She could feel the baby wriggling away and she clearly wasn't screaming in labour yet, so surely there was nothing to worry about . . . Right?

Molly slipped back into bed with Tom as gently as she could manage. He stirred a little, and moved an arm round and on to her belly before drifting back into a deep sleep.

She smiled and closed her eyes. Whatever was going on could wait until morning. Proper morning that wasn't actually the middle of the night, that is.

Having a baby on her thirtieth birthday would be a pretty amazing birthday present though . . . wouldn't it?

Tom's phone screamed out a shrill and irritating alarm sound as it woke Molly abruptly from her broken sleep.

Tom wearily grabbed his phone and set it to snooze before pulling himself closer to her. She placed her head on to his bare shoulder and slowly began to force herself out of sleep. She wasn't ready to open her eyes fully yet. She just wanted to enjoy lying there with him for a few moments . . .

As she woke up a little more, Molly became aware of

the deep pressure that persisted on her pelvis. Still feeling strange.

'Happy birthday, beautiful . . .' came Tom's husky morning voice as he stroked her arm with his fingers.

'Thank you,' Molly managed, still not fully awake.

'How you feeling today?'

'Actually, a bit weird.' She forced herself to open her eyes. 'Everything's kind of shifted down. I think things might happen a little earlier than planned, maybe . . .'

'Wow. Really? Are you okay, though? Do you need me to stay home today?' Tom said, sounding a little concerned.

'Only if you want to. I haven't heard back from the midwife yet, so who knows. Let's just stay in bed and see what happens. It's my birthday. I demand it.'

'I'm cool with that,' Tom said, relaxing again. 'Play your cards right and you might even get a special birthday present . . .'

'Well.' Molly hoped that he meant that as sexily as she heard it. 'You're definitely staying home today with me now . . .'

Tom had decided to work from home for the day just in case . . . but annoyingly he had actually been 'working' . . . so things hadn't gone quite as Molly had hoped . . .

In fact, they'd mainly gone into yet another morning of sofa-based bed rest following the extreme discomfort that comes with a human headbutting you repeatedly in the pelvic tract.

Molly had spoken to her midwife now, who'd booked

her in for an appointment tomorrow morning. Her main advice was to relax and not worry unless things changed, as it seemed like the baby was engaged and that could mean everything or nothing, apparently . . . which was pretty unhelpful.

Molly could feel consistent tightening now. She'd remembered Emily talking about Braxton Hicks and the few false alarms she'd had so she wasn't particularly worried.

She was happy letting Tom run around after her, while she partook in yet another rock-and-roll afternoon of decaffeinated tea, Netflix and chilling, although in this case, 'chilling' really did mean chilling . . . Maybe she'd go really crazy and have some Marmite on toast in a bit. Nothing like living life on the edge . . .

At least the 'happy birthday' messages flooding in on her phone and on her Facebook timeline were keeping her preoccupied.

> **Emily**
> Happy Birthday my beautiful,
> wonderful, kind, happy and brilliant
> friend!
> I'm SOOOO gutted we can't see you
> today ☹
> Hope you're holding up okay xx

> **Molly**
> Thanks sweetie!
> I'm okay xx

Feeling a little odd today but think
it's just boredom mixed with the baby
starting to engage.
Hopefully I don't have to deal with a
human head hanging down between
my thighs for too long!

Emily
Oh wow – already?
Hope you're not too uncomfortable!
We'll have a post-birthday celebration
as soon as you're feeling better
and I'm feeling a bit more up to it!
Currently can't sit down without the
assistance of a doughnut cushion . . .
I'm not exactly party material as it is!
Lol
Have an AMAZING chilled day.
Miss you!
LOVE YOU!
Happy birthday again xxx

Liz
And from me!
Happy Birthday awesome lady ;)
Relax and let that boyfriend of yours
run around after you!
And do the cooking.
I think that's really best all round . . .

Molly
Thanks ladies!
I couldn't cook even if I wanted to!
Eating parsnip crisps and
watching Tom Hardy films . . .
Reckon that'll get things going ;)

Liz
Gets me going.
I'm not even pregnant.

Emily
If I wasn't so exhausted and
didn't have a fanny that looked
like badly stitched taxidermy
I'd be getting going too . . .

Molly
Well . . . that's the sort of mental
imagery every girl needs on their
thirtieth birthday! Ha!
Thanks, girlies.
We'll celebrate properly soon.
Miss you both so much xx
Can't believe I'm turning thirty sat in
maternity pants on the sofa watching
Mad Max . . .
Wouldn't have it any other way
though!
Love you both too xxx

Molly smiled and scrolled through the last few WhatsApp messages from her friends. They always cheered her up.

She became aware of Tom messing around with something awkward and heavy behind the sofa.

'What are you doing back there?' Molly said, frowning a little.

'Setting up a sex swing,' Tom replied.

'Lovely, I'll hop on later . . .' Molly said, laughing. 'But now would you like to explain to me what you're really doing so I don't have to put my crisps down?'

'I'm setting up the birthing pool.'

Molly smiled to herself. It was sensible to get it ready, she guessed. They'd already decided she'd have the baby right there at home. She'd been completely insistent. She knew that's what she wanted and she'd been told so long as there were no further complications, she was all clear to give birth right there at the flat.

That was exactly the way she pictured it in her head. Tom there with her and their baby brought into the world in the place they would call home . . . it felt right.

And right now, she'd be pretty happy to give birth with Tom Hardy in the background and still stuffing her face with vegetable-based snacks. Why not?

Molly felt suddenly very sick.

Next to her on the sofa, Tom turned his head as she lurched forward trying to get her breath back. It felt like every muscle in her stomach was suddenly cramping all at the same time. Not pain, necessarily, just incredibly intense tightening. It was like nothing she'd ever felt before.

It had taken her completely by surprise. She let out a small strained cry as she managed to sit herself up, and became aware of Tom next to her. Talking to her. Rubbing her back and making sure she knew he was right there with her.

'I'm calling the hospital now,' Tom said, his voice urgent and direct.

Molly couldn't find the strength to respond to him. She was completely consumed by the intense sensation her body was going through. She nodded and breathed as deeply and slowly as she could.

She was aware of Tom talking on the phone but it felt like a blur. This wasn't the way she expected it. There were no waves of increasing pain, she just felt a relentless and powerful sensation that was so strong it was pushing the air out of her lungs.

She searched her mind for the breathing techniques she'd learnt on her hypnobirthing CD. She knew this was it. This was labour. It was happening. She could feel it.

And she was going to hypnobirth the shit out of it. It had probably been the best £1 she'd ever spent . . .

She just needed to remain calm until the midwife arrived and helped her get her baby out.

Behind her, Tom was filling up the birthing pool and placing towels down everywhere as she concentrated on not letting the pain consume her.

He helped her carefully into the warm pool. She was

still wearing her pants and one of his T-shirts. She didn't really care what she was wearing right now, she just wanted to breathe. And not think about the idea of the baby coming before the midwife arrived . . .

The warm water was easing the pain in her lower back and relaxing her. She was surprised how okay she felt, not a bit like the squealing, screaming agony she was expecting after Emily's experience . . .

She could do this.

She was going to have her baby. On her thirtieth birthday. In a Guns N' Roses T-shirt. In a paddling pool in the middle of the living room in Tom's first-floor maisonette. While *Mad Max* played in the background.

It was perfect.

Chapter 79

WEEK ONE. DONE.

William was a whole week old.

Emily felt a little sad about that . . .

She was terrified she had been too exhausted to pay attention and appreciate him fully. If she could just get more than twelve minutes' sleep in a row, she might be able to relax and enjoy him a bit more, but she knew that wasn't going to happen.

She was so desperate to be a good mum. She'd read the books, done the courses, researched, observed and paid attention to everything she could to prepare herself, but the truth was that nothing could have prepared her.

The last week had been a total shock to the system. Suddenly, she wasn't just 'her' any more. She existed almost entirely to service this tiny, beautiful little person she made with her body. She had to give him everything, all of her, and any moment she stopped, even just for a few minutes, and let someone else take the burden for a while, she felt this bizarre and irrational sense of intense guilt.

And that was exactly what she was experiencing right now.

Paul had taken William out for a stroll around the park

so she could have a shower, blow-dry her hair, and generally try to feel a little more like her old self again – if she was honest she didn't know when she last changed her pants. And she'd been in her dressing gown for about three days straight now. She could actually smell herself – that couldn't be good.

She stepped into the shower and felt the hot powerful water wash away days' worth of emotion, exhaustion and slightly crispy underwear . . . she was beginning to feel a little restored at least. Even if she only planned to go from one set of well-worn dubiously stained pyjamas into a fresh clean set. Without any puke on the left shoulder. (For a little while, at least . . .)

She stepped out of the shower feeling revived, but missing William quite desperately, even in the half an hour he'd been gone . . .

Her boobs felt heavy with milk already. It wouldn't be long before the next feed. It couldn't be. Otherwise she'd literally have to milk herself . . .

Emily wrapped a cool towel around her and made her way to the bedroom to source some fresh PJs.

She got dressed carefully. Everything still hurt so much. And made her way back down to the comfort of her living room. She took her familiar spot on the sofa close to the baby bouncer, the remote, a stack of muslins and baby wipes, and a big box of biscuits . . .

She felt a little better.

She looked around at the almost overwhelming display of cards, gifts and flowers. The house was full of blue baby boy cards, and so many bunches of flowers she'd run out of vases. Currently, most were stuck in the sink . . . where they'd probably stay until they got to that weird furry-stemmed stinky stage.

Hopefully Paul would deal with that.

It wasn't really a priority for her right now. She couldn't sit down without the use of her piles cushion and her stitches stung so much every time she went for a wee her eyes watered. This was not quite the glamorous latte-drinking cafe lifestyle she'd imagined having a newborn baby would bring . . .

No. So far she'd spent most of motherhood crying, eating biscuits, trying not to think about what her vagina looked like, and, thanks to her bowel still being in spasm, hadn't had a shit for two days . . .

Emily tried to relax a little. She knew Paul and William wouldn't be long now. She should try and enjoy her remaining few minutes of peace.

Paul had been nothing short of wonderful the last week. He could see this was a big adjustment for her . . . not that he didn't feel it too . . . but then he didn't have a baby latched on to his plate-sized areolas for at least twelve hours a day . . .

He was honestly an amazing father, and he'd been an even more amazing husband. He'd done everything he could – cooked, cleaned, made late-night dashes to the twenty-four-hour chemist for lanolin cream, painkillers, nipple shields and cold packs, anything to alleviate the pain of blocked ducts and cracked nipples. He was also probably some kind of VIP member on Deliveroo by now. Every time Emily so much as looked like she needed chicken ramen, thirty-seven minutes later it would miraculously appear . . .

She was aware that he looked almost as exhausted as she felt. It probably wasn't the way he'd imagined fatherhood either . . .

She hoped he knew that she knew that.

Her blog had been an amazing source of comfort too. She never expected that would happen. Sometimes, during the relentless night feeds, it was the only thing that was keeping her going . . .

It was bizarre how late-night tweeting with total strangers could make her feel so much better, knowing hundreds of other mums were right there with her too: veiny, overinflated boobs, being drained by a tiny milk vampire in the twilight hours while dreaming, hoping when their babies had finally had their fill, that you could somehow transfer them back to the Moses basket without them waking for just an hour's uninterrupted sleep. Knowing you weren't alone made it feel less lonely.

Emily smiled.

Despite how much of an exhausting, guilt-laden, tear-filled adjustment this had all been, she was still utterly in love and incredibly happy.

It was a strange contradiction.

And something you would never be able to understand or explain until you became a parent yourself; she felt like the latest member of a secret club. One you only got access to once you had released a human from your fanny . . .

Emily decided to write something.

She opened up her laptop and began tapping the thoughts in her head down on her Facebook page:

An Ode to a Labia

Thank you, dear August,
for bringing me my baby, yeah.
I've said hello to sleepless nights,
and waved goodbye to my labia.

I've learnt not to swallow,
when there's faeces in my mouth.
I've learnt not to cry,
now my nipples point due south.

I'm powered by coffee,
hoping breastfeeding will make me thin.
So I'm free to eat chocolate,
and down pints of gin.

I'm lying on Facebook,
Saying my life is so fucking sweet.
When it's constipation and wailing,
and leggings for a treat.

So thank you, dear August,
for the joys you have revealed.
This year I'll mostly be drinking,
And keeping my fanny mostly sealed.

#byebyelabia
#hellogin

Chapter 80

MARLEY

Molly

Hey girls.

So guess what . . .

This will probably come as a bit of a shock but . . .

I JUST HAD A BABY!

Here's Marley.

He can't wait to meet you xx

Liz

WHAT???

OMG – that's insane!

You pushed him out pretty bloody quick!

Is everything okay??

Did you manage to have him at home?

Molly

Yes. We're both doing great.

I'm tired but fine.

I actually feel so much better for having him!

It was like hell being on bed-rest.

And yes, I had him right here at home.
He was in a rush! Clearly!
I would have told you he was coming
but he didn't even give me a chance!
I've only just found my phone down
the back of the sofa . . . lol

Liz
That's seriously amazing.
Well done.
Massive congrats to you and Tom.
He is a total cutie.
Can't believe both my best friends
have made such beautiful boys a
week apart!
I feel left out!
(JOKING. My womb is totally cool
being empty. Thank you.)

Emily
AARRRGGGHHH!
Just seen this! Sorry!
W was latched to me for an
hour straight!
Molly – this is so amazing!!
I'm so happy for you!
He is completely stunning.
You are amazing!
Huge congrats xxx

Molly

Thank you, ladies.

It's still a bit surreal.

I was actually a bit worried going into it,

but Tom set up the home birth pool,

the midwife arrived and within forty-five

minutes he was here . . .

It didn't even hurt really.

It was more powerful than painful, if

that makes sense . . .

I did my hypnobirthing CD and just

remembered to breathe . . . It was mad.

Still can't quite believe I've

just had a baby . . .

Emily

I hate you.

Liz

lol

That's so crazy . . .

Guess it's true labour is totally

different for everyone!

Main thing is you both have beautiful

healthy boys. And I'm now an

unofficial auntie – TWICE.

Molly

You are!

I know it's quick but I honestly think

we should meet up this weekend!

I want to meet William!
And I miss you girls.
It's been forever since I've
been outside of this flat!
That okay with you guys?
You feel up to it Emily?

Emily
I'm knackered.
I've only managed two and a half
poos in a week.
And my tits hit my chin
when I sit down . . .
But I'm cool.
I wouldn't miss it for the world.

Liz
Me neither xxx

Molly
Perfect.
Will see you and mega-boobs
at the weekend then!
Love you xxx

Chapter 81

GIZ IS BACK

It had been an exciting and unexpected end to a previously ordinary Wednesday, Liz thought as she began shutting down for the day.

Liz was so proud of her friends. Both of them.

How utterly mad was it that both of them had had babies within days of each other. It was hard to even process it. Life had changed so incredibly in the last six months.

They had all hit thirty years old and they were all exactly where they were supposed to be.

Perhaps she and Gerald should go for a drink tonight to celebrate Marley's early entry into the world. She was sure Molly would appreciate her going and getting drunk on her behalf. People who'd just had babies on their thirtieth birthday loved that stuff, right?

She'd message Molly later with pictures of her doing shots and toasting her excellent baby-producing birthday vagina. She'd love it.

She looked up as a little series of taps sounded at her office door, and Gerald pushed it open a few inches with his usual kind smile on his face. 'You ready to go?'

'Sure,' Liz said, getting to her feet and gathering the

last few bits into her handbag as she lifted it on to her shoulder. 'Do you fancy a drink? I've just heard from Molly . . .'

'Oh?' Gerald said, lifting his eyebrows inquisitively.

'Yes,' Liz said, moving towards him and smiling. 'She's had the baby! A little boy. Marley. Seems like she had a pretty easy time of it, to be honest – he was clearly keen to get out of there.'

'That's amazing news!' Gerald said, stepping forward to hug her. 'Send her and Tom massive congrats from me. Wow. That's such good news.'

'I have,' Liz said, leaning into his embrace. 'Yes, I know. Totally wasn't expecting that today! It's her birthday too. How sweet is it that she gets to celebrate her birthday with her little boy from now on? I know she'll love that.'

'Shall we go have a drink to that then?' Gerald said, grinning a little as Liz looked up at him.

'Absolutely we shall. It's our duty,' Liz said, laughing as they began to make their way out of her office. 'We'd be totally shit friends if we didn't go and get drunk right now to celebrate everyone popping humans out of their uteruses. Wouldn't we?'

'Couldn't agree more,' Gerald said, still grinning and walking close to her as they strolled down the corridor together.

'Let's go get shit-faced in the name of childbirth . . .'

*

Liz sat happily perched on a bar stool with a cocktail in front of her, as Gerald stood next to her, taking a glug of something long and frothy looking.

Liz had had something playing on her mind the last few weeks. They'd been slowing things down again ever since 'Proposal-Gate' and it had been amazing.

The pressure had been off. They'd got back to laughing and enjoying each other's company. And loving each other.

She really did know that she loved him now.

The last few weeks had proven it. If they could bounce back from where they were to things being better than they'd ever been before, then this really was love. In every sense.

So she'd begun to wonder how they might take a small step forward again, without anyone making insane marriage proposals or talking about babies. And she had thought of something. Something that she knew would make him really happy. Prove to him how much she loved him. And how much she wanted to be with him.

Yes. It was time to take a little step forward. As she looked at his face, his kind eyes, how his eyes always lit up when he saw her . . . she knew it was time.

'So,' Liz said gently, pushing her drink a few inches away from her. 'I've been thinking . . .'

Gerald turned his body towards her, smiling with anticipation.

'I've been thinking that it seems a little silly how much time you're spending at mine. And it does seem ridiculous how much you're spending getting trains and cabs back at the weekends. And half your stuff is at mine anyway . . . I mean, I washed three sets of your pants on Sunday. If that's not commitment, I don't know what is . . .'

Liz became aware she was rambling. She just wasn't very good at putting herself out there. She needed to stop acting like a giddy teenager asking a boy to the school disco . . .

She took a deep breath and tried to ignore Gerald's ever-increasing grin as she composed herself.

'So what I'm really saying is, that I've had a word with the cat. And Jasper's cool with it. So the two of us would very much like you – if you're interested, that is, and don't mind washing your own pants from now on – to . . . move in with us.'

Liz was aware that she was holding her breath, but didn't seem to be able to resume breathing again until he answered her.

Gerald's grin spread into a full beaming smile across his face. He leaned in and kissed her, deeply and lovingly. She knew in that moment she'd made him so happy. And that made her happy too.

'Well. That certainly came as a bit of a surprise,' he said softly, gently smiling. 'But in the few seconds you've given me to deliberate, I would like to absolutely accept. And let you know that I will be more than happy to wash my own underwear from now on, and I'll be more than happy to resume primary lap rights for the cat. I know it's what he would want.'

Liz laughed. It was true. It was absolutely what the cat wanted. It would make his little furry kitty dreams come true . . .

'I love you,' Liz said suddenly. Feeling so happy she'd done this.

'I love you too,' Gerald said, kissing her again. More passionately this time.

Perhaps it was the cocktail taking effect but Liz was pleased she was sitting down as her legs felt weak.

She was so happy.

They were back and better than ever.

Giz was back.

Chapter 82

BABIES

Liz sat waiting patiently for her two friends in the little cafe off Wycombe high street that they'd met in when Emily had first found out she was pregnant all those months ago . . .

It seemed fitting.

Fitting that the three ladies would meet there for the first time since two of them had brought their babies into the world.

Liz smiled about how far they'd all come since that day. How different things were just a few months ago. She had got rid of 'him' and had lovely Gerald in her life, Molly and Tom had had their wobbles but were even stronger now, and Emily had somehow survived nine and a half months of the longest, hardest pregnancy in the history of time, and still managed to keep her Pinterest boards updated. It had been quite a journey for them all.

Just then, Liz spotted a mass of blonde curls heading towards her from behind a well-designed pushchair . . .

'Hi!' Emily mouthed, as she fought her way through the tables, and made her way to her friend.

'You look amazing!' Liz gushed, as Emily headed her

way towards her. 'I expected you to be a wreck but you look stunning . . .'

'Ha. Putting my face on makes me feel human – trust me when I tell you behind these four layers of Touche Éclat are dark circles like coffee rings . . . and the complexion of a *Walking Dead* extra.'

'I believe you . . .' Liz said, hugging and squeezing her friend's arms. 'But you honestly do look amazing . . . And. CONGRATS!'

'Awww, I know! I can't believe they actually sent me one! I thought it was never going to happen and then the courier turned up last week . . .'

Liz looked puzzled. 'Are you talking about your son?'

Emily laughed. 'Oh God no! Sorry! My iCandy – the pushchair?' she said, gesturing towards it. 'After I had a small breakdown while two weeks overdue and wrote that blog post about what pregnancy really feels like, you know, when you've not seen your vagina since April and your husband can no longer "roll" you out of bed because you're too heavy etc., etc., well, anyway . . . It went *viral*! And loads of brands got in touch . . . it was amazing!'

'Well, I meant congrats on the birth of your offspring, but I can see there's more important things going on here,' Liz said, laughing.

The two friends sat down, and moments later, Molly appeared with about twelve metres of fabric wrapped around her, with her baby somewhere in the middle, identifiable only as a tiny head poking out the top.

'Ladies,' Molly said, as she took a seat.

'Wow. That is a lot of material,' Liz, said, kissing her friend on the cheek.

'Hey. I'm not quite in the market for an iCandy, and he seems to love it. Even though it does take about an hour to hoist him up in there . . .'

'You look so well!' Emily said. 'I'm covering up how shit I feel with as much make-up as I could fit on my face, but you are glowing. I hate you!'

'Ha!' Molly retorted. 'I think I've just been lucky. It's actually been pretty easy so far. He seems to like sleeping quite a lot, so you know . . .'

'I don't think I can actually hear that. And, more importantly, I *need* caffeine. And lots of it,' Emily retorted.

'As the only person here whose cervix has not released a human in the last couple of weeks, I'm on it,' Liz said, wandering off to fetch some drinks.

'Congratulations, sweetie. I can't believe we both did it! Can I see him?' Emily said, smiling at her friend.

Molly pulled the edge of the fabric down to expose his tiny face. 'Here he is. Here's Marley . . .'

'He's so beautiful,' Emily said, stroking the downy crop of hair on top of his head.

'Is William sleeping or can I take a peek?' Molly said.

'He is, but you can still have a look. Quietly. It's the first time he's stopped crying in about three days so I am going to enjoy this . . .' Emily gently moved the blanket down a little so her friend could get a good look.

'He's beautiful too,' Molly said, just as Liz arrived back with some very strong-looking coffees.

For a few moments, the three friends just looked at the babies.

'What is that furry thing you've got him in?' Molly said eventually.

'It's a lambswool buggy liner. It regulates his temperature,' Emily responded a little snottily.

'It looks like he's made a bed out of the fur of all his enemies,' Liz interjected quickly as Molly fell about laughing.

Emily ignored it. She'd had forty-five minutes' sleep since she gave birth a week and a half ago. Not the ideal state to manage a sense of humour.

'So, Liz. How are things with Big G?' Emily said, changing the subject.

'Well, they'd probably be a lot better if you never ever called him Big G ever again . . .' Liz smiled at her friend. 'But, it's amazing actually. Really really amazing. I feel like a schoolgirl. It's made me realise what a pile of shit every other relationship I've ever been in has been. And, err, I've asked him to move in with me.'

'Wow. That's brilliant news! Nice one, sweetie. Lizzy-tits all loved up. Who would've thought it, eh?' Molly said, laughing into her coffee.

'Okay. I think we all know exactly how I feel about using the L-word, thank you!' Liz snapped back at her. 'But, I'm . . . happy. Properly happy. For the first time in ages . . . And I actually do love him. I really do . . .'

The three ladies grinned at each other. Like they had so many times, in so many places, at so many stages of their lives.

'I'm so happy for you,' Emily said. 'So it won't be long until you decide to join the mummy club yourself, then?' she said, raising her eyebrows and rocking William's buggy a little to settle him.

'Er . . . no offence, but after listening to Molly talk about having her placenta dried out and made into pills, and then hearing you describe your birth as "like shitting a giant pineapple with fingernails" . . . I think I'm cool. Thanks,' Liz responded as her friends laughed.

And as she watched her two friends smile and coo over their newborn babies, Liz did secretly envy them a little. Perhaps having one of those herself actually wasn't too bad an idea after all? Perhaps it'd suit her? Perhaps it was what she wanted. It probably didn't hurt that much, right?

But now she came to think about it . . . her period hadn't started yet. That was strange. She'd been so busy at work recently she'd not had the time to notice. She was never late. She should have started a few days ago, for sure. Oh God. She couldn't be, could she?

SHIT.

ACKNOWLEDGEMENTS

Thank you so much to my wonderful husband, family and many friends for all their love, support and laughter. (Along with providing me with some excellent material for this book!)

A special shout-out to my NCT girls – hopefully you're all still talking to me!

A huge thanks to everyone who reads my little blog and has followed me on this crazy journey we call parenting for the last few years. Without you I would never have got here, and I am so grateful for all your support and solidarity – thank you for reminding me daily that we are all winging it together.

Thank you to my brilliant agent Madeleine Milburn, and her team, for the wonderful support and advice. I'm so excited for what the future holds and can't wait to continue working with you on this project and hopefully many others.

Thank you in turn to the entire team at Hodder who have been so kind, so helpful, and taught me so much in the lead up to my debut novel launch.

And finally – a really special mention for my amazing editor Kate – you found me, took a chance on me, and I feel so incredibly lucky that you did! You've changed my life and I will be forever thankful for that – thank you so much.